M000199824

Letters
from
Jacob

Other Books in this Series
by H. C. Hewitt

Letters from Jacob

— a novel by —

H. C. Hewitt

Printed in the United States of America

Published by Author Academy Elite
PO Box 43, Powell, OH 43035
www.AuthorAcademyElite.com

Identifiers:
LCCN: 2019914427
ISBN: 978-1-64085-948-7 (paperback)
ISBN: 978-1-64085-949-4 (hardback)
ISBN: 978-1-64085-950-0 (ebook)

Available in paperback, hardback and e-book

Book design by Jetlaunch. Cover design by Debbie O'Byrne.

acknowledgments

"With man this is impossible,
but with God all things are possible."
(Matthew 19:26, NIV)

First and foremost I would like to thank Jesus! He is my rock, my saviour and my creator. He has given me many gifts, answered countless prayers and blessed me far more than I deserve and for that I am grateful.

To my husband and children, your love and support mean the world to me. You all have busy lives of your own, but always have time for your wife and mother, such a blessing. To my mom and dad, your love and support are appreciated.

Lorraine, you are an amazing supporter of my books. You believed in me from the very beginning with my first book. The countless edits and proofreading you have done - I can't imagine the time you have spent with every draft. To you Cathy, thank you for all the time you spent reading and giving your advice. Thank you, Laura, for proofreading my manuscript after the editing process.

W.O. Dan Flynn (ret'd), thank you for putting up with the endless questions regarding World War One information. You have helped me more than you will ever know and I appreciate the time you took to help.

To my editor, Gwennie Simpson, thank you! God blessed me with you. I couldn't have finished this book without you. I appreciate all you did for me. You went above and beyond for me and I can't thank you enough.

To my friends: your tremendous support means everything and you all are always faithfully there for me.

Tony and Debbie Photography: Thank you for the wonderful author photo.

Thank you to Kary Oberbrunner, Nanette O' Neal, Brenda Haire, Abigail Young, Emily Myers and everyone at AAE for all the help you gave to publish my third book. It's been a new experience and I look forward to publishing many more books with you. Thank you to Debbie at Jetlaunch for your incredible designing skills. The time you spent with me to get the "right" cover has been amazing. It was a pleasure working with you.

Thank you, the reader, for giving Jacob and Abigail the opportunity to leave a little part of their lives with you by following their journey. God Bless!

chapter one

Abbington Pickets, January, 1915

> *...the days are long and nights are extremely bitter. We take turns doing night duty. Everyone dreads it when it's their turn. It rains more often than not, but enough about that.*
> *I miss you Abigail, more than words can say. I think about our baby, a little boy or little girl. I am thrilled for either and I know our child will be beautiful like his or her mother...*

"Abigail!" sounded a voice from outside The General Store. Abigail looked up from the letter she was reading. *Who was hollering like a banshee?* The curly haired brunette wondered as she quickly folded and tucked the piece of paper into her floral apron pocket. Abigail had a beautiful poise, and her wavy locks set off the loosely held bun piled on her crown. The ankle-length, floral tone-on-tone burgundy dress swished as she moved. Wishing she still could be reading Jacob's letter, she walked toward the door.

"Are you here?" The sound became clearer as it neared the inside of the building. "Abigail!"

"What is it?" Abigail met her sister-in-law in the doorway. The frantic look on her face gave Abigail a scare.

"What's wrong, Jane?" Abigail grasped Jane's upper arms with both hands. The coat she wore was slightly big for her and hung down to her knees, revealing the grey dress underneath. Jane's mousy-coloured hair, usually in a tight, neat bun, was falling out of place, with strands of hair that fell down on either side of her face. Her naturally serious expression was even more stern. Not only was Abigail startled by her sister-in-law's appearance, she was even more surprised she was here in Abbington Pickets, since it was quite a long drive from Crocus Flats. It was also wintertime and Claude, her husband, usually did the shopping in the cold weather.

"I just came from Doc's," Jane gasped trying to catch her breath.

"Come, sit down." Abigail led her toward the chair beside the tea table in the corner of The General Store. It was where Abigail sat with all the ladies who came for tea and biscuits while she worked at the store, which was the majority of her time.

With Jacob gone to war, she had to keep busy and besides, the village needed her. She supplied all the space needed to store the items sent to the men at war. She wanted to do all she could for the war effort so her Jacob could come back home safely. She wanted him to be proud of her. She wanted to show him that she could handle everything at home while he was gone. She did have help when she needed it. Charles' father, Mr. Edwards, stopped in everyday to see if she needed anything or to make sure she was alright. In fact, everyone who knew Jacob called in to check on his wife. Everyone in the village knew how Jacob had struggled for the life he had, and the fact that he had to leave his beautiful Abigail with child to serve his country was heart breaking.

Abigail sat across from Jane, she leaned over toward her. "Now what is it?" Abigail asked. "Have you calmed down enough to tell me what it is?"

Jane took a deep breath and closed her eyes. It was obvious she didn't want to make eye contact with Abigail. It was as though she was ashamed and angry at the same time.

"I am going to have a baby," Jane blurted out matter-of-factly.

"Well, that's great news." Abigail threw her hands in the air.

"No, it's not!" Jane stared at her.

"Of course it is," Abigail insisted, trying to make her feel better, knowing full well the way she felt when she found out that she herself was expecting.

"I can't be a mother."

"Why not?" Abigail's happiness turned to confusion.

"I am not ready to be a mother," Jane stated. "We're not ready to be parents." Jane's blotchy red face frowned with wrinkles across her forehead.

The all too familiar feeling crept up inside Abigail tingling the tips of her nerve endings as if they were lightning bolts. Abigail silently recalled the day she learned she was expecting. It was a cloudy morning in September, right after their third anniversary, and soon after she found out Jacob wanted to go to join the army. When she began vomiting, she thought she had influenza. Each day she woke up with the same thing. Not wanting to worry Jacob, she hid it well, but finally took a walk down to see Doc, who revealed the shocking surprise that she was with child.

"I can't have children!" She exasperated.

"I can assure you, Miss Abigail," Doc replied, "you can, you are."

"What am I going to say to Jacob?" She panicked. "I- I mean- never mind," remembering with whom she was speaking, at the same time remembering the conversation she had so seriously with Jacob about not having children. Truth was, she did want to have children. She didn't want to have to tell her love, the one whom she was about to marry, that she couldn't have children. Abigail thought she couldn't conceive. When she went back to England to marry Patrick, she got measles and because she was already in her teens the doctor told her it was very unlikely that she could ever have children. Abigail would rather tell Jacob she didn't want to have children than to admit she couldn't. It was like admitting that she wasn't a real woman, or a complete woman. It broke her heart to see the look on Jacob's face when she told him that she didn't want to have a family. Abigail knew it was the best thing to do. If only she could explain that to him now. Instead she had to write it in a letter telling him he was going to be a father, and when he was on his way to war, no less. Oh, if only she could see his face, touch his hand, feel his strong arms wrapped around her right now! She looked down at her swollen belly. Abigail rubbed both her hands over her round front. *Oh, Jacob, how I miss you*, she thought.

"Abigail?" A sharp voice shook her into the present. "Are you even listening to me?" Jane waved her hand in front of her face.

"Of course," Abigail answered her as if what a thing to say, "I am listening."

"Well, then?" She asked

"Well, what?" Abigail looked confused.

"How am I going to tell Claude?"

"He will be thrilled," Abigail assured her. "Believe me, every man wants to have children with the woman he loves."

"Are you sure?" Jane was still not convinced.

"Mark my words," Abigail confidently informed her as she patted Jane on the shoulder. "Claude's shirt will be bursting at the seams." She imagined how Jacob looked when he read the letter Abigail wrote him. She knew he would be grinning from ear to ear and it would give him that much more to live for. She wished she could have been a fly on the wall at the time.

"I hope you are right," Jane frowned.

"I know I am." Abigail added, "now, this isn't making the baby a new dress or mending the old one." She grabbed the broom and began to sweep, trying to cover up the tears welling up in her eyes.

"What?" Jane looked confused. "What baby, what clothes, you don't have a baby yet."

"It's an expression, Jane. My grandma always used to say it," Abigail laughed, "you know, when you aren't doing any work and you should be."

"Oh." Jane shook her head.

"Now, you better fix yourself," Abigail scolded. "Here comes your husband now." Abigail could see the top of Claude's head as he walked toward The General Store.

"He must be finished at the blacksmith shop." Jane wiped her tears with the white hanky she pulled out of her pocket, then patted her hair on each side above her ears, feeling it to make sure it was in place.

"Don't worry," Abigail hugged her. "Everything will be alright, God is in charge and he doesn't make mistakes."

"Thanks, Abigail," Jane half smiled. "I can always count on you."

"Of course you can," Abigail grinned. She did wish that the burden of carrying a baby and looking after The General Store was something she didn't have to do alone. But, she knew God was with her, and she wasn't alone as long as she had faith in Him. Since Jacob left, she had decided that looking after The General Store and living in the home quarters of it would be easier than keeping up two places in the cold, hard winter. She closed up Jacabig Place and brought the belongings she would need while Jacob was away. It was hard keeping two fires burning and this way when deliveries came to the store she was always there. This also made it easier to be there for the drop-offs for the war effort.

"Bonjour!" Claude walked through the doorway as he took off his hat. He nodded to Abigail, and smiled brightly at Jane as though she were the only one in the room.

"Are you ready to go, mon petit chou?" Claude asked.

"I am," Jane said certainly as she brushed her dress downward with both her hands. She quickly glanced at Abigail.

"What does that mean?" Abigail whispered.

"I don't know," Jane smiled, leaning in close to Abigail, "but I love it." She blushed.

Claude walked closer to them and held out his arm to Jane. She slipped her arm in his. They began to walk out the doorway.

"It was lovely to see you," Abigail called out after them.

Jane turned her head and lightly smiled back at her, as a communication to the secret they both now shared.

Abigail continued to sweep the floor, humming the familiar tune she loved as a child, 'London Bridge is falling down.' She thought about the man in Claude when Jacob and she first met him. He had a chip on his shoulder and a bitterness in his heart. Abigail's heart warmed as she thought of the man he has turned out to be and how he loved Jane and doted on her endlessly.

She noticed a horse-drawn sleigh that pulled up. She walked over to the white four-pane window and watched her father carefully climb out of the sleigh, then turn back around to help her mother out. To her surprise, he reached into the back of the sleigh and pulled out a leather suitcase.

What's going on? Abigail wondered to herself. She reached the door before her parents and waited for them to approach. "This is a surprise!" Abigail exclaimed as she opened the door for her ma and pa.

"Abigail, you are radiant!" Her mama gushed as she reached forward to hug her. "You have so much colour in your cheeks and look even more beautiful." Her mother still looked concerned. Abigail hugged her father as well.

"What's with the suitcase?" She questioned.

"Well, dear," her mama looked at her, "you will need someone here with you sooner or later..."

"You see, Abigail," her father interrupted, "your mother has been worrying herself sick."

"About what?" Abigail shook her head with confusion. "I am fine."

"You are going to have a baby soon," her mother pointed out.

"Not until April," Abigail argued.

"Well, it's January, honey," her mama continued. "You shouldn't be lifting anything. Besides, anything could happen."

"You need your mama," her father added. "Or your mama needs you," he grinned.

"Mr. Edwards checks in every day," Abigail explained, "and so does half of the village." She laughed. "Oh, mama!" Abigail hugged her ma. "I am grateful for your help, but what about pa? What's he going to do without you for three months?"

"Don't worry about him, dear," her mama winked. "Your aunt Gladys has everything under control."

"Just let your mama help you out," her father finally stated. "It will be good for both of you."

"Well, it sure will make the nights a little less lonely," Abigail admitted, "but I have been working on a little baby quilt and that keeps me busy."

"You shouldn't be lifting anything right now, anyway." Pa glanced at her.

"I feel great, pa." Abigail did adjust to pregnancy well. Once the morning sickness stopped, she felt good, and recently had more energy than usual. "And I don't lift anything anyhow," she added. "Mr. Edwards has been more than helpful with that, believe me. In fact, everyone in the village has been wonderful to me."

"I don't want you wearing yourself out." Mama looked sternly at her daughter.

"You worry too much," Abigail smiled. "Now, let's have some tea."

chapter two

Winter went by quickly and March came in like a lion at Abbington Pickets. It was much windier than the past two months. There wasn't as much snowfall but the temperature dropped to a bitter cold. Jacob always said nothing prepares you for a hard cold winter than weathering it out the first few weeks of a cold snap, then you are able to conquer the crisp frost first thing in the morning.

"Good morning, mama," Abigail shuffled into the kitchen. "Did you have a good sleep?" Her mama was pouring coffee into two cups. Abigail could hear bacon frying in the pan on the cookstove.

"Good morning, honey." Mama smiled as she set the coffee pot down. "Breakfast is almost ready."

"You are spoiling me, mama." Abigail picked up her cup, blew on the surface, and slurped in the steaming liquid. "Mmm, good coffee."

A knock from the store door sounded vaguely in the room.

"Who could that be? It's still early!" Mama frowned.

"Could be almost anyone." Abigail pushed her chair back away from the table, much further than usual due to her huge round stomach. She slowly stood up and headed toward the store front. "Coming, coming!" she called out as she waddled closer to the door. She stretched her arms out and grasped the long piece of wood that was cradled on either side of the door in metal hooks. Mr. Adair had handcrafted this sort of door lock to keep unruly drunken men from coming through the door in the middle of the night, since the Empire Hotel was so close at hand. The knocking got louder the longer she took.

"Hold your horses." Abigail called out as she set the piece of wood down and leaned it up against the wall. She unlatched the door and opened it up for whoever was outside.

"Abigail." Claude was pale as a ghost, his clothes wrinkled, and his shirttails weren't tucked into his trousers.

"Come in Claude," Abigail backed up from the doorway to let him in out of the cold. "What's going on? Why are you here so early?" Claude stepped through the door, took off his hat and held it in his hands in front of him. His black hair was standing on end, the five o'clock shadow told the story of his long day and night. Abigail could plainly see he looked exhausted.

"It's Jane." Claude took a deep breath. "It's not good."

"The baby?" Abigail held her breath waiting for his answer. Claude nodded slowly, tears welled up in his eyes.

"I am so sorry," Abigail reached out and touched his arm. "I really am, Claude."

"I know." Claude wiped the tear that had rolled down his cheek. "Jane isn't doing very well."

"Where is she now?" Abigail asked.

"Doc's," Claude began. "The bleeding wouldn't stop, I was so worried. I drove the horses as fast as I could."

"I should go be with her," Abigail said.

"She's resting." Claude rubbed his eye with his left hand. "Doc sent me away to let her sleep."

"Is she going to be all right?"

"I don't know," Claude put his hand on his hair and combed it back with his fingers.

"You better get some sleep yourself," Abigail told him.

"Non, non," Claude argued shaking his head, "I couldn't possibly sleep right now."

"Alright then, come to the kitchen." Abigail looped her arm in his arm and tugged him along. "Mama has breakfast made, you look like you need some nourishment."

"Mama, set another place," Abigail called out as she shuffled with Claude, both slowly making their way to the table.

"Good morning, Claude," Mama smiled. "What brings you here this early?" Abigail's mama asked. The three of them sat at the table quietly, as Claude told Abigail's mama about Jane.

"I am so sorry, lad." Mama reached over and placed her hand over the back of Claude's hand. "Abigail and I are always here for both of you."

"After dishes, I am going to go with Claude back to Doc's to check on Jane," Abigail explained. "Can you manage the store?"

"Of course," mama nodded. "But don't you be walking that far," she scolded.

"Don't worry, ma'am." Claude spoke up, "I have my horse and wagon."

"Are you sure you can even get into the wagon?"

"I think your mama has a point." Claude looked at Abigail.

"Oh, come on," Abigail looked surprised. "I am not that big." Abigail looked down, not able to see her shoes.

Both Claude and her mama looked at her with eyebrows raised.

"Alright, alright," she gave in, "so I can't see my shoes." Abigail didn't realize that being pregnant meant getting this big. She still had two months left. At least that's what Doc told her.

"I will tell Jane you would have come if you could." Claude told her.

"No." Abigail said plainly. "I am going."

"Abigail." Her mama glanced at her firmly.

"Mama." Abigail turned to her, "I am going, I will walk there. You know how poor Jane will be feeling. She needs another woman to talk to, she needs the next best thing to Jacob. I am going."

"But..."

"No buts," Abigail interrupted "I will be walking."

"It's cold." Claude added.

"I will bundle up."

"You know," Claude scratched his head, "I never knew you to be so stubborn."

"Well, you don't know me that well, then," Abigail laughed. "But if you would like to help me out, stop by and pick up the mail." Abigail was hoping for a new letter from Jacob. It had been weeks since she received that last one.

"Will do." Claude agreed as he stood up and walked over to the basin. "I will get cleaned up and take my time. You and Jane can have some time alone."

"I will do the dishes," mama said earnestly. "If you are going, then get going." Abigail knew her mama wasn't happy with her, but she had a duty to do. She understood how she would feel if this was happening to her; the loss of a baby when you have prepared your mind, body and life around it, then to have all that taken away. Abigail knew if Jacob was here he would be the first one over there giving all sorts of advice and words of encouragement. God gifted him with that. For her on the other hand, it didn't come as easily, but she wanted to do what Jacob would do and if that meant walking down there to comfort his sister, so be it.

Abigail reached the door front of Doc's house. She rapped on the door swiftly.

The door opened slowly. Mrs. Johnson smiled kindly to Abigail, letting her in without any words spoken. Abigail knew she was being quiet for Jane's sake.

"Come dear, sit down," Mrs. Johnson finally spoke. Doc's wife had a remarkable face and a beautiful physique. She directed Abigail to the tea table and chair that was in the sitting room area next to the kitchen. "I will make some tea." She went into the kitchen, poured water into the kettle and placed it on the cookstove.

"You're looking very well, Abigail." Mrs. Johnson spoke low. "Your baby must be a happy one," she smiled. Abigail smiled politely but anxiously.

"How is Jane?" Abigail cut to the chase.

"She is still sleeping." Mrs. Johnson informed.

"Claude said she was...well...you know...there was so much..." embarrassed by saying the words out loud, but Mrs. Johnson knew what she meant.

"Jane will be fine," Mrs. Johnson said with confidence. "She will need time to heal."

"And children?"

"She will have more children."

"Are you quite sure?" Abigail was still skeptical.

"Doc said she will still have many more children, Abigail," she explained. "Not to worry. She has to rest and take time to heal."

Mrs. Johnson poured each of them a cup of tea. She took homemade almond cookies out of a silver square tin, and placed them on a rose-painted serving plate.

"Help yourself," she nodded at Abigail.

Abigail picked up a cookie and took a bite. Her mind was anxiously thinking of Jane.

"Do you suppose Jane could be awake?" Abigail prompted.

"I will go check on her." Knowing what was on Abigail's mind, Mrs. Johnson stood up and went into Doc's patient room and came back quickly.

"You can come in."

"She's awake?" Abigail pushed her chair away from the table and placed her hand on the hard surface to help her to stand up. She walked as quickly as she could.

"Don't be too long," she warned, "Claude will be back soon." She squeezed Abigail's hand. "I will let you two visit."

Abigail wasn't sure what to expect. Jane was curled up on the bed like a small child. Her eyes swollen from crying, her mousy hair matted on the back of her head from lying for so long. Her face almost matched the white sheets she lay between. It broke Abigail's heart to see her in that weakened state.

"Hello, Jane," Abigail entered the room with a smile and slowly walked toward Jane. She reached out, picked up her hand and placed it in hers. Jane's lips quivered as she saw her sister-in-law approach. Tears flowed from her eyes once again, she turned her head with embarrassment. Not always do words need to be spoken in moments such as this. Abigail sat down in the white wooden chair beside the bed.

"It's going to be alright," she reassured Jane quietly as she listened to Jane weep softly.

"How was Jane?" Abigail's mama asked as she walked through the doorway. "I hope you didn't catch cold or play yourself out."

"Oh, mama, I am fine." Abigail spoke as she took off her hat and hung it on the hook by the door. Her mama helped her take off her coat as she told her how Jane was doing.

"She will be back to normal in no time," Abigail spoke optimistically as she put on her oversized apron for the rest of the working day.

"I left as soon as Claude returned," Abigail continued. "I believe he is taking her home today."

"The poor girl."

"You know, mama," Abigail began, "I couldn't help but feel so much guilt as I sat there with Jane."

"I know, dear." He mama sympathized as she swept the floor.

"I was supposed to be consoling her with words of wisdom, just as Jacob would have if he were here." Abigail continued, "but all I did was sit there, and say 'everything will be alright' while feeling extremely guilty for still being with child."

"Oh, dear." Her mama stopped sweeping and walked to her and gave her a big hug. "Don't feel that way, everything happens for a reason. It's God's plan." She smiled, "Do I have to turn into Jacob now?"

"I know, I know," Abigail shook her head, "but I can't help feeling this way."

"You need to worry about yourself, now," she reminded her, "you are getting close to becoming a mama and soon you will be giving your own advice."

"I don't think I could possibly be as great a mama as you," she grinned with a wink.

That night Abigail sat down at her desk that was next to her bed. She lit the lamp with a strike of a match and covered it with the clear glass chimney. She then picked up the box which held her lavender coloured paper. She took the lid off the ink well, dipped her black-stemmed ink pen into the dark liquid and tapped it against the side. She began to write.

Dearest Jacob,

*It's been so long since I have heard your voice,
and felt your touch. I am missing you terribly,
today especially. I sure could have used your help*

and so could your sister. You see, today Jane and Claude lost their baby. Oh, Jacob, I feel so remorseful. We are going to have a beautiful baby and your sister will not, at least not this time. I tried to comfort her, but all I could do was sit there. If only you were here to give the well-deserved advice that was needed. Poor Claude, you should have seen him. He was lost and heartbroken.

How have you been my darling? Wherever you are, be sure to know that I love you with all my heart, body, mind and soul. And soon we will be parents and have a little person to love with each of our beings.

I am praying for you Jacob, and Charles too. Reverend Young has been having weekly prayer meetings to pray for all the local soldiers who have left their families to go to war.

I am waiting for the day you walk through that doorway and hold me once again.

All my love,
Abigail

Abigail folded the letter in thirds, slid it into the envelope, then licked the flap and pressed it closed. She wrote Jacob's name and address along with her return address in the top left hand corner. She held the envelope close to her heart, closed her eyes and whispered, "I love you, Jacob. God speed you home." Just then Abigail felt a strong pressing in the side of her belly. The baby had kicked, she smiled as she placed her hand on the moving spot. *If only Jacob could feel this right now, he would be thrilled,* she thought to herself.

Abigail stood up and walked past the end of her bed toward the east window. She pushed the parchment-coloured curtain to the side and revealed the darkness with only the moon shedding light. The snow blew around the already white ground and gusts burst around the trees outside her window pane.

"Oh, Jacob, I pray you are safe and warm somewhere," Abigail spoke out loud. She took in a deep breath and released the curtain.

Prayer. That indeed was what she didn't do. Abigail sat down on her bedside and began to pray.

chapter three

My darling Girlie,

I was sure happy to receive your letter, but I am so sorry to hear of Jane's miscarriage. It's a terrible time for her without her ma to help her through this difficult time. She is tough though, and I know she will bounce back. Claude is a good husband and understanding to her nature. There will be other babies. The Lord wasn't ready to make her a mama yet. I guess he needed his angel in heaven. Jane and Claude are in my prayers.

I wonder if ever you see much of Peter? I thought maybe he would drop me a letter or two before now. I realize how busy he is farming and helping out the neighbours while their son fights along with us. I do think of him often and wonder how he and his family are doing. I did receive a letter from Sarah. It was good to read her news. She must not be keeping in touch with Jane, as she didn't say anything about Jane's condition.

We are continuing to dig trenches. Many seem to take so long. The rain pours, and some days it defeats the purpose of digging, when all it does is fill in as fast as we can get it out. So sorry my letter is dirty, it's so hard to keep the stationery clean around here.

I have to go my darling, I love you and miss you every day. I pray for the day that we will be together again.

Miss you with all my heart,
Jacob

Abigail held the letter close to her heart after she finished reading it. As fast as she read it, she was already longing for another. It was good to read his words and know that he was alright.

It had been quite some time since Jane's miscarriage. Abigail thought about her and Claude each day. When she looked down at her large belly, holding it, feeling her baby kick sporadically, it made her heart hurt all the more for her dear sister-in-law. As she swept the floor of The General Store, the bell hanging above the door rang. Abigail looked toward a familiar face.

"Good morning, Claude," Abigail smiled as she stood still with the broom in her hand. She noticed his unkempt hair when he removed his hat, and the dark whiskers covering his face. His eyes were tired as he smiled faintly.

"Bonjour, madam." He stepped closer to Abigail.

"How are you doing?" Her concerned eyes watched him as he bowed his head and looked at the floor.

"I am alright, but Jane-" he stopped.

"Is she-" Abigail began as Claude continued to tell her.

"She is taking this really hard." He looked straight at Abigail. "She won't eat, she won't sleep and she won't get out of bed either." He shook his head.

"Oh, dear," Abigail's eyes narrowed, "what can I do?"

"I don't know if there is anything anyone can do." He brushed his hand over his forehead. "Reverend Young has been out to Crocus Flats. Doc has come and checked on her and even Mrs. Ford has tried to talk to her."

"Maybe if I go and talk to her."

"I wish it were that easy." Claude rubbed his chin. "I am worried sick about her. With the chores and the house, I am not sure what to do anymore."

"I will get my coat," Abigail turned around and walked toward the kitchen. "I will let mama know I am going with you," she called over her shoulder.

"Are you sure-" Claude called back to her, but she was already telling her mother.

"Mama, I will be back tonight." Abigail explained as she gathered her bag and put a few items in it.

"Where are you going?" Her mama's concerned face stared at her as Abigail hobbled from room to room and explained what she was going to do. "In your condition?" Her mama asked.

"Oh, mama," she smiled, "in my condition?" She repeated humorously. "I am having a baby not spreading a disease."

"But the wagon ride," she persisted. "It could cause-"

"It will be fine mama," she patted her arm reassuringly. "Doc says I am as healthy as a horse, I feel good and Jacob's sister needs me."

"I know honey, but-" she tried to think of another reason she should stay home.

"I will see you tonight." Abigail kissed her mama's cheek and Claude helped her put on her coat. She sat down on the chair near the door to put on her boots. The huge bulge in the front of her made it hard to bend over. She managed her footwear on her own, but she did accept help from Claude to get up onto the wagon.

The ride was cold and long, but Abigail didn't think about how frozen her feet felt or how rough the trail was. She was wrapped up in the blanket Claude gave her and thought about the words she was going to say that would make a difference in Jane's life. What would Jacob tell her? What would he do?

As the horses pulled the wagon down the Crocus Flats lane, Daisy, their dog, came running to greet them. She jumped excitedly as she got closer to the horses, happy to see her master return home.

"Bonjour," Claude called out as he set his hat on the hook and continued on into the kitchen. "I am home," he continued to holler. "She must be still in bed." He looked at Abigail as she took off her coat and hung it on the back of the kitchen chair.

Abigail reached out, caught Claude's arm and stopped him from moving forward.

"Let me go alone," she whispered. Claude nodded, as he stepped aside and watched Abigail walk to the bedroom.

Abigail reached the bedroom door, it was partially open. She lightly knocked, and slowly pushed the door open.

"Jane?" She said, and walked into the room gingerly. "Hello? It's me, Abigail."

Abigail looked about the room. Clothes were scattered across the floor, shirts were draped over the back of the chair and socks were piled on top of the chest of drawers. The curtains were closed shut with a hair pin that kept the sun from shining through the crack between the panels.

The quilt was bunched on top of the bed with the sheets twisted into a long row. Jane laid on the bed next to the lump, still dressed in her long white nightgown with her housecoat wrapped around her tightly. She stared at the wall adjacent to the bed, without even moving or acknowledging that Abigail was there.

"I know you're hurting, Jane," Abigail began as she picked up the clothes from the chair which was next to the bed. She held each arm of the chair and slowly sat down. Jane kept staring. Her hair was strewn every which way and hadn't been combed in days. "I can't say I know what you're going through."

"You're right," Jane continued to look forward as she spoke, "you don't." Her voice broke as she wiped her nose with the back of her hand.

Abigail didn't expect the cold response that she received from Jacob's sister. She thought a few kind words, a pat on the hand and a sweet smile and Jane would be back to her normal, former, serious self. Honestly, she didn't think it would be quite that easy but she thought it maybe was going to be a little less awkward than it was at this moment. Probably the fact that she was expecting herself didn't help matters. Abigail didn't think of this. She remembered how Jacob was with people. He always had the right words, the right sentiment and always seemed to make everything alright with the world again.

Abigail took a deep breath and said a silent prayer under her breath.

"No, I don't know how you feel." Abigail looked at Jane as she spoke quietly. "I won't pretend to know, and how could I? Truth is, I can't imagine what you are going through."

Abigail shifted in her chair trying to find a comfortable spot. Jane continued to stare straight ahead. Abigail reached out to Jane and placed her hand over hers. Tears filled up Jane's eyes and spilled out down her cheeks. Abigail wasn't sure what else to say.

"I-," Jane sniffed, "I didn't know-" she stopped.

"It's alright, you don't have to say anything." Abigail softly rubbed the top of her hand. "I only want you to know, that you are not alone, that we are here for you, always."

"I didn't know it would hurt this much," Jane finally said. "It's not like I was-." She let out a small cry.

"It doesn't matter how far along you were," Abigail looked at Jane's expressionless face, "it was still your baby, and it hurts no matter what."

"I know, I am being foolish." Jane's eyes met Abigail's. "But for some reason, I can't stop feeling-"

"You are in mourning, Jane, it's natural to feel sad and for your heart to hurt."

"I don't even want to get up in the morning, or any part of the day for that matter."

"It takes time."

"Claude has been so good about everything." Jane wiped away the tears from her jaw line.

"He's worried about you."

"I know, but I don't know what to do."

"Can we pray together?"

"No- I mean- I don't feel like praying."

"Do you want me to pray with you?"

Abigail still hadn't become a confident prayer warrior. Jacob always led the prayers in their home. Other than her own private prayers, he did it all. Despite her nervousness to pray out loud in front of anyone, she persevered to help Jane.

"It's a little late for that now!" Jane snapped.

"Your baby is in heaven, Jane," Abigail reassured her, "Praying will give you peace and comfort."

"I am sorry, Abigail," Jane pulled her hand away from Abigail, "but I am not feeling well."

"I will go make you some tea, and something for you to eat." Abigail gripped the chair arms as she pushed herself up and tried not to make her "condition," as her mama called it, so obvious. *What was she going to tell Claude? That she made no headway? That it wasn't as easy as she thought? That Jane had given up hope in God, and in Life? She couldn't do that, she couldn't let Jane give up!* She made her way to the kitchen using the back stairway that ran down the other side of the main staircase. It was a shortcut from the front of the house to the back.

"Well?" Claude quickly stood up from the table when Abigail entered the room.

"I am going to make her some tea and a bite to eat." Abigail walked to the pail of drinking water.

"I have taken her more tea than any one person can drink."
Claude's voice grew suddenly louder. "How much more tea
does she need to make her better?"

Claude abruptly sat down, shaking his head.

"I am sorry." He ran his fingers through his hair then held
his head in his hands. "I don't know what to do."

"She will be alright." Abigail filled the kettle with water
and placed it on the cookstove. "You both will be alright. It
just takes time."

"I hope you're right," Claude looked over at Abigail. "I
sure hope you're right."

"Why don't you go out and do your chores and I will make
us all some lunch."

While Claude was outside, she took a cup of tea to Jane.
She fried scrambled eggs and bacon with sliced potatoes.

"How about you come into the kitchen and eat, Jane."
Abigail stood at the bedroom doorway. "You will feel better,
and Claude would be happy to see you out and about." She
coaxed.

"I don't feel like it," moaned Jane. "I just-"

Abigail was beginning to think kindness wasn't working.

"You aren't the only one who lost your baby!" Abigail
snapped.

Jane looked back at Abigail in disbelief.

"Don't you think your husband is hurting?" Abigail put
her hands on her hips feeling like her mother at this point.
Jane looked away.

"Not only has he lost his little boy who would walk in
his footstep or his baby girl who may resemble her mama,"
Abigail stood up straight, slid her hand from her hip to the
small of her back and rubbed it gently, "Claude is slowly losing
the love of his life -- the woman he vowed to spend the rest
of his life with, through sickness and in health, for richer or
poorer." Abigail's voice softened as she walked into the room

and sat on the edge of the bed opposite to Jane. "He needs his wife back."

Jane turned over in the bed toward Abigail, her face stained with wet tears.

"There will be other babies," Abigail encouraged. "You will be blessed with a little one someday." Abigail rubbed the side of her abdomen as she felt her own baby push its feet against her side.

"Come to the kitchen to eat?" Abigail held her breath hoping her firm prose worked. Not that she didn't mean every word -- she certainly did. She felt guilty for speaking that way to her, but she didn't know what else to do. Jacob wasn't here so she needed to do things her way.

Jane slowly moved and she swung her legs over the edge of the bed. Standing up, she retied the housecoat ties and began walking toward the door. Abigail got up and followed her to the kitchen.

Without a word, Jane sat down in front of the place setting at the table while Abigail put a plate of food in front of her.

"Thank you," Jane softly said and looked down at the scrambled eggs. She picked up the fork, moved the food around for a few seconds and finally scooped up a forkful and put it in her mouth. Abigail set another cup of tea in front of her. *According to Jacob, Bert says tea cures everything,* Abigail thought to herself.

"How about you sit in the living room and enjoy the sunshine when you're done eating." Abigail pushed it.

"Alright." Jane didn't argue.

Abigail went back to the bedroom and picked up the quilt from their bed. She took it to the chair that sat near the east window.

Jane ate everything on her plate and finished the tea, then she got comfortable in the chair Abigail prepared for her. Jane thought about the countless days her mama spent sitting in this exact chair after Lucy disappeared. She would sit weeping for hours, and then she would stare out the window, looking at nothing. There were many times when she slept there as well. *I wonder what mama felt like after losing Allie?* Jane thought to herself. *And she must have been beside herself when Lucy disappeared. Oh, what a fool she was being, what a burden she was being to her dear Claude, who loved her unconditionally.* She thought about her family. Her mama had died not knowing what happened to Lucy, her pa had begged forgiveness before he passed away and her dear brother Andrew had died from his injuries in an accident a couple of years ago. Through all her family's tragedies, Jane had always been there for everyone, and yet this is what put her over the edge. This is what broke her. She was the one who kept the family together during the hard times and yet this loss took her peace, her joy, made her self-centred and depressed while she thought only of herself.

While Jane was absorbing the sunshine, Abigail took the opportunity to strip their bed and make it again with clean sheets. She tidied up the bedroom. When she was finished, Abigail began to clean up the kitchen. Claude walked in the doorway while she was washing the dishes.

"Smells good in here." He took off his coat and hat. When he looked past Abigail, he saw Jane sitting in the living room and his eyes widened. Abigail smiled.

"But how?" He whispered.

Abigail shrugged her shoulders as she dried a plate with a tea towel. "Just give her some time," she suggested.

Claude slowly walked through the kitchen and into the living room. Jane turned toward him, slightly smiling. Claude walked quicker and fell down to his knees beside her chair, scooped her hands up in his and looked up at her without saying a word.

"I am so sorry, Claude," Jane sobbed. Claude wrapped his arms around her and pulled her close to him. "I have been so selfish, so terrible to you."

"There, there," Claude soothed. "It doesn't matter now."

Jane shook her head against his chest.

"No, it's not right," she continued to wail, "not right."

"It's forgotten." Claude stroked the back of her hair.

Abigail smiled as she witnessed the love between a husband and his wife blossom into a bond that not every couple experienced.

Claude and Jane talked for quite a while in the living room. Abigail kept busy with household chores and started supper for that evening.

"Thank you, Abigail," Jane smiled at her sister-in-law who was standing at the table ready to leave.

"Will you be alright while I am gone, mon petit chou?" Claude held Jane in a long hug before leaving.

"I will be fine, Claude." She didn't want him fussing over her so much. It embarrassed her. "The quicker you go, the quicker you will be back."

"Touché," he smiled, happy to have his wife back. Realizing it wasn't always going to be easy, but as they talked before, Jane was going to try hard to move forward and be a wife again. They both hoped there would be more babies. They had a lot of time and their family would grow one day in God's perfect timing. They prayed together, wept together and just held each other in silence. But they both knew it was going to take time and a huge effort on both their parts.

"Now, get out of here." Jane flapped her hands in a fanning motion to get them to leave.

Again Claude helped Abigail onto the wagon and covered her up with quilts. Abigail was cold and tired, that was for sure, but she felt warm in her heart. Her head bobbed as the wagon shook from side to side while the horses loped along the trail back to Abbington Pickets.

"Merci, Abigail." Claude helped her down off the wagon. He held her hand as she stepped down, first to the step then to the ground. "I can't say it enough," he smiled. He had already told her more than five times on the ride home.

"We are family," Abigail smiled. "You would have done the same for me or Jacob." Claude smiled though Abigail saw concern in his eyes. "Don't worry, but pray about everything."

"Merci." He repeated and nodded to her. He watched her waddle her way back to The General Store. He climbed back into the wagon, turned the horses around and headed back to Crocus Flats. He didn't want to leave Jane any longer than necessary.

As Abigail reached the door to The General Store, she thought about the letter she was going to write to Jacob before going to bed this evening.

chapter four

Morning came far too quickly for Abigail's liking. She had stayed up late writing to Jacob and told him about his sister and Claude.

> *...Jacob, you would have been proud of your*
> *wife. I was strong and assertive, but loving and*
> *kind all at the same time. I know you would have*
> *maybe handled this a little differently but God*
> *spoke to me, Jacob, He gave me the words to say...*

Abigail continued to tell Jacob of her day with Jane and how Claude came to see her, grateful for her help. She explained how her mama had watched out for her and helped her so much with the housework while she worked The General Store and did other odd jobs around the house.

> *...Mama is here helping me until the baby*
> *comes. I am grateful to have her.*
> *You asked me about Peter, he was in for some*
> *goods a couple of weeks ago. I don't see him often*

but I know he has been helping his neighbours as you said. They are short handed since both sons and their field hand went to war. I believe Claude has all he can handle, and I know with Jane on his mind so much he will be glad to have his wife back. I haven't heard from Sarah lately and Jane has never mentioned anything of her either. All are busy with their own lives and doing what's necessary for their families by making many sacrifices.

Oh, Jacob, I miss you so much, Jacob, it hurts. I thrive on every letter you write. I need you to come home, my darling, we are all praying for your safe return.

So much love,
Your Girlie.

Abigail tossed and turned and didn't sleep well. Her mind was full with thoughts of Claude and Jane going over and over in her head, Jacob in another country as she tried to keep a handle on The General Store, expect a baby and pay the bills that keep coming in. Her swollen belly seemed larger than usual and extremely uncomfortable, which contributed to her intense discomfort when lying in bed.

She needed her energy for the day she and mama had planned. They were going to get some things ready for when the baby arrived. Abigail had made a new skirt for the bassinet that Jane had given her. Each of the Hudson children had spent the first few months in this bassinet. Abigail felt a little guilty for having it when she found out about Jane expecting, but Jane assured her it was fine. Jacob would be so thrilled that his son or daughter would be cozily wrapped in the same bed he slept in as an infant. She added that Claude wanted to build their first baby's cradle anyway and start a new tradition for their family. Abigail understood and knew that if Jacob was here, and there was no war going on, he would in fact be building his own baby's crib.

She had also made baby sheets and a little quilt to match. Abigail felt very blessed, as several neighbours stopped by over the past few months and brought her baby clothes. She was so grateful and happy to receive such wonderful gifts. Everything helped, more than they knew, but maybe they did know.

Mama and Aunt Gladys had hand sewn small bibs and two bonnets. One was for good and the other for every day. Abigail pulled out a small washstand with a top drawer and two doors below. She thought it would make a nice dresser for baby clothes until the baby was older.

Today Abigail and her mama were going to set up a temporary area in the dining room for the 'baby's room' with all the items he or she would need until a few months older. Later the baby would have its own room upstairs.

"There," Abigail smiled as she stepped back from the bassinet after she put the skirt on and made the small bed. It had a little pillow with the word 'baby' hand embroidered on it for a decoration. "That looks great if I do say so myself," she beamed alongside her mama.

"This baby is one blessed child." Mama put her arms around Abigail. "And to have parents as wonderful as you and Jacob she will be one special baby."

"She?" Abigail looked at her mama wide eyed. "Do you know something I don't?" She giggled.

"Well, of course, it's going to be a girl." She informed her daughter.

"What makes you so sure?" Abigail raised an eyebrow.

"Well, my dear," she grinned, "it runs in the family."

"Oh, really?"

"Yep, look at you," she pointed out. "Your father and I had you - a fine young lady. My mama and papa had your Aunt Gladys and I, and their mama and papa had three girls..."

"Alright, alright," Abigail laughed, "I see your point. But what about papa? He had three brothers. And Jacob, his family was made up of half girls and half boys."

"It's going to be a girl." Mama stood firm on her statement as she crossed her arms in front of her. Nobody was going to change her mind.

"Well, I guess it won't be too long before we find out." Abigail shook her head as she took the dishcloth and wiped the washstand.

"I will line the drawer with some paper." Mama opened the drawer, looked inside and squinted up her face. "I will wash it out first. Do you have some paper Abigail?"

"I think there is some in the office." Abigail passed the cloth to her mama. "I will go and look." Abigail stood up straight and stretched her back as she rubbed her hip. She waddled toward the store office.

She struck a match, lifted the chimney of the oil lamp and held it to one side as she lit the wick with the flame. The room illuminated as she placed the chimney back on top of the lamp and adjusted the knob to the right amount of flame.

Abigail walked over to the big closet against the wall where the Adairs had left it. Jacob and Abigail hadn't changed much in the store when they took over after the accidental death of Mr. and Mrs. Adair. There wasn't really much time. First with the store so busy, then they built their home, then Jacob went off to war.

Abigail opened the double doors to the closet and revealed six shelves full of boxes, books and tin cans full of odds and ends. There was a wooden box which held an alphabetical index of cards with customers' accounts. There were rolled up maps stacked neatly to one side on one of the shelves.

Abigail pushed aside the tin cans to see the back of the closet. She thought she had seen some flowered paper in there somewhere. She moved the tins back and looked on the next shelf above that one. Abigail stretched her arms to reach what she thought was the paper. She felt around with her hands more than she could see, but to no avail. There was a broken lamp and a chimney standing up next to it. She wondered why they would keep a defective item like that. Not finding anything on the upper shelves and the ones that were level with her, Abigail finally resorted to the last two at the bottom. She had left them until last as bending down wasn't easy for her.

Abigail strained as she grabbed a chair near the desk and dragged it to the front of the cupboard. She sat down slowly and gripped the arms as she finally rested on its seat. She leaned forward and moved books, small boxes and paper bags filled with paperclips. Abigail took in a deep breath. *Well, maybe I was wrong, maybe there isn't any decorative paper here like I thought,* Abigail said to herself. The last shelf held more stationary items, such as ink, paper, receipt books and things of that nature. Abigail was going to give up. *I guess I will have to use the brown paper from the store,* she told herself.

Abigail was about to sit up straight when something caught her eye. It was a small stack of papers clipped together, but what got her attention was the name on the top sheet, 'Mr. Rodgers.' *There were no other Rodgers in the area, were there?* She asked herself. Abigail picked up the handful of papers and placed them on her lap. Above her father's name there was a red stamp which read 'PAST DUE', but further down, it said in black 'PAID IN FULL.' She saw the date on the top right hand corner.

"Why, this is before pa had his stroke," Abigail whispered out loud.

There were groceries and goods listed on the paper and the ten or so pages that were behind it. Abigail flipped through further back and there were more recent accounts of food and supplies for the ranch. At the top, it no longer said Mr. Rodgers. It said 'Jacob Hudson.' She continued to look at each sheet and the items purchased. Each one said paid.

Abigail continued to read each bill, engrossed with each page.

"Abigail, what's tak-" her mama walked into the office up to her daughter.

"Mama, what's this?" Abigail held out her hand full of papers. Mrs. Rodgers stopped in her place, her face dropped and turned a little pale. "What does this mean?" Abigail grabbed the chair arms, pushed herself up and stood before her mama.

"Let me explain." Mama's eyes narrowed as she stepped back. She didn't need to look at the papers Abigail was holding. She knew perfectly well what they were. "We didn't want to tell you."

"Tell me what?" Abigail's cheeks reddened.

"It was quite a while ago," stuttering her words slightly as she tried to explain. "And Jacob was-"

"Why didn't you tell me?" She insisted.

"Your pa, I mean we..." mama licked her lips, "we were ashamed." She whispered and put her head down.

"Your pa had just had his stroke," she began. "I didn't know what to do. I spent more nights walking the floor knowing we owed money to the Adairs."

"You could have shared with your own daughter," she argued.

"You were so worried about your father," her eyes met Abigail's. "You spent every waking moment with your pa."

"But-"

"Jacob was there one night. I poured my heart out to the young lad," she continued. "Your Jacob was a gift from God. I begged him not to tell you, Abigail. We didn't want to bring shame to you and Jacob obliged my request. He was so gracious."

Abigail breathed in and looked away from her mama. She didn't know whether she should be mad or happy.

"That's Jacob," she whispered.

"Not only did he pay the outstanding debt, he paid for everything every month since until your father was better and back on his feet." Mrs. Rodgers wiped the tears from her face.

"But our wedding-" Abigail looked back up at her mama, "our house-" she shook her head, tears welling up in her eyes.

"To be honest," her mama sniffed as she played with the handkerchief she held in her hands, "I don't know how Jacob did what he did. It was like a miracle." She put the hankie back in her apron pocket. "He even found Claude, hired him to work for your father and paid for him every week."

Abigail gasped at the thought of how Claude had given him such grief because of her the first few months he was there. The hurt it must have caused Jacob. Oh, my poor, sweet Jacob. The sacrifices he made for my family, for our love and happiness and still he was happy. The love Abigail felt for this honest, hardworking honourable man tripled in size, if it were at all possible. Her heart swelled with pride to know he was willing to take care of his in-laws before they were even related.

"Oh, mama," Abigail stepped toward her. She reached out, pulled her close and hugged her like there was no tomorrow. She petted the back of her neck, soothing her. She knew that her heart must have been aching over this these past few years. That the shame she harboured had caused her to lose that weight when she was so weak while her pa was sick. Jacob had worked so early every morning until so very late every night. She thought back. Now it made sense, everything began to go together like a puzzle. But the biggest blessing to her was the fact that her husband honoured her parents in a way no one had ever done before.

"I am so sorry, Abigail," her mama sobbed into her shoulder as they remained embraced.

"You have nothing to be sorry for, mama." Abigail pulled back, her eyes met her mama's. "I wish you would have told me," she smiled weakly.

"Would it have made a difference?" Mrs. Rodgers asked. "I could have got a job in the village."

"Then who would have looked after your father and me?" Her mama pointed out.

Mama was right. What would she have done? She spent all her hours sitting with her pa, and when she wasn't doing that she was helping her mama. There was no time to be in town for work. If she had, her mama may not be here right now to help her get ready for her little baby.

"Let's go make some tea." Abigail put her arm around her mama. They walked slowly together toward the kitchen.

"Oh, and I guess it's going to be brown paper lining for the drawer for the baby," Abigail smiled. "For the life of me, I couldn't find the fancy paper I was looking for." They both laughed.

"It's alright, dear," her mama reassured her, "it will be clean just the same, flowers or no flowers."

She was right.

chapter five

"Abigail, come quick." A voice lingered in Abigail's mind while her head was hazy with dream-filled slumber.

"Abigail." The voice repeated.

"I'm awake." Abigail's eyes opened and immediately squinted up at her mama who stood at her bedside standing over her. She was still in her housecoat, her wavy brown hair with sparse strands of grey accented her long braid draped down over her shoulder.

"Sorry to wake you so suddenly," her mama's expression spoke volumes.

"What is it?" Abigail picked up her covers and threw them back. "What's wrong?" She tried to pull herself up, but the huge ball in front of her prevented her from sitting up. Her mama reached for her arm and pulled her forward, helped her land her feet on the floor and stand upright instantly. "Tell me, what is it?" she insisted as she looked for her slippers. Her mama grabbed Abigail's housecoat and held it up as Abigail put her arms in one at a time, while talking.

"Ernest is here," she bluntly informed her as she cracked a smile.

"What?" Abigail's eyebrows raised up into her forehead as she grabbed the ties of her housecoat and looped them through one another to tie a knot. "Where is he?" Abigail couldn't wait to see what Ernest looked like. The only thing that went through her mind was Jacob. *If Ernest appeared in good health, then Jacob also has to be alright, right?* She asked herself. She reached for the knob of her bedroom door and waddled as fast as she could go to reach the store.

"He's waiting at the front counter." Her mama followed, talking behind her, hardly getting a word out before she reached Ernest.

"Ernest." Abigail exclaimed as she walked up behind the soldier who stood and leaned against the counter. He still had his coat on, and held his hat in his hand. He slowly partially turned around and gave a shy smile.

"Abig...ail." Ernest hesitated as he watched her come closer to him. "You are...well...look..." He put his head down and coughed as he breathed in.

"You meant huge, didn't you?" Abigail laughed. "It's alright, I know it and you don't have to be embarrassed." Abigail reached out to hug Ernest, he reluctantly reciprocated. As she got near him, he looked toward her and that's when she noticed the patch over his eye. She pretended not to notice as she embraced him.

She could hardly wait to ask about Jacob but undoubtedly noticed Ernest didn't look well. His face was pallid and thin, while his good eye was dark and sunk in. His dirty blonde hair appeared more dirty than blonde and longer than he would usually keep it. His regular bare fresh face was covered with dark bristles. Abigail worried, *how could six months bring a man to this state. It must be worse than she feared. Poor Jacob, poor Charles.* Her heart pounded anxiously, not really knowing why, but she couldn't help but feel much more helpless now that she has seen what she feared the most.

"I apologize," Ernest took a breath, "for coming in so early this morning." Again he tried to take another breath but began to cough hard into his hand as he explained. The clock rang four times. "But I got in on the train at Pickets," he spoke in between breaths, "and there was another young lad… offering me a ride, as he was driving through Abbington Pickets." Ernest took a moment to catch his breath.

It was obvious why he was back so soon. Although Abigail still worried about it, she didn't dare ask and Ernest could see the questions on her face.

"I got sick leave." Ernest coughed again, almost uncontrollably, as he hunched down heaving over and over.

"Are you alright?" Abigail began to get really concerned. "We will go get Doc."

Ernest shook his head as he buried it into his arm, coughed, then raised his arm in an attempt to stop her from leaving. He dug into his pocket and pulled out a dingy white hankie.

"Mama," Abigail looked at her mama, "go get Ernest some water." She turned back to Ernest.

"I think you need to sit down." She held onto his arm and walked him toward the living quarters of the store which were located in the full width of the back, adjacent to the office and pantry. The sitting room was in the same room as the kitchen which was on the northwest end of the building. The main bedroom was in the northeast corner and the other two bedrooms were up the stairs, along with a storage room. There was a potbelly wood stove in the centre of the store to keep that part of the building warm and a cookstove in the kitchen to warm the home part of the building. Abigail helped Ernest sit down on the couch and her mama brought him a glass of water. He took the glass from her with his shaky hand and took a sip.

"Take your time," Abigail encouraged. He looked up at Abigail gratefully and gave her a nod. "You should see Doc once daybreak comes. Do Bert and Alice know you were coming?"

"No, ma'am." Ernest shook his head, but didn't argue about seeing the doc. "I was in an English infantry hospital with pneumonia at first," Ernest explained between breaths. "Once the fever broke...they sent me back out...that's when a grenade... blew through a window... close to where I was..."

"Take your time, Ernest." Abigail smiled anxiously.

Ernest took another short breath before continuing.

"Glass was everywhere... including in my eyes." He shook his head. "... the glass scratched... the lens of my left eye. I am blind in my left eye... While I was recovering... fluid set in my lungs... the pneumonia came back in full force. Ernest was played out by this time.

"Jacob?" Abigail looked intensely at Ernest.

"He's alright, Charles too." Was all Ernest commented on. He struggled to reach into his inside pocket, he fumbled and dug deep, so it seemed, but was successful for what he sought.

"He sent this to you," Ernest handed Abigail a ragged envelope. The corners were worn and dirty from being hidden in his pocket since the night Jacob had handed it to him.

"Thank you, Ernest." Abigail took it slowly from him. Inside her heart leapt for joy. She didn't want it made known that she couldn't wait until she was alone to read it.

Mama made breakfast, Abigail went back to her bedroom to get dressed. She then stoked both stoves and filled them with chopped wood. The bell over the door rang and Abigail looked to see who came through the doorway.

"Doc!" Abigail closed the door of the round stove. "Just the person we want to see."

"Well, it so happens the missis was out of coffee for breakfast this morning."

"Ernest," Abigail began, "you know, Bert's brother-in-law." She walked over to the counter, reached for a tin of coffee and set it on the counter. "He's back from the army. He needs your help."

"Yes, I know who you mean," Doc answered. "Is he hurt? Wounded?"

"Blind in one eye and pneumonia, he can hardly breathe."

"He's lucky that's all that's wrong with him," Doc stated gruffly. "Where is he?"

"He's in the kitchen with mama, having breakfast."

Doc placed eight cents on the wood counter top then followed Abigail to the back of the store into the kitchen.

"Good morning, my boy," Doc approached Ernest.

"Hello, sir," Ernest nodded, then began to cough once again.

"Let's take a look at you." Doc sat down in the chair next to him.

"We will leave you alone," Abigail told them. "Mama, I think we have some dusting to do in The General Store."

"I think you're right." Her mama took off her apron and hung it on the pantry door knob. They both left Doc to examine Ernest.

It wasn't too long before Doc came into The General Store. "I don't think Ernest should go home," Doc informed Abigail and her ma, "at least not yet."

"We can make the couch up for him," mama suggested.

"Nonsense," Abigail interjected. "I can sleep upstairs, he can have my room."

"I beg your pardon, dear," her mama argued, "but you can barely walk as it is. You can't expect to go up and down those stairs."

"Your mama is right," Doc agreed. "The couch will be fine for him."

"Oh, alright." Abigail threw her hands in the air, "you two win, but not for lack of my trying." She cracked a smile.

"He shouldn't be doing stairs either. In fact, he shouldn't be doing much of anything, but sitting up a lot. The pneumonia is still there, and I don't want it to get any worse. I will check on him each day. I want to keep an eye on him before he goes home. He would be too far away from a doctor."

"We understand," Abigail said matter-of-factly.

"I know you will take good care of him," Doc looked at Abigail. "After all, you helped your father get better."

"Oh, no, Doc," Abigail proudly grinned, "that was all God and Jacob."

"Well, whatever it was," Doc put on his hat, began to put on his coat and head toward the door, "it was a miracle."

"Indeed," mama agreed.

"Jacob doesn't give up, nor did he let The Lord give up," she continued to boast. Abigail loved any time she could pay a well-deserved compliment to Jacob. He taught her how to love God, be faithful to Him and to count her blessings. She watched as Jacob's continuous faith brought real miracles. Things weren't always easy but with The Lord and Jacob by her side, she never felt alone. With Jacob gone, her faith was being tested.

"Don't worry, Doc." Abigail walked to the door, "we will take good care of him."

"I have no doubt." The wind blew in the doorway as Doc opened it and stepped outside. The gust of snowflakes felt cool on Abigail's warm face. It made her think of Jacob who trained for war in this bitter cold weather with nothing but a soldier's uniform to keep him warm. *I know Jacob is strong, strong at heart, strong in body and strong in his faith. Is he strong enough to handle this war?* She asked herself.

Abigail turned from the door after it closed.

"I know, mama," she began, "we shall start a women's group."

"For what?" Her mama looked at her strangely.

"For the war effort, of course," she announced as if her mama was silly for not knowing what she was talking about.

"And what exactly will you be doing?" Her mama was still no wiser to the idea that Abigail pitched.

"Sew quilts, knit socks, scarves and possibly sew shirts," Abigail listed one by one, "whatever it takes to keep our men warm."

"I have some yarn at Goldenrod," her mama began to see her vision.

"Perfect. Mrs. Adair kept some old bolts of fabric upstairs, we can start cutting squares for quilts."

"I can..." Ernest slowly entered the room. "...help"

"That would be wonderful." Abigail smiled, she knew it was something he could do at his own pace. "I will g-"

"You will not go upstairs for that fabric," her mama interrupted.

"But..." Abigail began to argue.

"You are not going up those stairs in your condition," she looked seriously at her. "No buts, I will go upstairs for you. Just tell me where the fabric is."

"Oh, Alright," Abigail huffed. "The bolts are in the wardrobe in the northwest bedroom, I believe."

"I will head up there and fetch the bolts now." Her mama headed toward the staircase that was behind the front counter back wall.

"I will begin to make posters to hang here in the store." Abigail went into the office to retrieve supplies to begin her project.

"I will make the tea." Ernest turned back toward the kitchen.

Abigail was smiling to herself for most of the afternoon. She felt proud of herself for thinking up such a good idea. It made her feel like she was actually doing something for this war, not just sitting at home waiting for her husband to return. Anyone who came into the store was told about the idea, and if they were men she sent notes with them for their wives at home. If the women came in, she sat them down for tea and explained her brilliant plan. Abigail even made a date for their first meeting to work on each of their own projects.

That night Abigail sat down on her bed and reached into her pocket for the letter from Jacob. That was the one thing that kept her going all day as she read his words into her heart.

She tore open the envelope, pulled out the folded piece of paper, unfolded it quickly and began to read.

My dearest Abigail,

I received your letter and anguish over the thought of you working so hard. My darling, it was never my intention to leave you with so much work in your condition.

Things here aren't as everyone thought they would be and I regret to say we will probably be away from home much longer than expected. To be honest, Girlie, I don't know what I expected, but needless to say it's far worse than one can imagine.

I am happy to hear your mama is helping you and that pa's doing well. Having the neighbour boy to help with the chores is an answer to prayer. It makes my heart happy to know that your father is feeling better each day. God is good and I pray every day for continued good health for both of them, as I pray for you and our little one.

Charles has made a few friends here. You know him - he seems to fit in well with some of the good-natured lads. We have met young men from all over Canada. It's interesting to see how we all come from different places but in reality we are all very much the same. Please keep praying for us, Girlie, we do need it. We were not quite prepared for the cold and wet, but we are doing our best.

I miss you dearly, more than I thought my heart could handle. I think of you every moment

*of every day and dream of the day I will see you
again.*

*With love and prayers,
Jacob.*

Abigail sat down at her desk, reached for her stationary
and placed it down in front of her. She began to write...

My darling Jacob,

*It was so good to receive your letter. I read
it over and over, I couldn't get enough of your
words. I tried to inhale every sentence. My heart
skips a beat when I receive an envelope from you.*

*Don't you worry a bit about the work I am
doing here. It's nothing compared to the sacrifice
you are making for us all. I can't complain, when
you are knee deep in mud, freezing in rain, not
to mention fighting for your lives. We get the
newspapers, it paints an all too dreary picture
none of us want to imagine. Oh, Jacob, I am sick
with worry for you, praying doesn't seem enough,
I feel so helpless!*

*Poor Ernest, it's so hard to see him so weak. He
will be staying with us until he is strong enough
to go to his farm. He won't be joining you over
there. Doc says that with his wounded eye, the
army won't take him back. I could see the sadness
on his face.*

*Please, love, know that I love you, I can't seem
to say it enough. I miss you so much.*

*Your loving wife,
Abigail*

chapter six

Abigail's women's group was a huge success; every woman in Abbington Pickets and the area wanted to do her bit. All who could, met every Tuesday at The General Store. The women brought potluck dinner and stitching, crocheting or knitting for the men they knew and loved. Gathered around the kitchen table, with a fire burning in the cookstove, a pot full of tea and a plate of homemade ginger snap cookies, the women chatted eagerly among themselves. Each one had her own story about her beloved soldier, whether it was her son, husband, nephew or grandson. Ernest was still there recovering. He helped with store chores and customers during the women's gatherings. When it was slow in the store he also helped to thread needles, cut squares and any other things the ladies needed. Ernest was really itching to go home and be more useful there, but this made him feel somewhat helpful. Doc wanted him to continue to stay a little while longer. It would probably be until the beginning of May before he could head for home.

A.P.L.G.

Abbington Pickets Ladies Group

WHEN:
Every Tuesday
10:00 am - 4:00 pm

WHERE:
The General Store

WHAT:
Making socks, shirts
quilts and scarves to send
to our soldiers

POTLUCK DINNER

The bell over the door jingled as the door swung open. Ernest stood up from his chair and walked over to greet the customer who came in.

"Good morning, Ernest," Mr. Edwards took off his hat and wiped off his boots on the mat.

"Good morning, sir," Ernest nodded. "How are you today?"

"Doing alright," he half heartily smiled at him.

"What can I do for you?"

"I only came in to check on Abigail."

"Oh, she is hosting the 'A.P.L.G.' today," Ernest explained.

"A.P.L.G.?" He looked confused.

"You bet, it's for the war effort," he began. "Abigail thought about how cold the men are, and believe me, I know all about it, and she wanted to help. The ladies get together once a week to work on their projects to send to the soldiers - socks, quilts, scarves and anything else that can keep them warm. The Abbington Pickets Ladies Group - "A.P.L.G." he explained.

"That's what the missis has been coming here for! Good idea," Mr. Edwards perked up. "Abigail is always thinking of everyone else."

"She sure is." Ernest reflected on the couple of weeks that he had been there, how kind she and her mama had been to him as they helped him get back on his feet. "Got time for a game of cribbage?" Ernest asked.

"Well, I don't know," Mr. Edwards, hesitated as he looked toward the door.

"Come on, a couple of games won't hurt," Ernest encouraged. The truth was he missed a bit of the 'men talk.' "The women will be busy all afternoon."

Mr. Edwards sat down at the table that held the crib board. There was a chair at each end next to the potbelly stove. Ernest tried to talk anyone who came through the doorway into playing crib with him. He liked the challenge and felt cooped up like chickens in a henhouse.

"Fifteen two, fifteen four, fifteen six..." Ernest counted his points as the women entered the store.

"Is Ernest beating you?" Abigail grinned as she walked up to the little table and noticed one set of pegs considerably further ahead of the other. Mr. Edwards threw down his cards in front of Ernest and shook his head with disapproval.

"Of course," Ernest smirked, as he sat proudly shuffling the deck of cards.

"He's pretty good at that," Abigail looked at Mr. Edwards then to Ernest. "You could be nicer to the guests, Ernest," she teased.

The women each put on their coats and boots, as their husbands rode up to take them home. The afternoon wore on and the warmth of the sun began to fade. Some of the ladies came in groups and left as such. It was a very productive meeting and Abigail was encouraged as there was much to be done for the war effort. She smiled at the success all evening and thanked God in her prayers as she went bed.

Abigail abruptly awakened. As she lay in her bed the noise that disturbed her got even louder. She pushed herself up into a sitting position. It was pitch dark. She felt for the wooden matches on her bedside table and by feeling, she struck the match and ignited it right away. The little gleam of light lit the area around her as she took the glass chimney off the oil lamp and held the lit match to the wick until it glowed. She turned down the flame and replaced the chimney. Abigail then swung her legs to the edge of the bed and slowly stood up. With both hands she pushed herself up from her bed and grabbed her housecoat that was hanging on the back of her bedroom door. She slipped an arm into one arm hole and then the next and tied the ties in front of her huge stomach. The noise continued. Abigail picked up the lamp and carefully walked into The General Store. The racket escalated. She placed the lamp on the counter top to illuminate the room so she could reach the doorway. She peaked through the window and discovered two men outside rustling around, shouting and throwing something about. Abigail couldn't quite see what it was.

"Abigail," a whisper came from behind her. "What's happening?" Abigail turned around to find her mama behind her.

"I don't know what's going on."

She lifted the piece of wood that locked the door.

Mama grabbed her arm.

"What are you doing?"

"I am going out there and see what's going on." Abigail threw over her shoulder.

"No, you're not." Her mama held onto her wrist, "you can't."

"Oh mama, they are only drunk," Abigail shrugged as she opened the door.

"How about keeping it down out there!" Abigail put her hands on either side of her mouth to holler out to them.

"Abigail, come back in here." Ernest had come to the door when he heard voices.

"It's alright, Ernest," Abigail turned around and whispered. "Get back in the house, before you get sick again."

"Well, look who it is," one of the men spoke sneeringly. "Jacob Hudson's wife." It was too dark for Abigail to see her tormentor. She couldn't see the dirty, torn clothes or the scruffy face but sure could smell the extreme odour.

"Oh, you mean," the other one laughed, "that farm boy that thought he could take us, Thomas?"

"You got it, Willie," he continued to laugh.

"Well, where is he now?" Thomas asked sarcastically.

They were beginning to make Abigail a little uneasy, and besides that, they were starting to make her mad.

"He's where you two should be," she sternly told them, "fighting for our country."

"Oh, Hudson's trying to be a hero." They both laughed simultaneously. They were still throwing something around, and at each other.

By this time Ernest had put on his coat and boots and came outside.

"Who are you?" The two scruffy men sneered.

"Someone you don't need to worry about," Ernest answered. "Go about your business and go home."

"Woo! Look who has a boyfriend," again laughing at their own jokes, "but I am sorry to say mister," they stumbled even more as they got closer to Abigail and Ernest, "she seems to have a problem," Thomas whispered. Then they both burst out laughing as they pointed, referring to Abigail's condition.

"Alright, that's enough!" Ernest raised his voice. "You're in the presence of a lady"

"Oh, really? Says who?" Willie asked.

"Says me." Ernest wasn't as tall as these lads but his build was more muscular. Presenting himself with confidence spoke louder than words.

Without warning a loud crack sounded through the dark night. The sound came from the direction of the two men, but at the moment no one knew what the sound was.

Abigail suddenly felt an oozy feeling come over her, and then she began to feel cold, she could feel something was crawling down her arm, tickling her hand.

"Abigail?" Ernest looked at Abigail, "are you alright?" Abigail stumbled as she began to walk forward.

"I didn't mean to," Thomas yelled.

"Honest, it was an accident." His face turned white in horror as he shuffled around. His drunken state had turned sober in a hurry.

"Let's get out of here!" Willie grabbed his friend's arm giving it a big tug. The two of them ran toward the stable north of the Empire Hotel.

"What's happened?" Her mama ran out toward Abigail and Ernest. She had stood at the door and watched the whole ordeal. "What was that noise?"

"Keep calm, Mrs. Rodgers." Ernest spoke collectedly. "We need to get Abigail into the house and get Doc right away."

"It's alright, mama, but Ernest is right." Abigail was as calm as Ernest. As Ernest and Mrs. Rodgers both supported Abigail they slowly walked back into The General Store. The door slammed shut behind them. They shuffled to Abigail's bedroom past the kitchen. Abigail sat down and her mama lifted her legs and helped her lie down.

"Oh, my Lord! You're bleeding!" Abigail's mama gasped.

"Abigail's been shot," Ernest calmly pointed out.

"What?" Her mama cried.

"There's no time to explain, we need to stop the bleeding. I will go and get Doc. You get a sheet and press on the wound hard to stop the bleeding," Ernest directed, then ran out the doorway.

Mrs. Rodgers then ran to the bedroom, returned with a white cotton sheet, placed it on Abigail's upper arm and pushed hard.

"I am sorry, mama," Abigail winced in pain. "You were right. I should have..." Abigail fell unconscious.

"Abigail? Abigail?"

Abigail squinted as she began to open her eyes and heard vaguely the sound of a strange voice calling her name.

"Abigail?" The voice repeated. "Are you awake?"

"Is she alright?" A familiar voice sounded from the other side of her. Abigail turned her head to see who it was. It was her mama. "What about her... you know... condition."

"She appears to be awake," the Doc told Mrs. Rodgers. "But as far as her being alright, I am not quite sure. I stopped the bleeding, but the bullet went clean on through her biceps brachii and she lost quite a bit of blood. We need to keep her quiet and still as her baby may be at risk."

Abigail could hear the talking but didn't seem to be part of the conversation. Her mind raced with questions but she couldn't seem to get the words out. She scowled as she looked around the room and listened to the words spoken.

Baby? Suddenly Abigail remembered clearly, she was with child and she had been wounded. Fear began to well up from deep down inside, her heart started to race and she clutched her belly as she felt a stabbing pain in her front side. She groaned in pain and pressed her upper body down toward her stomach.

"What's wrong?" Mrs. Rodgers demanded of Doc.

"It appears that Abigail is beginning labour." Doc announced. "Go get Mrs. Johnson," he directed Abigail's mama.

Mrs. Rodgers ran into the kitchen to retrieve Mrs. Johnson, who was cleaning up from stitching Abigail's wound.

There was a brief knock at the kitchen door.

"Yes, who is it?" hollered Mrs. Johnson as she swiftly made her way back to the room where Abigail was lying in terrible pain.

The door opened and Ernest stepped through the doorway. He was being extra polite. Usually the door to the kitchen was kept open, but during these unusual circumstances there was a need for privacy. Mrs. Rodgers was back in the kitchen since Doc's wife was assisting him.

"How is Abigail doing?" he asked Mrs. Rodgers. His voice was quiet and low. He had been keeping The General Store going while Doc was tending to Abigail's injury.

"Oh, Ernest, it's not good," she quickly darted toward him. "Abigail is going to have her baby...soon."

"Now?" His grey eyes grew wide. "Isn't it too soon?"

"Yes, it's too soon," Mrs. Johnson was distraught as she stood there and wrung her hands. "Please, keep the home fires burning."

"Will do, Mrs. Rodgers," Ernest said confidently. "Anything you need." Ernest slowly closed the door and headed back to the store. Mrs. Rodgers raced to the door, opened it again and called out to Ernest.

"There is one thing you could do for me," she began. Ernest turned on his heal back toward her. "Could you go tell Reverend Young of Abigail's situation?" She looked down at the ground, "...well, the more prayers, the better."

"Of course, Mrs. Rodgers," Ernest promised her, then put the closed sign up on the door and headed to the church.

"Mrs. Rodgers," Mrs. Johnson peeked out from Abigail's bedroom door, "could you put a big pot of water on the stove please?"

"Certainly, is everything alright?" Abigail's mama asked.

"Yes, of course," Mrs. Johnson reassured her.

Abigail had never experienced pain as she was feeling at that moment. The bullet wound barely compared to the sharp pain in her side and the dull backache that radiated across her lower back. *If only Jacob were here, he would know what to say.* Despite her mama being here during this difficult time, Abigail couldn't help but feel a sense of longing, as if she were homesick. With Jacob not being there in a time of crisis, even in everyday life, she missed him dearly and didn't feel whole without him. As another piercing pain filled Abigail's body she couldn't help but groan loudly in agony.

"Oh, Jacob," she yelled, "why... did...you...leave...us?" She cried under her breath as tears welled up in her brown eyes, poured out of the corners and rolled down the side of her head.

"It's alright to yell." Mrs. Johnson placed a cold cloth over her sweat beaded forehead. "If you breathe through your nose and out through your mouth it helps with the pain." Mrs. Johnson demonstrated as she told her.

"I knew this was going to be painful," Abigail winced. "I remember Alice giving birth."

"Yes, and remember, Abigail," Mrs. Johnson began. "Everything turned out well." She explained, "once that new little baby was born, all that pain she felt all disappeared immediately and nothing else seemed to matter."

"I hope you're rig-." Abigail again reached for her stomach and bent her upper body toward her middle as another labour pain began.

"Abigail, breathe," Mrs. Johnson reminded her as she rubbed her back.

"Can mama come in here?" Abigail asked. "Tell her it's all right if she comes in."

"Well, you see, dear," Mrs. Johnson tried to explain, "not all mamas like to see their daughters in pain."

"Oh... I see." Abigail tried not to show her disappointment.

"Your mama will feel like she is doing more for you by keeping herself busy."

Abigail smiled faintly in time to start another contraction.

At that moment Doc walked back through the doorway. He had been out on a quick call while his wife kept Abigail calm. He knew she would be in labour for many hours.

"I want to check your wound, Abigail." He began to unwrap the bandage as she laid uncomfortably flat on her back on the bed. Abigail barely felt Doc hold and tug on her arm as he unravelled the strips of cloth. Although it was annoying, it wasn't nearly as excruciating as each labour pain.

"It appears that the bleeding has stopped." Doc looked down his nose through his glasses. "Could you bandage it back up again, Mrs., please," he motioned to his wife.

For the rest of the day Abigail persevered through labour pains and breathing, and prayed mercifully that The Lord would take the pain away. Mrs. Johnson was there to hold her hand, rub her back and wipe her brow. Abigail's mama made tea, boiled water and made small meals. Doc checked on Abigail and kept saying that it was not time yet. The Reverend and his wife came and sat in the kitchen and kept Mrs. Rodgers company while praying that Abigail and the baby would be safe and well.

Ernest popped his head in the doorway every now and then to check on Abigail. The last time he did, Mrs. Rodgers sent him to Goldenrod to tell Mr. Rodgers so he knew what was happening, making sure he wouldn't worry but to know that he would soon be a grandpa. Ernest came back with Mr. Rodgers in tow. He wouldn't stay home. He knew there was nothing he could do but this was his only child. Mrs. Rodgers was secretly happy; after all, her sister, Gladys, was there to keep the fire burning.

Once evening came, Ernest was done working at The General Store and came and sat in the kitchen with everyone else. Even Mr. Edwards rode right over to see how Abigail was once he heard she had been injured and started premature labour. By then, most of the village had heard as well, and some stopped in to see how she was doing. There were quite a few local men who got together in the search for Willie and Thomas. There was a price to be paid for almost killing Abigail and possibly her baby. The village was aghast with the news about Jacob's wife.

Mrs. Rodgers made supper for all who were there, as everyone patiently, but worriedly, waited outside Abigail's door. Ernest and Mr. Rodgers played countless games of cribbage to pass the time. Pot of tea after pot of tea was drunk and each male jumped at the chance to get up and put wood into the stove or look out the window.

By the next morning, even Mrs. Johnson was beginning to get worried. She had assisted with a lot of births, but this appeared to be taking too long with little progress. Abigail has been in pain for quite a long time, but Doc reassured her that everything was coming along fine and she was getting close to giving birth.

Reverend Young and his wife had gone home for the night but came back first thing in the morning just as Mrs. Rodgers was serving breakfast. Ernest swept the floor. Mr. Edwards walked through the doorway. He took off his hat and wiped his shoes on the mat at the door.

"How are things this morning, lad?" Ernest shook his head. He knew what that meant. "I brought Abigail a letter." He handed it to Ernest. He also had a basket over his arm.

"Thank you, sir," said Ernest as he took the letter in his hand. "I will give it to Mrs. Rodgers. Come in for a cup of coffee."

"Oh, alright." He followed Ernest to the kitchen where everyone was gathered around the table. The room was small but the love in there was as big as a castle. Small space didn't seem to matter to anyone. They were all there for the same reason - for Jacob and Abigail. With Jacob's absence, it appeared there was a greater need for everyone to gather.

"Good morning," Mr. Edwards spoke, as he placed the basket on the table. "The wife sent over a pie and some biscuits."

"How kind of her," Mrs. Rodgers took the basket and took the items out of it. "We appreciate this very much," she smiled. Mrs. Rodgers was beginning to look run down. Her tired eyes, untidy bun and wrinkled clothes from sleeping in the chair, spoke volumes.

"I will get you a cup of coffee," she told him as Ernest found him a chair.

There was very little noise coming from Abigail's bedroom.

"Here," Ernest passed Mrs. Rodgers the envelope. "Maybe this will help Abigail along."

"Oh, my." A big smile formed on Mrs. Rodgers face. "I will take it to her now."

She lightly knocked at the door and slipped inside, barely opening the door.

"How are you doing, honey?" She looked at her daughter sympathetically. Her long wavy hair was soaked in sweat and her sleep deprived eyes sadly looked at her mama, anguish on her face.

"A letter from Jacob," she grinned, hoping this would keep her mind off of the pain for even a moment.

Abigail's eyes lit up. Her mama could see the colour come back into her face for a split second, right before another contraction came. Abigail cried out. The pain was sharper and there was barely a reprieve in between contractions.

"Please read it to me," she whispered under her breath and gritted her teeth. She then breathed deeply into her nose and out her mouth as Mrs. Johnson had shown her.

"Maybe this should wait..." Mrs. Johnson interrupted.

"No, I want..." Abigail breathed in again. "...to hear Jacob. I need to..." Again another pain, tears rolled down her cheeks as her eyes spoke to her mama, begging her to start reading.

Abigail's mama cleared her throat as she opened the envelope and unfolded the paper, she began to read.

My dearest Abigail,

Abigail closed her eyes and smiled, she imagined Jacob in the room speaking to her. She felt his presence.

> *How are you darling? I think of you daily and miss your smile, your laugh, your squeal when I tease and tickle you. I would do anything to hear your voice at this very moment.*
>
> *Charles and I are doing well, considering. How is Ernest? He was sure a sick lad here. When he was struck with that grenade, they had no choice but to send him home. To be honest I was so relieved. We have seen men here die of pneumonia or influenza. I have been praying extra hard for you lately, as I know you are getting closer and closer to becoming a mother. I pray to Jesus that you and our little baby will be safe. Each night, especially when I am on night watch, I can talk to God about how I miss you and how I need to be even stronger to endure this time away from you. I feel I can fight any battle with much strength, but when I think of you suffering in labour, it breaks my heart and brings me to my knees with weakness.*
>
> *Please know, Girlie, that you are with me wherever I go and I look forward to every letter you send to me. It makes the time here go by faster knowing there is word coming from you. It brings*

*a piece of home to me and I tuck it in my pocket
and carry it with me until the next one arrives.*

*Please don't worry about me. Take care of
yourself and your ma and pa and that little one
inside you. I am not sure where my next letter is
coming from. They are sending us somewhere, I
can't say of course, but I will write as soon as I can.*

*I love you forever, Girlie,
Love and Prayers,
Jacob.*

Abigail held in every bit of pain she could to be able to listen to the very end of the letter. Finally, at the word 'Jacob,' she allowed herself a huge scream and lifted her head up from the pillow as far as she could.

"Alright, ladies," Doc started, "I believe this is it. Mrs. Rodgers, more hot water, please, and the cotton sheets."

"I will, Doc." Mrs. Rodgers left the room, barely opening the door. The faces she saw on the other side of the door were concerned. She knew they had heard Abigail scream at the top of her lungs. Every man in the room was speechless. In fact, Mr. Rodgers couldn't bear to hear it anymore and was in The General Store with Ernest, trying hard to keep busy.

"I will pray," Reverend Young informed everyone as they bowed their heads to pray. "Dear Jesus, we give up this young lady to You. May Your hand be upon her and her baby, Your angels surround her, may the armour of Jesus be upon them, in Your mighty name. Amen."

Everyone simultaneously said, "Amen."

"Quick, please fetch more wood," Mrs. Rodgers asked of the men who sat at the table. She poured water from the pitcher into the biggest pot and placed it on the cookstove. She opened the door of the stove and stoked the wood inside. Mr. Edwards brought in an armful of wood. He crouched down and placed one piece in at a time until the stove was full, then he closed the door. Another scream came from the bedroom and everyone looked at each other. Mrs. Rodgers scurried around even more, trying to remain calm while busy. She left the kitchen and climbed the stairs to the upstairs bedrooms to locate more sheets. In the armoire in the northwest room she found enough sheets for ten beds. As she stood up on the creaky hardwood floor she heard a faint noise of a crying, not a scream, but a crying. She dropped the sheets, and proceeded to climb downstairs, practically running into Mr. Rodgers and Ernest once she reached the kitchen door.

"Was that..." She felt excitement yet fear in her heart as her eyes met Mr. Rodgers. They both walked into the kitchen and anxiously waited for Doc or Mrs. Johnson to appear from the bedroom. Reverend and Mrs. Young were smiling, and Mr. Edwards as well.

"Why has the crying stopped?" Asked Mrs. Rodgers.

"I am sure everything is fine," reassured Mrs. Young. She had been making tea when everyone filled the room.

"But babies usually cry longer than that," she persisted.

Another long cry came from the other side of the door, but it wasn't a baby's cry. It was Abigail.

"I can't stand the suspense," Mr. Rodgers spoke. He had been pretty quiet up until that point.

The door squeaked slowly open and there stood Mrs. Johnson with a tightly wrapped bundle in her arms.

"Why don't you come in, Mrs. Rodgers." She smiled and stepped back into the room. Mrs. Rodgers looked at her husband then quickly followed in anticipation.

She walked in and closed the door behind her. She looked at Abigail propped up with a pillow nursing a small baby. Then she realized Mrs. Johnson was still holding a baby. Wait. She looked at Mrs. Johnson, then back to a smiling Abigail.

"Twins?" She burst out.

"Yes!" Abigail could hardly contain her excitement.

"Thank you, Lord!" She clapped her hands together and looked upward. Mrs. Johnson passed her the baby that she cradled in her arms. "That was so fast after I left the room."

"I guess all I needed to hear was Jacob's words of encouragement," Abigail beamed. "Won't he be thrilled to come home to a baby girl AND boy?"

"One of each?" Mrs. Rodgers almost did a dance. "I have to tell everyone who is waiting outside."

"We have to finish up with Abigail," Mrs. Johnson explained, "so you show off that little boy."

Mrs. Rodgers opened the door with her free hand and beamed as she walked into the kitchen to show her brand new baby grandson.

"Congratulations, grandma." Mrs. Young smiled.

"Praise The Lord!" Reverend Young shouted.

"Here, grandpa." Mrs. Rodgers placed the bundle into his arms. He turned a little red and moved his arms awkwardly as he tried to get comfortable with the baby.

"Jacob will be so proud." Ernest stood leaning against the doorway of the kitchen.

"He sure will be." Charles father piped in.

By this time, Mrs. Johnson had stepped out of the bedroom, the sound of a crying baby flowed with her.

"What?" Mr. Rodgers looked at his wife. She couldn't keep it in any long, she nodded her head up and down with a big grin.

"Twins." She stated matter-of-factly. "A girl AND a boy."

"What a miracle," Mrs. Young added.

"It sure is," Mrs. Rodgers beamed. "One of each, who would have thought."

"Alright," Mrs. Johnson's stern voice rose. "All you men scat. Us women have important things to do." She was referring to the mess that came with birthing.

"We are going, we are going." Mr. Rodgers passed the baby back to Mrs. Rodgers and headed into The General Store, along with Ernest, Reverend Young and Mr. Edwards. Mrs. Young stayed and helped.

Indeed it was a blessing-filled day. All the community were part of it, supporting and witnessing a true miracle. It was a day Abbington Pickets would not soon forget. Not only was a baby born, but two - the first twins in the village.

chapter seven

My darling Jacob,

How are you my love? I hope you are well and keeping yourself safe from whatever harm can come to you. I think of you daily and dream of you at night.

I am delighted to send you blessings from home. Your babies were born safely and healthy. Yes, that's right! I said babies! Jacob, you are a proud father of twins! We have a precious little boy and a wee small girl who share your likeness, baring a sweet little dimple on both cheeks for little Danny and one for Josie. I hope you don't mind. Of course we didn't get to speak about names, but I thought I would name Daniel Andrew after you and your brother and Josephine Lucy after our dear friend and your little sister.

I won't go into details but the twins were born a little early. But the most important fact is, they are here and even their mama is doing *wonderful. With a little rest she, too, will be fit to churn butter!*

Mama and Ernest have been very helpful, working extra hard to make it easier for me. Ernest says he is going to stay until planting season begins. God has sent us a blessing when he brought us Ernest.

I have diapers to fold and babies to feed, I am going to sign off now, my love. I pray every day and night for you to return safely home to us.

Love,
Girlie

Abigail remembered the words she penned to Jacob last month after the birth of the twins. She was anxiously awaiting his reply, envisioning Jacob receiving the letter and thinking of how he would feel while he read it.

"Abigail," a voice came from the kitchen.

"I am in here," Abigail called out to her mama from her bedroom where she sat at her desk beside her bed. The twins were down for a nap in the sitting room. Abigail thought she would take the moment to write Jacob another letter, but words seemed to escape her. She wanted to be honest with Jacob about why she had the babies early, but she didn't want him to worry about things at home when there was nothing he could do about it from where he was. It took her several weeks to get some feeling back in her arm from the bullet wound, not to mention giving birth to two babies. She didn't feel run down or tired - it was quite the opposite - she felt full of energy and wanted to put it to use. But as she looked at the empty piece of paper, her mama jogged her out of her daydream.

"You're supposed to be resting, Abigail," her mama scolded her. "You will never let the arm heal if you don't quit using it."

"I am fine, mama," Abigail stated. "Besides it's hard to rest an arm when you have two babies to hold and feed," she laughed. "And my arm feels so much better. It's been two weeks since they were born."

"You are overdoing it." Mrs. Rodgers leaned against the doorway as she dried her hands with a dish towel.

"Your mama is absolutely correct." A new voice appeared in the room behind her mama.

"See, there you are," mama turned around to find Doc standing behind her. "The doc has spoken," she smiled in satisfaction.

"Oh, not you, too." Abigail rolled her eyes. "Come on, I need someone on my side."

"I came to check on you and the little ones." Doc stood holding his black leather bag.

"I am fine," Abigail insisted.

"Well, that's for me to determine," Doc said firmly.

"The twins are sleeping," Abigail pointed out.

"I guess we start with you," Doc stated plainly in his no nonsense attitude.

"I guess I am at a loss." Abigail frowned looking at her mama smiling.

"I will make some tea." Mrs. Rodgers went back into the kitchen to put the kettle on the stove.

Doc checked Abigail out from giving birth, as well as her wounded arm, he then looked at the twins. Afterward each of them sat down for a cup of tea.

"Give our best to Mrs. Johnson," Abigail smiled as she cradled little Daniel with her good arm.

"Sure will." Doc set down his empty tea cup, stood up from his chair and picked up his coat and hat.

"You all take care." Doc put on his coat as he carried his hat. He left the kitchen, walked through The General Store, put on his hat and left the building.

Ernest swept the floor and Abigail put baby Danny in his bed in the sitting room next to his sister. While they slept she thought she would help in The General Store.

"Is there anything I can help with, Ernest?" Abigail asked. The past couple of weeks she had let Ernest do all the work as far as The General Store was concerned.

"I think everything is caught up," Ernest smiled. "I put away the freight that arrived this morning, and even hung up the war posters."

"What are war posters?" Abigail looked confused as Ernest pointed toward the wall behind the counter. There hung a picture of King George V pointing, with the words 'Your country needs YOU!' 'You' being capitalized in huge letters. Abigail stared at the poster for several minutes.

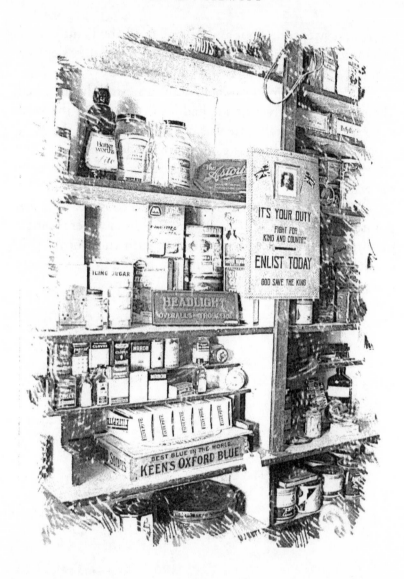

"What is it?" Ernest asked as he watched the look on her face.

"I can't believe he or anyone would encourage young men to run to their death." Abigail shook her head. "Did you read the newspaper lately?"

"Yes," he said quietly as he looked away, knowing full well what Abigail was talking about as he thought about the headline 'CANADIANS KILLED WITH POISON GAS!'

"Well?" She studied his face as Ernest began to speak.

"It's the honourable thing to do." Ernest looked directly at Abigail. "If Doc wouldn't have declared me too sick to return to duty, I would be back there in a minute."

"Why?" Abigail looked confused. "To risk your life in another country," a frown line fell across her forehead, "and miss your family, and maybe never see your sister, Bert, and your nieces again?"

"It's about honour, Abigail." Ernest's face turned placid but serious."

"But the fact is, you could die and who would care?" Abigail shook her head. "Besides, of course, your family. No one is going to care whether you died out on the battlefield or died in the infirmary from pneumonia. The point is no one else will care, besides your loved ones back home, who wished you had never gone in the first place."

"I will care, Abigail." Ernest didn't back down. "No one wants to die, but to live a coward for the rest of your life... I would rather die alone in the battlefield."

"I don't understand the way you men think," Abigail firmly stated. "Your family needs you and all you care about is your stupid honour."

"It's not only our honour," Ernest tried to explain. "It's our family's heritage."

"What?" Abigail' eyes narrowed, she didn't understand his meaning.

"Well, when you think back to your great-great-granddad," Ernest tried describing the picture, "you want to say that he was a wonderful, hard-working honest man, with integrity and so on and so forth. Just think, if he ran away from the war, or any other act of dignity, what would you think of him? You wouldn't say, 'well I got to see him live.' And truth is, you didn't because that was too long ago. But you will remember the legacy he left because it will be passed down from generation to generation."

"I see your point, Ernest." Abigail admitted. "But it doesn't mean I like it." She huffed. "Now, are you going to deal the cards, or am I?"

"I didn't know you played, Abigail." Ernest looked dumb founded.

"Jacob taught me," Abigail stated. "Of course he always won, but I do know how to play the game."

Abigail thought back to last winter when there was quite a lot of snow on the ground and it was still blowing hard. Jacob had done his chores for the day and even sanded six tables in the shop. There wasn't much he could do outside since it was already dark by five o'clock. Abigail's thoughts turned into a daydream...

"Let's play some cribbage." Jacob suggested.

"Well, I am not very good, remember," Abigail had reminded him, "I only learned last month."

"Practice makes perfect." He grinned.

"Alright," she retrieved the crib board and deck of cards from the small drawer inside the tea table in the living room. They sat at the kitchen table where it was cozy and warm as the wind gusted against the west window. Jacob won the first game, then the second. By the third, Abigail was beginning get very annoyed.

"That's not fair!" She piped up.

"What isn't?" Jacob looked confused, and slightly amused that he was getting her dander up.

"You are always pegging points."

"Well, that's what you're supposed to do."

"When I try and get points for doing that, you say it's not right."

"It isn't right."

"Well, then why are you getting away with it?"

"Because it's not the same as what you're doing."

"Oh, really? How!" Abigail's face was flush with anger.

"When I put that three down, then you put the two down, I put down the ace, because it's a run, I get three points."

"I did that last time," Abigail frowned, "you said it wasn't legal in the game.

"That's because we had already added up to thirty one..."

"That's not fair." Abigail wasn't usually a sore loser but this time, Jacob got the better of her and she felt like he was playing unfairly.

"It is, sweetheart." He grinned sheepishly. He knew she was mad. They played another hand. Again Jacob made a run while pegging and Abigail did the same.

"Sorry, you don't get a run this time," Jacob objected.

"What? But you can?" Abigail raised her voice, "the rules only apply to you, don't they?" She threw her cards down. "Only when it's convenient for you."

"But you had a card in between the run," Jacob tried to explain. Abigail jumped up, shoved her chair under the table, ran to their bedroom and slammed the door. She was so mad, the tops of her ears were burning. She gruffly undressed, snatched her night dress out of the top dresser drawer and banged it shut. She changed for bed. Besides, it was close to bedtime wasn't it? She lit the oil lamp beside her bed, crawled in between the sheets, grabbed the book off the table and started to read. Her heart was racing a mile a minute, even sometimes felt like it skipped a beat. How dare he cheat in crib. Of all the nerve, I am never playing with him again. She told herself.

Jacob let her cool off a bit before he came to bed that night. He went out to feed and water the horses and brought in an arm load of wood and a pail of water for the night. When he walked into the softly lit room, he kept his guard.

"Are you still mad?" He cheerfully asked. Several minutes passed with only the sound of each of them breathing heard in the room.

"Yes," Abigail firmly scowled, as she tried not to look at him. Jacob sat on the edge of his side of the bed and began to take off his socks.

"I guess we won't be playing that game anymore?" Jacob tried not to sound too sarcastic and began laughing.

"I guess not," she bluntly said, trying to hold in her own laughter. Jacob turned to her as she pretended to read. His stare down got the better of her and she burst out laughing and threw her book down. Jacob moved toward her side of the bed.

"I am sorry, I have never been a sore loser in my life," Abigail laughed, "but you made me so darn mad, I wanted to scream."

"I know," Jacob laughed just as hard. "It's so much fun."

"Oh, it is?" shouted Abigail as she pretended to be even more angry. She play punched him in the arm. "We shall see about that."

Abigail was no match for Jacob as he grabbed her hands and pulled her close to him. He kissed her forehead, then each cheek. He pressed his lips against hers…

"Abigail? Abigail?" Ernest sat across from her and snapped his fingers. "Are you alright?

Abigail shook herself back to reality. She didn't want to leave the vision she played in her head about Jacob. She missed him terribly and wondered what he was doing at this moment. *I will always play crib with you Jacob Hudson, and you can win every game, as long as you come home safe to us,* Abigail told herself and vowed she would never be a sore loser again as long as she lived.

Ernest had already dealt the cards while Abigail was daydreaming.

"It's my crib I guess," Ernest told her as he waited for her to cut the cards.

"Oh, right." Abigail tried to remember the rules of the game. "Sorry, you will have to bear with me; it's been awhile." She smiled, as if she had changed personalities as she remembered her love.

The store was quiet while the two enjoyed playing game after game. Mama was baking coffee cake in the kitchen and the babies were still having their nap. The outdoor wind could be heard from inside but it was cozy warm in the middle of The General Store. Ernest would get up every now and again to load the stove with another log or two as well as keep Mrs. Rodgers' cookstove steady for her baking.

"Mmm, that smell," Ernest took a deep breath, "reminds me of my mum. She baked the best treats." He smiled, reminiscing.

"Do you miss England?" Abigail asked. She knew she missed it somewhat but not like she missed her mama and papa, since they came here together.

"Yep, I do," Ernest looked down, "but not as much as my Nellie."

"Is that your sister?" Abigail was curious.

"My girl."

"Ah, I see." Abigail had heard from Alice about this young lady who broke Ernest's heart. "I am so sorry."

"I thought I was going to share a good life like Bert and Alice, and Jacob and yourself, but I guess that wasn't in the cards for me." He shook his head.

"How so?" Abigail prompted as she shuffled the cards. She could see the pain in his eyes and the sadness on his face.

"She wasn't the per-, the lady I thought she was." Ernest slowly picked up the cards Abigail dealt. "Or should I say, she wasn't the lady I expected her to be."

"I guess everyone has their differences." Abigail wasn't sure what to say. "Tell me about her." She smiled wanting to know a little more about the ever-so private Ernest.

"I met her while riding my bike," Ernest continued as he cut the cards to begin the game. "My little sister, Gracie, was ill and I went to fetch the doctor. I almost ran her over. Instead I ended up on my head."

"Oh, my," Abigail's eyebrows rose. "Ten." She laid down a card.

"You should have seen her face." Ernest's eyes lit up as he spoke of his love. "Fifteen for two." He placed a five on the table, then he pegged his points in the cribbage board. "She was so angry, but I didn't care. I had to get to the doctor's house."

"Twenty for two," Abigail smiled as she laid down another five, hoping that Ernest would fall for her trap. Usually no one would place a ten down if they could help it.

"Twenty-five for six." Ernest placed his five down calmly, not missing a beat.

Abigail drew in an irritated breath.

"Ugh. Go." She grunted under her breath as she rolled her eyes, as her idea didn't go as planned. He had made more points without blinking an eye. *Why is this game easy for everyone but me?* Abigail asked herself. Ernest put down four, then pegged one point for his go. "Eight." She placed her second last card down.

"We met up again later. Fifteen for two." Ernest continued his story as he placed down a seven and pegged two points. "She wasn't nearly as mad, but not really friendly either." He smirked. "It took some doing, but she did, in fact, come around."

"What did she say the next time you saw each other?" Abigail raised her eyebrow.

"Twenty-four," Abigail smiled as she proudly placed her last card down - as the count of four included last card in the hand. "For four points." She grinned with satisfaction.

"Oh, you again," Ernest laughed. "I stopped by her house a few times, she finally smiled, wasn't long before we spent a lot of time together, riding our bicycles and doing homework together. She helped me through a difficult time.

"What does she look like?" Abigail asked as she shuffled the cards again.

"She has medium brown hair, with a natural curl," he began, "you know the kind you create using rags?" Living with four females in the house, Ernest got to know the ways of the women, their beauty secrets and such. "Despite her plain, petite appearance, she has the most piercing blue eyes, the kind that take your breath away. Her voice can calm a screaming baby in a moment."

Ernest put down his cards, dug deep into the pocket of his britches and pulled out his brown wallet. He separated the leather pockets, lifted out a picture, leaned over and handed it to Abigail. She took the photo from Ernest and looked at it intently. *So this is the woman who broke this poor man's heart. Ernest is a kind and gentle soul and works hard, he would do anything for anyone. How could she do that to him,* Abigail asked herself?

Ernest described Nellie to a tee. As he spoke of her, Abigail could hear in his voice how much he had loved her and still loves her. She sure wasn't pretty but Ernest's kind words made her sound beautiful.

"She is quite a gal." Ernest put the picture back in his wallet and shoved it in its special place.

"I am sure she is," Abigail smiled. Even though she didn't know Nellie, she decided she didn't like her. In one way, she wished she hadn't pried into his personal life as it was difficult for him to talk about, but on the other hand, Abigail thought that it was good for him to talk to someone.

Abigail and Ernest were in their sixth game when a sound came from the sitting room.

"I guess that's my cue," Abigail smiled. Abigail put down her cards and began to stand up. Just then the store door swung open and the wind gusted in as a large figure came through the doorway.

"Abigail?" the voice shouted, "where's Doc?"

"Well, he's not here." Abigail ran up to the person standing in the entry way. "Oh, it's you, Mr. Edwards," Abigail could tell he was in a panic and didn't want to wait long.

"He isn't at home and his wife thought he may be here," Charles father explained.

"He was here earlier this morning," Abigail informed him, "but I don't know where he was going next. Why? What's wrong?"

"The train brought in sick soldiers," he explained in one breath. "Some even with amputations. They need him now."

The first thing that came to mind when Abigail heard the word "soldiers", was Jacob. Her heart skipped a beat and she brought her hands to her heart and stepped back.

"Jacob?" Her whitened face fell, she let out a deep breath, worried she would hear bad news.

"No, or Charles, either," Mr. Edwards stated. "Believe me, it was the first thing I checked."

Abigail should have known he would have looked for them. She didn't know if she was relieved he wasn't wounded or sent home dead, or disappointed that he wasn't wounded but home for good. She could still hear the babies crying in the sitting room as her mama tried hard to console them. Her mind was so filled with mixed emotion that she barely noticed them crying.

"I better get to my babies," she told Mr. Edwards, "excuse me. Ernest, maybe you can help Mr. Edwards find Doc."

"I sure will." Ernest grabbed his coat that was hung on the hook by the door and he reached for his boots. "We can try the blacksmith shop. I heard that the blacksmith got burned the other day, perhaps we will start there."

Both the men left as Abigail tended to the babies. She couldn't help but think about the wounded soldiers sent home. *Do they know where Jacob is? Do they know if Jacob is alright? When will this war be over!* She screamed in her mind.

chapter eight

Finally the letter Abigail had been waiting for...

My dearest Abigail,

I am delighted to have heard the good news of our tiny miracles. God is sure faithful and good to us. Imagine two little babies, I can't even fathom it and I am still in awe since I read your letter. I had to read several times because I couldn't believe my eyes. I was happy to be able to share with Charles as I could hardly contain myself. I must admit my shirt buttons were popping off. I am so proud of you, Girlie, and what you have been through on your own. I know you will be the most amazing mama in Abbington Pickets. Our daughter will beam her mother's smile, and our son will bear mine.

I am going to be quite frank, my Girlie. It's not good here. I can't tell you details, I wouldn't want you to know even an inkling of what's happening. I need you to understand that it isn't as

*easy as I thought, heck, I didn't think it would
be easy but I at least thought it would be simpler.
Men are dying on either side of us, literally as
we try to make it through each day to win this
war. Each moment feels like hours long, every
day, feels like weeks. We are far from conquering
our enemies and I fear this will take much longer
than everyone anticipated. I only pray to God,
our Father, that each man, must he die, know
Him personally.*

*My dreams are filled with you and our babies
and the day we will see each other again. God
bless and keep you.*

*Girlie, continue to pray for us.
I love you forever, Jacob*

Abigail realized now that her letters were taking longer to
reach Jacob and his letters were definitely taking longer to get
to Abbington Pickets. Did this mean he was getting further
away? Perhaps closer to the front line? Abigail didn't know
which was worse - the pain of not knowing or the worry of
knowing everything.

My dear Jacob,

*I just finished reading your letter, darling. I
fear what you are going through and each letter
makes me apprehensive. I can hear the anguish
in your words as I read them. It's getting worse
each time.*

*Men are coming home wounded, just like
Ernest. They are sick and Doc only has so many
hours in a day. He looks so tired and I know his
wife helps as much as she can.*

*Danny and Josie are already two months old
and are growing so fast. I fear if I blink, I will
miss something. I only wish you were here to see
them. Their chubby cheeks and gurgling noises
they make, I've never seen anything like it as I
hadn't been around many babies in my life, being
an only child and no other small relatives.*

*Remember when you taught me to play crib?
Well I am getting over being a sore loser. Don't
laugh, but it's true. Ernest has been very gracious
and patient with me as we have been playing cribbage to pass the time while he was so ill. You will
have a run for your money when you get home.*

*Ernest has gone back to his farm and we
miss him. He was such a help in the store, very
good with the customers too. I think he enjoyed
it as well.*

*As much as I don't want to, I must sign off
now, my darling. I will kiss the babies for you and
I tell them that their papa loves them so much
and will be back home very soon.*

I love you Jacob.
Your Girlie

Spring had come in like a lamb. Wounded soldiers came
by train weekly. Doc tended to them the best he could, along
with the doctor from Pickets and another neighbouring town.
They sent the men to the doctor nearest to where they lived in
hopes the local physician had the space to keep them, if that
was needed. Most men went home, which meant the doctors
made house calls. They were long days for Doc and he even
requested help from the city. A young doctor came all the way
from Regina to Doc's aid. He boarded at the Empire Hotel
in the space in the back where Jacob used to stay. He could

have stayed in one of the Hotel rooms but Doc felt that he could set his place up as a doctor's office as well. Lord knows they needed extra medical facilities.

Newspaper headlines read dreadful news each time it was delivered. Most recent was 'BOMBING IN LONDON! 28 DEAD!' Abigail wondered where her Jacob was, if he was alright. It wasn't pleasant, but it was all most people talked about. It was a conversation of who was right, who was wrong, when it would be resolved and when the troops would be coming back home. Most folks had their own opinions. Abigail refused to listen or discuss it.

Ernest had gone back home when Doc had given him a good bill of health. Even though he didn't want to leave Abigail and the babies to fend for themselves, he needed to begin sowing his crop. Abigail was grateful for his help and knew he was an answer to Jacob's prayers. Despite Ernest's reluctance to stay home from the war, he decided to devote his time to help all he could while his brothers in arms were fighting for our country. Bert and Alice were managing quite well despite calving season having started before Ernest returned home.

The twins had grown like weeds and demanded much attention from their mother. Abigail's mama had to go home to help Aunt Gladys. It seemed that her aunt was under the weather. Mr. Rodgers came to get Mrs. Rodgers and said it was likely that Aunt Gladys worked herself into a state of sickness. This worried mama. Now she had to think about Abigail alone with the babies and Aunt Gladys sick at home, not to mention worry whether Jacob was ever going to come home again.

"No use worrying yourself into anemia, mama," Abigail warned the day her mama left. "I will be fine, there is always someone I can ask if I need help." Abigail kissed her mama goodbye.

"But the problem is, Abigail," her mama looked at her sternly, "you don't ask for help."

Abigail wanted to ease her mama of any of her own worries and only smiled.

"I will if I need it, mama, I promise." Of course she didn't want her ma and pa to know how worried she was herself about being alone, and whether she was able to handle every day chores and the babies too, as well as run the store. But she did have confidence with some apprehension. *I can do this,* she told herself. Besides, the villagers were kind and compassionate, and if she needed help she could count on them, not to mention the daily check-ins that Mr. Edwards made.

Abigail hadn't heard from Jacob since his letter after the twins were born. She was silently worrying, but he had said he wouldn't be able to write for a while. She kept that in mind, but it didn't lighten the load of concern on her mind.

Abigail continued her weekly women's group. They had already sent three crates of goods to the soldiers overseas. Reverend Young prayed over every crate, pray that each item would help a soldier in need and bring each safely home. Maybe even Jacob and Charles would end up with something from Abbington Pickets.

It was now the beginning of July and Abigail had learned many new tricks to keep her children occupied while dealing with customers. Even the men held the babies while she filled their wives' orders. The community did well to have compassion for Abigail and the children, along with every other woman from the south-east corner of Saskatchewan who had a husband at war. Local men would cut extra wood and anonymously leave it in Abigail's woodshed. Abigail suspected who it was but never said a word. People pulled their weight and then some, to help their fellow neighbour - especially the women left behind. It was a stressful time with each family worrying about a son, husband or brother at war, food for the family's table and money to pay the bills. It was tough on the village and surrounding area. Not only was there a shortage of labour workers, there was also a shortage of money because no one had work to make an income. Rationing became a household word. Everyone had to do it. Folks had a certain amount of ration stamps they could use in a month to purchase what they needed, especially sugar, flour, eggs and butter, and Abigail was required as a store owner to follow specific rules. No one person or family was allowed to hoard any of the food; it all needed to be shared.

The General Store door swung open. A tall, lean figure came through the doorway. He removed his hat and held it in his hands as he stepped through the doorway.

"Good day, miss," A deep masculine voice sounded.

"Good day," Abigail looked up from the open door of the pot belly stove. She was stoking the coals before throwing a few logs in. The very well dressed young man stood fifteen feet away from her. He had slick black hair and fine features, with sharp narrow eyebrows and a very thin moustache that stretched across his upper lip. "What can I help you with today, sir?"

"Well, I am new to town."

Abigail listened as she finished placing the logs in the stove, closed the door and stood up. She brushed her skirt with the palms of her hands.

"And I am in need of a few groceries."

"Oh, you must be Dr. Parker?" Abigail presumed. She remembered Doc telling her he was coming to town. "What can I get for you?"

He pulled open his suit coat, reached into the breast pocket of his white cotton shirt, pulled out a folded piece of paper and held it out to her.

"Everything I need is on this list, I'll be back to pick it up in an hour," he stated.

"Oh, of course," Abigail hesitated, almost wanting to say "yes, your majesty" instead. She was reluctant to reach for the paper but did anyway. She scanned the list to make sure she had everything in stock.

"Perfect, miss- uh what did you say your name was?" he asked.

"I didn't." Abigail raised her left eyebrow, "and it's *Mrs. Hudson.*" Abigail didn't know what it was about this fellow, but she felt she had to explain herself to him, at least that she was married. He made her feel slightly uncomfortable, almost like she was committing a sin while speaking with him. *He sure is very presumptuous to assume she would get his supplies as if she were his maid, how dare he? Who does he think he is? He may be a doctor but he sure has a lot of nerve,* Abigail said to herself. *I bet he was spoiled and his mother didn't teach him any manners,* she continued to think.

He put on his hat, walked out and slammed the door behind him. As fast as he came in, he left. Abigail was curious about the strange doctor and ran to the window to watch him leave. To her surprise he climbed into a metal machine she had never seen before. It had metal and rubber wheels instead of wooden, and there were no horses. It was partially enclosed with doors at the sides and glass in the front. Abigail had heard of these kinds of transportation, and read about them in the newspaper, but hadn't actually seen one in person.

As he drove away there was a popping noise and it began to roar louder as the contraption accelerated. Abigail had never seen anything like it. At that moment a baby's cry came from the sitting room.

"Coming." Abigail spoke out loud as if the babies knew what she was saying. Abigail tried to hurry before one twin woke the other, but by the time she reached their bassinets, they both were wailing, one as much as the other.

While Abigail was consoling little Danny, baby Josie cried as she laid in the bassinet and kicked her feet and waved her arms.

"Calm down, little ones, I only have two hands," Abigail said audibly. She began to nurse Daniel as she sat in the rocking chair next to Josie, using her right foot to push the rocking chair while her left foot pushed the bassinet back and forth.

Danny calmed down as he gulped mouthfuls of milk, and Josie's cry turned into a low whine. Abigail slowly leaned her head back against the back of the rocking chair and breathed a sigh of relief.

The store door flew open with a bang.

"Abigail!" A man's voice grew loud and clear. Abigail's head flew up and both babies began to scream. Abigail rolled her eyes, quickly tucked her blouse back in her skirt, stood up and reached down to pick up Josie. As she walked into the store with a baby on each hip, she blew at the hair that had fallen down in front of her face. She could see the person who was calling her. It was Mr. Edwards.

Over the shrilling noise of a baby crying in each ear, Abigail loudly spoke.

"Oh, hello, Mr. Edwards."

"Good day, Abigail, I see you have your hands full," Mr. Edwards appeared rather embarrassed. "I am sorry to bother you, uh..." The noise was even getting to him. "...uh but I thought you would want this." He handed Abigail an envelope.

Abigail turned her body sideways and reached for the envelope with her right hand as she clung onto Danny.

The blood drained from her face as she looked down past Danny's shoulder at the familiar stamped envelope. She grasped it tightly with her fingers.

"Thank you, Mr. Edwards," Abigail struggled to smile as she held back the tears. "So kind of you to bring it to me."

"Well...I knew..." he cleared his throat"...well...I just knew." He put on his hat as he quickly turned and left.

Abigail was so excited, she couldn't think about anything but to sit down and read that letter. The twins still screamed in her ears, but she didn't hear a thing. Quickly walking back to the sitting room, she sat down and began to feed Josie, as she rocked Danny on her other knee. She ripped open the back of the envelope and quickly pulled out the folded piece of paper. Her heart thumped loudly in her ears, as her trembling fingers unfolded the unlined paper. There on the paper was the familiar penmanship of her Jacob. Her stomach felt like it flipped inside her as she began to read.

Dear Girlie,

How are you my darling? I read your last letter and just had to write you as soon as I could, there isn't much time for writing letters and such but I do my best, and spend the few moments before sleeping re-reading letters from my beautiful wife. The other men here have the same trouble, we are all the same here. Doesn't matter if we are rich or poor, coloured or white, English or French, we all share the same burden of missing our family, wanting to be back home, but desire to win this war as quickly as possible. I am sure the enemy thinks the same way.

I am pleased Ernest has been helping you so much, it does my heart good to know that. I only pray you have someone else who will be there when he can't.

Charles and I have been separated and sent to a new location. I do pray he is alright, and keeps out of harm's way. Each day isn't a certain thing, one minute you're here, the next somewhere else. One day your friend is having dinner with you, the next he's gone.

The one thing that keeps me going is knowing what a wonderful family I am returning back to. I love you darling, I miss you every moment of every day. Praying every day for our soon reunion.

Your loving husband,
Jacob

Danny cried but Josie cooed and looked at her hands and kicked her feet. Abigail began to nurse Danny to calm him. She still stared at the sentences on the crinkled paper she held in her other hand. Her heart ached for Jacob, his strength, his touch. Her eyes yearned to see his dimpled smile and her arms ached to feel his touch. She never thought it would hurt this much to read his letters, see his inked words shed from his pen on the paper. She didn't know that the absence of her best friend, her husband, could be this hurtful. It didn't even feel this painful when she left for England and left Jacob behind. Maybe this was how he felt while she was gone. She imagined the heartache he felt when reading the letter she had sent him telling that she was to marry another. *Oh, my Jacob,* she thought, *the hurt I have caused you, the pain you must have gone through.* Her heart ached even more to know she caused him the same sorrow she now felt.

"Hello? Hello?" A male voice sounded from the store.

Abigail jolted out of her daydream. She realized an hour must have gone by and she hadn't even had a chance to get the doctor's order ready and here he was.

"I will be right there," She called out to him as she began to unlatch Danny from her breast so she could straighten herself to greet her customer. She hurried as the voice got louder; Abigail realized he was getting closer. She set one twin in his bed, then picked up the other and placed her down beside the first.

"Shhh," Abigail placed her forefinger to her lips. "I will be right back." She reached into her pocket and pulled out the list which she read as she walked toward the doorway. All of a sudden she stopped. There stood Dr. Parker. Abigail jumped back as she looked up; she almost ran into him.

"What are you doing?" Abigail angrily asked. "I said I would be right there." Abigail had wondered how long he was standing there and was he watching her? This angered her all the more.

"I figured you were busy," the doctor smiled mischievously "thought I could save you some steps."

"Well, not really when I have to come into the store anyway." Abigail's voice revealed her annoyance.

"I see you haven't gotten my order ready," Dr. Parker continued as he followed Abigail to the front counter.

"I apologize, but I didn't have time..." Abigail began to explain but then she realized, she had nothing to explain to this stranger. This rude, presumptuous, forward stranger whom she would rather serve the devil himself than to gather, count and bag all the items he requested.

"Well, I am kind of in a hurry..." He stated.

"Well, then I guess you could go to the store down the street," she smiled to herself.

"You're funny, as well as beautiful." He placed his elbow on the counter, leaned his head down on his hand, put his right foot behind his left leg and rested the toe of his boot on the floor.

Abigail huffed under her breath as she took the list out of her apron pocket, scanned it quickly, removed items from each shelf and placed them on the counter. Dr. Parker watched with great interest. What seemed to be hours, but actually minutes, Abigail finished the doctor's order, took his money and sent him on his way. She hoped his visits wouldn't be often.

After the twins were in bed for the night, Abigail sat down at her desk beside her bed. She reached out and opened the drawer to take out a piece of paper. Picking up the dip pen, she dunked the tip into the black liquid. As the pen touched the paper, ink began to outline the words Abigail spoke to Jacob.

My dearest Jacob,

Your letter couldn't have come at a more perfect time my love, just as you always are, with your impeccable timing. The day was not my best and missed you more than I can explain. The twins are healthy and growing quickly. They are good children but as all little ones, they both try my patience every now and then. You would be a proud papa, Jacob, as you said your boy bears your smile and your daughter, mine. They are anxious to meet their pa.

Things here at home are as good as can be expected. Everyone is putting on a brave face. I saw Mrs. Ford in the store the other day, I remember you telling me she was your mama's good friend. Her son came home but not the way she wanted. There was such pain in her eyes, sadness consumed her face. I didn't have the words I should have. Oh, Jacob, I hate this war!

I have met the new doctor in town. His name is Dr. Parker. I can't say that he will last long in our quaint little village but I guess we will see. I hope he doesn't stop in real often, he is a bit full of himself.

It brings me such pain to hear how horrible it is for you and all the other soldiers. I don't know how you can bear it, the cold, the fear, the anguish while watching your fellow servicemen die before your eyes. You don't have to keep things from me Jacob. There is talk in the village. I hear things. Not nice things but how men have come back and told others about what happened while they were there. I can't think about it too long or it will drive me mad.

*My heart yearns for you, Jacob, I never have
known such an aching in my chest. I pray every
day for this war to end and that you will be
coming back to us.*

I love you with all of my heart,
Your Girlie,
Abigail

Abigail placed the pen back on the clear glass holder and
laid it in the two indents that cradled the long instrument. She
picked up the blotter and rolled it over the ink on the paper,
then folded the paper in thirds, slid it into the envelope and
addressed it. She held it close to her chest and closed her eyes
as she took a deep breath. She let it out and looked upwards.

"Dear Lord, I know only You know what is happening
with the war, and where my Jacob is at this very moment."
Abigail didn't move as she prayed. "But I must admit, I am
losing faith." A tear rolled down her face. "I don't have the
hope Jacob had in You..."

Abigail stopped and began to sob. She dropped the letter
in her lap and brought her hands to her face as she loudly
cried out. As hard as she tried, even before Jacob and she were
married, she didn't feel the faithfulness Jacob did. She did her
very best and even at one point convinced herself that she did.
Tonight she realized she didn't have enough faith.

chapter nine

"Just a minute," Abigail hollered at the ringing of the bell as the door opened. "I will be right there." Danny was screaming loud and clear, with tears staining his rosy cheeks. His eyes resembled half moons as he looked up at his mama and reached up to her.

"I can pick you up in a minute, Danny," Abigail cooed as she gave Josie another spoonful of oatmeal. Josie slapped her hands together, smiled, enjoying her toothless chewing. For whatever reason, Abigail didn't care. She had to get to the store to help a customer.

"It's only me, Abigail," the gentleman's voice came closer to the kitchen.

Abigail bent over, reached for Danny and looked up to see Mr. Edwards.

"Good morning, Mr. Edwards." Abigail threw Danny on her hip, and bounced him up and down to console him. "Good to see you." Abigail thought it wasn't great timing as it was hard to speak when crying filled the air.

"I brought you a letter," Mr. Edwards smiled as he held out the familiar envelope to Abigail.

"Thank you." Abigail smiled back with tired eyes, as she took the envelope. *This would definitely put a spring in your step for the rest of the day,* she thought to herself.

"Do you need a hand with anything?" Mr. Edwards looked around at the empty woodbox, the piled up dishes, the laundry on the floor, not to mention the diapers hanging on a rope from one side of the room to the other.

"I am alright, Mr. Edwards." Abigail knew things were a mess, heck SHE was a mess. Her hair was not in place, her skirts weren't ironed and the beds still needed to be made. But she only had two hands, and they were filled with two children.

"Well, how about I fill the woodbox before I leave," Mr. Edwards nodded toward the stove.

"Oh, it's alright," Abigail wiped her forehead with the back of her hand. "I will do that while the twins nap," knowing full well there was a great possibility that the children wouldn't sleep at the same time. She didn't want to be a bother to Mr. Edwards.

"It's no trouble. I will fill both the one in the kitchen and the one in the store."

Before Abigail could argue, he was already headed out the doorway.

Danny finally calmed down and was content in his mother's arms. Josie was still happy in her chair, now playing with a small wooden spoon. Abigail looked down at the letter in her hand and couldn't wait to open it - in private of course.

Mr. Edwards hauled in several armfuls of wood, piling each woodbox as high as he could without the wood spilling over onto the floor.

"Thank you again, Mr. Edwards." Abigail stood at the door as her company left.

She briskly walked back to the kitchen, sat Danny in his chair with a toy, and she sat next to both twins pulled up to the table. She picked up the envelope, lifted the edge of the flap, and tore it open. She quickly scanned the words before she began to read.

My dearest Abigail,

I hope this letter finds you and the twins well. There isn't a day that goes by that I haven't thought of you a thousand times.

How are things in Abbington Pickets. I heard about Mrs. Ford's son. I was so sad to learn that he was killed in action. He was a good lad, I always liked him.

I met a young lad the other day, he was in another battalion. Quite the character, kind of reminded me of Charles in a way, always smiling and making jokes. Well he is from Eastern Canada, and wouldn't you know it, he has three other brothers, here. Can you imagine Girlie, being that mama of those boys, all four of them in this war? Please pray for all of them, my love. Pray they go home to their family.

Some days there is a lot of time spent waiting in these trenches, then others we are run off our feet, and there aren't enough hours of daylight. You would sure be surprised about how big these trenches are and how many men you can cram down in them, and still have room to play a game of cards. But I tell you, I would give anything to be back in Abbington Pickets cutting wood and kissing my Girlie.

One thing I sure miss, besides my love of course, is a good home cooked meal. Boy would I love to get my hands on your fried chicken and some half hour pudding! Makes my mouth water writing about it.

*Well, I have to go my love, I hope that you
are keeping well and give those children a kiss
and a hug from their papa.*

*Your loving husband,
Jacob*

Abigail pressed the letter to her chest for a moment and
thought about the words she had just read. *My poor Jacob, how
can he stand it being in another country so far from his family?*

"Delivery!" Came a voice from the store. Abigail had been
so preoccupied with Jacob's letter that she hadn't even heard
the bell above the door.

Abigail got up and headed to the store.

"Coming," she called out.

"Hello, ma'am." A skinny tall young lad stood before her
with a dolly cart with two crates on it. "Here are your papers
and a couple crates of goods," the delivery man stated.

"Thank you, sir," Abigail pointed behind the counter near
the office. "You can put them there."

The young lad left them where she had asked. She reached
down and read the headline of the Regina Leader.

'WILL WOMEN BE ALLOWED TO VOTE?' it read.

Oh, my, Abigail thought to herself as she read the article of
the women's suffrage on why women should be allowed to vote.

"And why not? Why shouldn't we be allowed to vote?"
Abigail whispered to herself.

Abigail grabbed a hammer to begin opening the crates
when she heard a loud squeal that turned into a cry. Abigail
threw down the tool and raced to the kitchen. She stopped
short when she entered the room to find Josie on the floor,
with blood streaming from her forehead. She rushed down to
the floor and scooped up the little girl. Josie was screaming,
mouth wide open, causing Danny to frown, then wail himself.
Abigail grasped the tea towel from the back of the chair and

placed it on her little girl's head. She wasn't able to hold it there very well, as she needed to pick up Danny so she could run to Doc's. Abigail's heart pounded in fear, as she held a screaming baby on either hip, running toward Doc's house. She heard a roaring sound come up from behind her as she went as fast as her legs could take her.

"Honk, honk." It scared the life out of her! She turned around to find Dr. Parker in his car behind her.

He stopped abruptly, got out quickly, and ran toward Abigail. He could see the blood that was now on both children and Abigail.

"I am trying to get to the Doc's."

"Here, get in," Dr. Parker reached out and opened the passenger door. Abigail was hesitant for a second but all she could think of was how badly Josie was hurt. She ducked down and climbed in awkwardly as she held onto both babies. The young doctor ran to the driver's side and drove as fast as his car would take them and pulled right up to the front door. It wasn't a far distance, but in an emergency, it felt like miles to Abigail.

Abigail didn't know how to open the car door. She searched fiercely to see how, as the two wailing children sounded in her ears. Dr. Parker ran to her side of the car and opened the door for her as she clutched the children while trying to step out of the car without dropping them. The young doctor steadied her as she placed her feet firmly on the ground and pulled herself up with a twin in each arm.

When they reached the door, Dr. Parker leaned past Abigail and opened it as he called out to Doc.

"Come through here." Dr. Parker held the door as Abigail walked through. He pointed toward the exam room off the living room. It was apparent that neither Doc nor Mrs. Johnson were at home.

"Let me see." He took Josie from Abigail's aching arms.

"She fell to the floor from her highchair," Abigail looked at her sweet little baby girl. Danny had calmed down as Abigail bounced him slightly on her hip. The most natural thing for a mother to do is soothe her young ones.

Josie still cried hard, as Dr. Parker looked at her split open forehead. The baby's tear-filled eyes searched the room to find her mama. Abigail tried to console her as she held her little boy. She stood as close as she could to Josie so she would know she wasn't alone.

"What happened?" Mrs. Johnson came through the doorway, "I can hear the crying down the road."

"Oh, thank goodness you're here!" Abigail almost burst into tears at the sight of the older lady. "Can you take little Danny please," and before she could answer, Abigail put the little boy in her arms.

Abigail walked back to Josie.

"Here, I will hold her." She scooped up the crying baby and sat down before the doctor. Abigail held the little one on her lap and rubbed her back to soothe her. She had her head facing forward so Dr. Parker could tend to it. Whenever he would touch the open wound, Josie would scream louder.

"She isn't going to like this," he told Abigail as he pulled out a needle and thread. Abigail squeezed her eyes shut and held Josie's head against her chest for the doctor. He was right, the poor little girl cried even harder than when she had fallen to the floor.

Abigail had to admit, Dr. Parker was quick in action and although it was painful for both involved, he was efficient and it was over before she knew it.

The doctor bandaged the wound and Abigail had her baby calmed down before Mrs. Johnson called out, "Tea time!"

"If she shows any signs of headache," Dr. Parker looked directly at Abigail, and for the first time she saw his serious side, "or if she starts vomiting, bring her here immediately."

"Of course, doctor."

"It's highly unlikely," he saw the fear in her eyes. "It's precautionary. Little Josie will be fine."

While sitting for a cup of hot tea, Abigail explained to both of them what had happened.

"There isn't enough of me to go around." Abigail sighed taking a sip of tea. Both twins happily played on the floor with the square wooden blocks Mrs. Johnson had given them.

"Well, I best be getting back to what I was doing." Dr. Parker stood up and pushed the chair back under the table. "I will come by the store and change the bandage." He looked at Abigail.

"Thank you very much, doctor," Abigail stood up as well. "I don't know how to repay you."

"Oh, I am sure you will think of something," Dr. Parker winked as he put his hat back on and left.

Abigail stood staring as she watched him from a distance, as he got into his car and drove away. *I wonder what he meant by that?* Abigail asked herself.

After she finished her tea with Mrs. Johnson, she gathered the twins and walked back to The General Store. She hoped no one had come while she was gone. She opened the door and saw the crate where it had been left. She reached the kitchen and looked at the big mess she had left.

"Oh, Lord, give me strength," she declared. "I really need it right now."

Abigail poured two bottles of milk and gathered the twins to lay them down for their nap. She needed to get a hold of this mess, and do it before anyone else came to see what a terrible housekeeper, not to mention terrible mother, she was. *How could she leave her babies alone, let them fall off the chair onto which they had climbed?* she asked herself.

Once Josie and Danny were fast asleep, Abigail tiptoed out of the room and back to the kitchen.

She picked up Jacob's letter, unfolded it, and read it again and again. It made her feel closer to him, and right now she needed to feel closer to him. Before she dove into bed herself, she penned Jacob a letter explaining the day's events.

...Poor little Josie, she cried her little heart out while getting her stitches. It was such a helpless feeling to watch my baby girl in pain such as that. Oh, Jacob, why wasn't I watching better? Why did I have to open the freight when I did? Oh, I can't figure out how it happened. It's like when you're a parent you need eyes in the back of your head, or at least in the other room, if that were possible! I need to do better!

Dr. Parker may be annoying, but he is a good doctor. Thank God he was coming back from a house call and could help because Doc was not home...

She finished the letter and dropped into bed after her exhausting day.

Just as Dr. Parker had said, he came by the next day to have a look at Josie's stitches.

"Already healing," Dr. Parker hollered over Josie's wailing as she sat on her mama's knee while he removed the bandage. "A bit swollen and bruised, but that is to be expected."

Abigail listened as she tried to console little Josie before she woke up her brother. It was difficult to bounce her up and down as he looked at her.

"Thank you," Abigail smiled cordially. Abigail was grateful for his help but there was still something about him she didn't care for.

chapter ten

"You want me to do what?" Abigail's eyes grew wide as her eyebrows almost raised into the top of her head.

"It will only be temporary," Doc Johnson put his hand on her shoulder, "until this Godforsaken war is over."

"And only God knows when that will be." Abigail's face began to redden.

"Abigail, I know what you must be feeling," Doc looked at her with concern. "But we have to be realistic here, life has to go on here, no matter what."

"I am sorry, Doc," Abigail's voice softened as she looked down and kissed the top of Danny's head as he sat in her lap. "I can't stop thinking of the day Jacob is going to walk through that doorway."

"I understand," Doc nodded his head. "This war has affected everyone in Abbington Pickets. You're not alone," he assured her. He grabbed his hat and walked slowly toward the door. He stopped as he reached for the door knob and turned around.

"Think about it," he put his hat on his head. "Don't take too long." He walked through the doorway and closed the door behind him.

Abigail slouched in the chair and pulled Danny even closer to her chest as if the baby was going to fall to the floor. Her mind was going a million miles a minute.

Jacob worked so hard to build their house, even when he hurt his hand so badly that Doc Johnson said that if he didn't stop using it, he wouldn't have a hand to use. How on earth does he expect me to give up the one thing that means the world to me by the one I love the most? she mused. *How could Doc ask this of me?*

"God? How much more can I take?" Abigail took a deep breath. "Why don't You answer me?" Her voice got louder, she looked up to the ceiling.

"Hello, anyone here?" An all too familiar male voice interrupted. "Helllllo?" He repeated.

"I am here..." Abigail stood up, lifted Danny and straddled him on one hip. She met Dr. Parker in the middle of the store by the potbellied stove. Abigail noticed his neatly pressed suit, bright white shirt and the fabric hat he held in his hand.

"What can I help you with?" Abigail cleared her throat.

"Well, I wondered if you were even here," Dr. Parker smiled, as he reached into his left breast pocket and pulled out a folded piece of paper. He reached toward Abigail.

Really again? When will this man realize I am not a maid, or his servant, Abigail thought. She lifted her hand, held it out palm side up, but didn't step forward. Dr. Parker smirked, walked up to Abigail and placed the note in her hand.

"I will be back in an hour," he said matter-of-factly and winked at Abigail. He put on his hat and walked back toward the door. He left and the door slammed shut.

Of all the nerve! Abigail huffed. *I can't believe him. He is so full of himself, he doesn't respect anyone, especially women! This is why women need to vote! So men like him won't walk all over them! Does he think he is the only customer I have? I am not his maid!* "Eeeek!" She screamed.

Crying came from the bedroom.

"Coming!" Abigail hollered out to Josie. With Danny still attached to her hip Abigail walked toward the loud sound.

Later that night after the doctor came back for his groceries, the store was closed and the twins were sound asleep. Abigail sat down at the rocking chair in the kitchen, picked up the nine patch quilt on which she had been working, and began to stitch the binding. With every needle stitch pushed through the fabric she thought of Jacob. It was a quilt she was making to send overseas, with the hope that a soldier like Jacob would feel the love and comfort that was used to hand make it.

Then her thoughts went back to Jacabig. *How could she say yes and let an arrogant doctor like Parker move in and run the hospital like he owns the place, and throw his arrogance around the room as he always does. It made her shudder. Then she thought of Jacob. She knew full well what he would do. He would be the first person to say, 'come on in, what's ours is yours, take what you need.' Ah, she knew what she needed to do, her heart told her 'yes,' but her mind is yelling 'no way!' Jacob built that house for her, and the selfish side of her wanted to leave it alone and to be there when he came back from the war. They would all live there together, one happy little family.*

The next day, Doc came by to pick up some coffee grounds. Abigail knew the real reason he was there.

"Doc," Abigail began as she tipped the tea pot filling his tea cup. "You gave me a lot to think about last night."

"I know." Doc smiled.

"I couldn't stop thinking about it." Abigail sat down across from him, lifted her tea cup to her mouth and slurped up the hot tea. "I know what I want to do." Doc's eyebrows lifted as he looked over his glasses.

"But I also know what Jacob would do." She set the tea cup down on the saucer. By then Doc already knew what her answer was going to be.

"I know what you think of Parker."

"What? Uh, what do you mean?" Not wanting to make it known.

"Abigail," Doc looked sternly, "I know."

"You know?"

He nodded.

"Well... Uh... Well," Abigail shifted from side to side in her chair.

"You don't have to like Dr. Parker," he smiled at her.

"I know." She looked down, embarrassed.

"It's not like he's the boss," Doc chuckled.

Abigail was relieved that Doc was able to understand her, but she also was relieved that she knew in her heart this is what Jacob would want.

"We will begin moving in as soon as we can get some volunteers." Doc finished the last swallow of his tea and set it down. "If that's all right with you."

Abigail nodded.

Even though Abigail had only written Jacob not long before, she needed to talk to him again. She wanted to tell him first hand about his hard work being turned into a hospital. She was confident Jacob will be pleased that Jacabig was being converted into a hospital. She wanted to tell him before anyone else penned him the news.

After Doc left, Abigail sat down at her desk, pulled out the white paper and began to write.

My dear Jacob,

I know I have just written to you, but I never tire of it. I hope you are safe and doing well. I hope to hear from you soon, I worry so much about you. Have you heard from Charles?

Darling, I have something to tell you. Doc Johnson came to me asking to use Jacabig Place as a hospital for the soldiers who come back wounded. I will admit to you Jacob, that I didn't want to do it. To let them change our beautiful home you built with your own two loving hands into an infirmary. I didn't want them to disturb the rooms, any part of it. I don't want that high and mighty Dr. Parker sleeping in our bedroom, living in our home. It's tearing at my heart. But after great consideration and thought, I told Doc they could use it for a hospital. I knew it would be what you would want. I want to help the soldiers who gave up their lives at home to fight in this war.

Danny and Josie are doing well and continue to grow. Josie's forehead is already healing well and she is almost back to her fun little self.

Claude and Peter should be harvesting soon. I know that most folks' crops are almost ripe. It has been extra hot and dry this month. What I wouldn't give for a nice pouring rain. Although the farmers wouldn't appreciate it right now.

I am going to sign off now, my love. I will keep writing, and patiently wait to hear back from you.

Your loving wife,
Abigail

chapter eleven

It took almost a week to change Jacabig Place into Jacabig Hospital, but Doc and Dr. Parker didn't waste any time. Almost all the men and women who were available to help from the village were there. Abigail's papa and hired help came into town to do their part. The first thing that needed to be done was to move all the furniture that they could upstairs. Anything, such as the piano, had to stay downstairs but was moved out of the way. The kitchen table remained because meals would still need to be prepared there.

Once the house was cleaned out, the men set up the furniture for the hospital. Some folks were able to donate extra beds that they had on hand and others gave spare sheets, blankets and pillows. Other items such as wicker baskets for laundry, small bedside tables, and lamps were also given. Each person who could, did.

Abigail's heart broke a little as she watched everyone touch their belongings and move stuff from one room to another. It was a good thing that she had cleaned out their personal things and took them to the living quarters of The General Store. It was bad enough Dr. Parker was moving into her home, but he would be using their furniture upstairs as well.

Thank goodness he wouldn't be sleeping in their bed, Abigail thought to herself. Doc was using that room for operating and procedures if necessary.

Abigail's A.P.L.G. began to make bandages for the hospital as well as sew white aprons for volunteers and hospital gowns for patients. It took a good month to get almost everything that the hospital would need to run efficiently. Before that, the doctors had to make do with what they had. Abigail tried her best to help the doctors as much as she could; she was their first 'nurse' besides Mrs. Johnson. She kept Doc's office running and Dr. Parker was going to run the hospital. They soon had to get a volunteer to sit with patients when Dr. Parker was away as Abigail wasn't always available.

Abigail served her customers during the day, tended to her babies and spent supper time and evenings making bandages and beds at the hospital. Sleep didn't seek her until well past midnight, and then she was awake again at five o'clock. It's not as though Abigail didn't enjoy sleeping, but the fact was, the less time lying in bed was less time to think about Jacob.

Finally she received a letter from Jacob. Her heart almost jumped out of her chest. She was so anxious to read his words, especially after the last three that she had sent him. She opened the letter with such anticipation.

My dearest love,

> *It was good to see your letters waiting for me when I got back for some shut eye. I read the letters several times I am sure, and still can't get enough of hearing from you.*
> *I am so pleased you said yes to Doc about the hospital. You were right to do so. I know you're hurting because it's our home, our first home together but sweetheart, a house doesn't make a home, God and the people who live in it do. I*

would build you three more houses if it would make you happy, my love. It's only temporary and believe me, you are doing the war a great service. Doc needs us, and I am happy to oblige. You are a kind and generous woman, and I know you will always do the right thing. God gave you to me, and I love you with all my heart. I thank The Lord every day for you and our children.

I know you will handle Dr. Parker the correct way. You are strong and have spunk. Do you remember the day we met? You sure told me. I trust you will have the words to say to him and he will surely get the hint to either leave you alone or wise up.

Did Claude, Peter and your father get harvest done? I always wonder what is happening back home, and miss everyone terribly. Next time you see them, please give them my best.

Kiss those babies for me love, and keep praying Girlie! We sure aren't looking forward to the cooler weather that is about to befall upon us.

All my love,
Jacob

Today was no different from any other day. Abigail was up to her ears in house work, children, business and anything else anyone could think of. She was working in the kitchen when she heard the bell of the door in the store ring.

"I am coming!" Abigail yelled out over her shoulder. She had one demanding child in the highchair and one at her feet, as she stood over the wash basin of soapy water and washed dishes. The kitchen table was full of dirty dishes and dirty clothes covered each chair. As Abigail grabbed the tea towel from over her shoulder to dry the saucer she held in her hand, an impatient voice sounded in the doorway.

"I said I would be right there." Abigail turned around. Her once neat bun loosened and strands of hair fell down in front of her face and around her ears. Her cheeks were red from embarrassment.

"I couldn't hear you," Dr. Parker smirked as he cleared his throat, "over the noise." He looked about the room and raised his eyebrows.

"I am sorry," Abigail wiped her forehead with the back of her hand, then scooped up Josie, and threw her on one hip. At that moment of silence, Danny felt the need to fill the one minute of quiet and began to sob loudly. Without thinking,

Abigail handed Josie to the doctor and he awkwardly took the toddler from her arms.

"Well...what..." He tried to say as the shrieking began again. Abigail quickly walked over to Danny and pulled him out of the highchair.

"If you want me to help you," Abigail talked as she walked past Dr. Parker, "you will have to work with me." The doctor followed her into the store. Both the twins were now in harmony with one another, with barely a second of breath. Abigail tried to jiggle Danny on her hip as Dr. Parker held Josie away from him as he walked.

"What can I get you?" Abigail yelled over the noise, as though she threw on her shopkeeper's hat.

"I need some supplies for the hospital." He handed her the list, which Abigail quickly skimmed.

"I have everything except the iodine."

"What? How could you be out of that? It's one of the most important things."

"I am sorry, Dr. Parker." Abigail tried to be professional under the circumstances. "I am expecting the order any day now." Abigail scurried around the store, putting each item into a brown paper bag. By this time Danny had quieted down with the movement but Josie was still crying due to the lack of attention from her holder.

"Bonjour," a new voice echoed in the store. Abigail turned her head to see Claude standing in the doorway.

"Good morning," Abigail smiled at the sight of a familiar face. "How are you today?"

"I am good and you?" Claude smiled.

"Great, now that someone else is here." Dr. Parker walked over as he held out Josie to Claude. Claude was as unfamiliar with babies as the doctor.

"Um... all right?" His confusion was obvious, as he glanced at Abigail then back to the doctor, but Dr. Parker still put the child in his hands. With that he walked over to Abigail, took the bag out of her hands, tapped the tip of her nose with his finger and gave her a wink.

"Can you put this on my bill, please?" He put his hat back on and walked out the door; the bang of the door closed behind him.

Abigail shook her head as she raised her eyebrows. She stepped closer to Claude. Josie stopped crying and began to play with Claude's hat.

"Wow!" Claude watched the door slam in disbelief. "Is he always like that?"

"Oh, he's harmless. How is Jane doing?" She knew that Claude was feeling sorry for her as she stood before him looking rattled and tired.

"She is better than she was." He smiled slightly. "I keep praying for her and our little one."

Abigail nodded in agreement. Jane was expecting a baby again and fearful of the same thing happening to her. She wasn't excited, she wasn't happy, she was only Jane before Claude. Abigail hadn't seen her very much since her miscarriage and only knew what Claude had confided in her. *Claude's faith in God was admirable,* Abigail thought, since her own faith had faded and left her as discouraged as Jane. Of course she didn't make that known.

"It will be all right, I am sure of it." Abigail smiled weakly. *How would she know?* She asked herself.

"I tell her that every day."

"A baby will be good for the two of you." Abigail watched Claude play with Josie. "You are a natural."

"Well, I don't know much about babies, but it's hard not to get excited about it." Claude began to swing Josie around in the air, and she giggled at the thrill of being thrown in midair.

"Lord knows we all need a little sunshine during this dreary time."

"How are you doing?" Claude's face sobered as he looked around the room, knowing things weren't as they usually were.

"It's sometimes a little trying," Abigail took a deep breath, "but we are doing all right." She pulled Danny tighter to her side as she spoke. "I received another letter from Jacob," she smiled.

"How is he?" Claude asked.

"He never really says, but he asked me to give his best to you and everyone." Abigail smiled faintly.

"Just like Jacob," he shook his head, "in the middle of this damn war, excuse my language, and he's selflessly thinking of everyone else."

"That's Jacob." Abigail knew it too. He was the most selfless person she knew, that was for sure.

"If there is anything you need help with..." Claude always offered and Abigail knew it was hard for him to help do anything. Not only was the trip to Abbington Pickets a long one but he was helping Peter with his chores. Now with Jane needing more attention he was up to his neck himself.

"I appreciate the offer," Abigail smiled, "but it's all right, really. Ernest will be here soon now that harvest is finished and I will be able to help at the hospital more."

"Ernest has been such a great help," Claude put his head down, "Jacob would be pleased to know-"

"What can I do for you?" Abigail interrupted. "I know it wasn't only for the visit," she laughed.

"We need some coffee, lard, a bit of sugar..." Claude read from his list.

"Do you have your ration coupons?" Abigail raised her left eyebrow.

"Yes, right here." He dug further into his pocket to produce the stamps.

"I will get everything for you," Abigail handed him the other twin as she set off to pick up a paper bag, opened it with a shake and began to put the items into the bag.

"Give Jane my best." Abigail reached for her children as Claude traded a twin for an armful of groceries. By this time the children were chatting baby talk which both could understand.

"I will, Abigail," Claude nodded as he walked toward the wooden door. "Merci."

Abigail walked into the kitchen and plopped down on the chair with both twins on her lap.

"Oh, Jacob, I miss you so much." Abigail squeezed Danny and Josie tight until they squealed to be released. She let them slide off her lap and onto the floor, and both crawled away to explore on their own.

Abigail couldn't stop thinking about Jacob, and how he has missed out on the twins' firsts. First smile, first tooth, first word and first everything. Not only did they miss and need him but Jacob's siblings needed him too. It was an overwhelming feeling of being alone, the desperation she felt every day. What if Jacob never came home. Abigail's heart began to pound, she could hear it in her head. She took a deep breath, and after several seconds she realized she was holding it. She let it out and closed her eyes as she leaned back in the chair. The panic seeped up through her stomach and into her heart like a freight train. Abigail remembered the last words she said to Jacob, she remembered his last touch, and also recalled how she felt as the train left the station that September day. Tears began to well up in her eyes, and spilled out down both cheeks. She couldn't help it, the helplessness overtook her. Abigail wailed as she hugged herself and rocked back and forth in the chair. The two children who had been jabbering and crawling about stopped and stared.

"I am so sorry, my babies." Abigail realized the worry on their faces, knelt down to the floor with both arms stretched out and scooped them toward her. She held them close.

"Hello?" A woman's voice sounded from behind Abigail.

"Oh, Alice!" Abigail turned around, quickly wiping the tears from her face with her fingers as she grabbed the arm of the chair to balance herself while getting up. She carried both twins as she walked toward the doorway.

"What are you doing here?"

Alice had her hair pinned neatly in a bun and wore a beautiful big brimmed hat which had flowers covering the front and sides, and a big bow on the back. She wore a long mauve dress that had an off-white collar and pearl buttons up the front. She held out her arms as Abigail embraced her briefly.

"Bert needed to meet a fellow in the village so I took the opportunity to come and see you."

"Where are the girls?"

"They are at our neighbours, the Rileys." Alice smiled "They have been so kind since we moved there, wouldn't know what to do without them."

"It's great when you have folks you can count on, like family." Abigail smiled back at her, knowing how they had been good friends to Jacob and her.

"Look at how big you two are getting," she looked the twins over and then took Josie from Abigail.

"Well, come in, come in." Abigail stood back to let her guest come further into the room. "Come, sit down at the table, I will make us some tea." Abigail put Danny in the highchair and poured water into the kettle, placed it on the stove top, then stoked the stove and added more wood. Alice held Josie on her lap and sang her a little song.

> Ride a cock horse to Banbury Cross,
> To see a fine lady upon a white horse.
> With rings on her fingers and bells on her toes,
> She shall have music wherever she goes.

"That's a sweet song." Abigail set the tea cups down on the table.

"It's an English song, my mum used to sing it to us when we were children." Alice continued to sing.

"I will have to remember that."

"We sing it to Grace and Annie as well." Alice laughed. "In fact Bert usually crosses his knee with one leg, puts the children on his foot and holding their hands bobs them like they're riding a horse. They beg him to do it all the time. My leg gets played out doing it."

"Sounds like a great family tradition." Abigail poured the water into the tea pot. She took biscuits from the cupboard, set them onto a plate and placed them on the table along with butter and jam.

"I haven't had time to bake any cookies." Abigail sat at the table, giving each twin a piece of biscuit and butter.

"This is great." Alice took a bite. When Josie began to cry, Danny mimicked and the two were en masse.

"Here we go again," Abigail picked up Danny and tried to console him by bouncing him, then rocking, then walking as she swayed from side to side. Alice did the same with Josie.

After what seemed like hours the twins were in bed for their afternoon nap. Abigail sat exhausted at the table with Alice. Alice reached out and put her hand over Abigail's.

"It's going to be all right."

"I don't know how!" Abigail blurted out. "Look at this place! I can't keep up with it, I can't keep the twins from screaming while I deal with patrons. Rationing food is not the easiest thing to deal with. Folks aren't happy but I have to abide by all the rules. It's not like they are MY rules." Abigail took a deep breath. "And not to mention that new doctor, he's on every nerve I have left, and you know that isn't very many." Abigail put her head in her hands and tried to stop the tears from welling up.

Alice patiently listened as Abigail vented.

"This would be so much easier if he were here. Why did he leave me all alone!"

"I know it's tough, and you have been so strong. God is your rock now."

"God?" Abigail raised her head. "How can God be here right now? I can't even begin to pray anymore. I feel God isn't listening."

"Don't say that, Abigail. God is always listening."

"Jacob had faith. I followed him. Everything seemed to work for him, but I don't have his faith." Abigail cried in her hands.

"Wasn't The Lord there for you when your babies were born?" Alice reminded Abigail. "Wasn't God faithful when the tornado took your home? What about when He restored Jacob's hand? God is everywhere, God is with us now."

"I am sorry, Alice, I don't feel Him as you do." Abigail shook her head.

"Let us pray together, Abigail." Alice bowed her head and began to pray, "Lord Jesus we come to You with heavy hearts. I lift Abigail to You Lord, please restore her faith, give her strength spiritually, mentally and physically. Please watch over and protect Josephine and Daniel. We also pray in Your name that You will keep Jacob safe and bring him home to his family soon. We ask this in Jesus Name. Amen."

Abigail wiped her tears with a handkerchief and tried to smile at Alice with gratitude.

"It's all right," Alice smiled back to her. "God is with you and He will get you through this."

"Thank you, Alice, I know you're right." Abigail half smiled, she really wasn't so sure anymore.

chapter twelve

Snow came, sooner than everyone was ready for. Ernest returned to Abbington Pickets to help Abigail once again. He cut wood, hauled water, worked in the store and even babysat the twins while Abigail helped at the hospital.

While Christmas was small, with only Abigail's mama and papa and Ernest, it was a nice get-together and Abigail was happy to see her family and her papa sure enjoyed the twins. Abigail couldn't help but think, while watching her father read to Josie and Danny, that if it hadn't been for the faithful prayers from Jacob and his persistence that her father was going to get better, that her papa wouldn't be here to enjoy these two blessings that giggled upon his lap.

The winter months sure didn't keep the Empire Hotel from being in business; the rowdy customers were as noisy as ever especially each Saturday night, that was for sure. Sometimes Abigail had dreams of that terrible night she went out to defend the quiet of the night from the two young lads causing a ruckus. Her dreams always consisted of her giving birth to the twins early but that they died and she would wake up in a cold sweat.

The war not only changed the way people lived, it changed the way folks thought. People lived for the day, not for what months would bring, because frankly, they didn't know. They knew their husbands may not ever come home. They knew that if their crops didn't grow well, they wouldn't have money for food or shoes for their children's feet. Many children didn't go to school and stayed home in order to help with the chores. Women had to do men's work and children had to do adults' work long before their time.

One day in March the newspaper came in with the headline 'WOMEN WIN THE RIGHT TO VOTE!' As of March 14, 1916, Saskatchewan women were given the right to vote. Manitoba were already given the right, where women attained the right to vote in January, 1916 and Alberta followed on April 19, 1916. Abigail knew it was a milestone in Canadian history, but all she could think about was whether her husband was going to come back from the war.

Abigail hadn't heard from Jacob since the letter she received before Christmas. It was a wonderful Christmas present indeed. She knew that God had sent her a gift and she accepted it with great thanks. She remembered his words...

> *...You are my gift from God, I will always know that. Merry Christmas, darling. Don't worry about me and what's happening, enjoy the day with our babies and love them extra hard for you and for me. Tell them papa will be home soon and kiss the top of their heads and pray to The Lord that our children will grow into God fearing, generous, loving adults.*
> *Goodbye my darling...*

Even though Abigail hadn't heard from Jacob, she still faithfully wrote once a week with Abbington Pickets news and updates of the twins. Writing letters felt as though she was really talking to Jacob as she looked for advice and understanding. She prayed less and less.

Working at the hospital gave her a satisfaction that she couldn't explain. It made her feel like she was helping Jacob in some way. Like he said in his letter, it was a service to our country, and Jacob honoured our country and hers. She was doing it for him.

"I am here." Abigail announced as she took off her hat and shawl and hung it on the hook by the door. She grabbed the full white apron that laid over the chair, slipped it over her head and tied the ties in the back. She rushed to walk toward the room of beds. What was once the dining room and living room now held the beds, one after the other in a row, at Jacabig. Abigail began to strip the dirty bed sheets off the first bed she saw.

"Good evening, Abigail," Doc Johnson was tending to a new patient. Abigail knew he was new because she had never seen anyone with bandages on the face before.

"Good evening, Doc. How are things today?"

"Well, two patients went home today," he took a puff of his pipe as he spoke, "but one more came this afternoon, and I am expecting two more tomorrow."

"I will get these beds made as soon as I can," she assured him as she piled the soiled sheets in her basket.

"I am not worried," he smiled. "Come, help me for a minute."

"Of course." Abigail walked to the patient Doc was standing over. The man's head was wrapped completely except for his eyes and mouth. His hands and chest were bandaged as well.

Abigail tried not to gasp. She had learned to stomach a lot of gruesome sights and this was no exception.

"Please help me roll him over." He held the roll of cotton bandages in his hand. "I have to finish his back." Abigail was scared to touch the man. He didn't speak a word, but watched through his mask. The raw flesh wept clear bloody liquid, the edge of which was raw, black leathery looking. It was the worst thing Abigail had seen so far. She didn't know where she could touch him without hurting him.

"Take this." Doc handed her the roll of bandages. She watched as he wiped ointment on the wound with a flat wooden tool. The soldier winced and groaned each time Doc touched him. Doc then wrapped him like a mummy as Abigail assisted him as she held the soldier's arms to keep him upright.

"There," Doc wiped his hands with a towel, "that should do him until tomorrow."

The mystery soldier's eyes didn't leave Abigail's face while she finished cleaning up. His stare followed her everywhere she went in the room. He watched as she stripped another bed, then made it with fresh clean sheets.

"Well, look who is here." The familiar voice of Dr. Parker reverberated the room.

Abigail ignored his comment and continued her work. She was nearly done and was going back home. She was only able to come over tonight as Ernest was at the store and the babies were in bed.

"All the beds have been changed and I made new bandages." She carried the basket of sheets to be washed to the front door. She took off her apron, put on her shawl, then felt someone come up behind her. The warmth of his breath stopped her in her tracks.

"I know what you're thinking," he breathed. "One day you will need a husband." His voice was deep with confidence. "And I will be here waiting for you." Abigail moved away from him abruptly, put her hat on her head and pinned it in place.

"Good evening, Dr. Parker." Not looking back, she picked up the basket and rested it on one hip. As she held it with one hand she opened the door with her other one. She couldn't get his voice out of her head. She shuddered thinking about it. He got bolder every time she met up with him. The audacity was unmistakable.

As Abigail briskly walked toward The General Store, she felt like steam was blowing out the top of her head. She fiercely threw open the store door.

"Abigail, you're back," Ernest said as he stacked wood into the wood bin. "I thought you might be gone another hour or so."

"I finished up early tonight." Abigail took off her hat. "How were the twins?"

"Never heard a peep out of them." Ernest wiped his hands together. "I checked on them and they were sleeping soundly."

"Thank you, Ernest." Abigail half smiled. "I couldn't do this without you. I don't know how I could ever repay you."

"Don't even think about that." Ernest shook his head. "I am happy to do anything to help."

"Well, you have gone above and beyond your call of duty for a family you barely knew."

"Any friend of Bert and Alice's is a friend of mine." Abigail smiled. *Why couldn't the world have more Ernests and a few less Dr. Parkers,* she wondered.

"Tea?" Abigail hung up her hat and headed toward the kitchen.

She made tea as Ernest locked up, filled both stoves, then sat down at the kitchen table.

"This came today," Ernest set the Leader Post down on the wooden surface. The headline read 'MANY DEAD, MORE WOUNDED AS WAR IN EUROPE CONTINUES!'

"I am so tired of seeing that everywhere." Abigail poured tea into each cup.

"I should be there with them." Ernest plopped his tea cup harder than usual.

"You are needed here, Ernest. You are serving here."

"It's not the same." He shook his head.

"You are serving our country, taking care of everyone here," Abigail stated. "Don't think for a moment that I don't know what you have been doing."

Ernest looked at her curiously.

"The extra stacks of wood, the extra pails of water in the house, the basket of eggs that magically appear on the counter. Should I go on?"

"You have me confused with someone else."

"You can't fool me anymore," Abigail laughed. "I know your secret. And I am pretty sure I am not the only one you have been helping."

Ernest shook his head again. "I don't know what you're talking about."

Abigail left it alone. If Ernest wanted his help to be kept a secret, so be it, but she didn't want him to think it didn't go unnoticed or unappreciated.

Ernest and Abigail sat in silence for several minutes. Abigail began to read the paper. She saw article after article about what was going on abroad. It made her heart pound in fear as she thought of where in that moment Jacob was. She read how men were freezing to death with the lack of clothing, how they were sick and dying from the cold. How the rain kept the trenches wet and muddy and that men's feet were rotting from being in the moisture.

"We have to do more," Abigail declared out loud. Ernest looked up at her and raised an eyebrow.

"Men are dying,"

"Ugh... I know..."

"No, I mean dying of other things besides by the enemy." Abigail stood up abruptly. "We need to do more."

"Like what?"

"We need to raise money." Abigail walked back and forth pondering her idea. "Money for more blankets, boots and things we can't make ourselves."

"It's a good idea, but what more can you do?"

"I've got it!" Abigail turned around, eyes wide. "A crib tournament!"

"What? Are you kidding?"

"No, I am serious."

"That's not very ladylike," Ernest stood up. "What will people say? The reverend?"

"So what? It doesn't matter what the village thinks," Abigail stated, "it's for a great cause. If it can help my Jacob, Charles and all the other soldiers stay warm in this wretched war, I am willing to do anything, despite what others think." Abigail walked into her room for paper and a pen to make a list of things she needed to do to get ready.

"Your mama will have a conniption," Ernest insisted.

"We will do it right here." She continued to write down notes.

"Here? But there's no room."

"We will make room." Abigail could hardly contain her excitement. "I will make posters tomorrow."

"When?" Ernest realized his argument fell on deaf ears.

"Next Saturday," Abigail stated. "The sooner the better." Ernest took a deep breath of defeat.

"If you make invitations, I will take them around to all the neighbours." Ernest offered.

"That would be wonderful," Abigail smiled. "Thank you." Abigail felt something other than helplessness for a change. It was different than making socks and shirts. She felt that she was mothering all the soldiers and making a difference.

chapter thirteen

It was Saturday, the day of the crib tournament. It was a beautiful day. The sun shone so bright, it was like a special invitation for all of Abbington Pickets to come out for the great cause. Men and women came to play in the tournament. Mostly men played while the women made and served chicken and beef sandwiches, with delicious homemade bread and freshly churned butter. Several kinds of cakes and loaves were brought, such as matrimonial cake, date loaf and different kinds of cookies and one of Abigail's favourites, ginger snaps, which was brought by Alice. It was harder and harder to bake because of the rationing of sugar, but each woman had her own baking secrets. The ladies who weren't serving and making lunch were knitting scarves, socks and hats - anything to keep the soldiers warm. Some left after they played and lost, some stayed to cheer each other on. The word heard most in the room was "fifteen". As in "fifteen this, fifteen that." There were several couples playing at a time, and the tournament went on as such. Four tables were set up for games. Each player paid a fee to play which was put into a pot in the beginning. In the end the winner would split the amount raised, half he could keep and half would be given to the soldiers' cause. The winner of each set would play against the other winner and so on and so forth. There was a lot of playful yelling and shouting as well as cheering. Abigail was so pleased at how the day was turning out. It was going to be a success, she knew it already.

Josie and Danny were a big hit for the day. The women held each of them on their knees and played with them, sang lullabies and told nursery rhymes. The twins were a growing concern and beginning to express their own personalities.

"I had an idea for you, Abigail," Mrs. Ford stirred her tea as she looked at Abigail.

"For what?" Abigail smiled as she bounced Josie on her knee.

"My daughter is twelve years old, her name is Elizabeth." Mrs. Ford took a sip of the hot liquid. "She loves children, she is good with them."

"Oh?" Abigail wasn't sure what she was saying.

"She would be happy to help you with your twins, do a little housekeeping and help with the meals."

"I couldn't ask her to do all that."

"Elizabeth would love it, really."

"I can't keep her from her school work."

"She is a smart girl, she does her studies at home." Mrs. Ford seemed to be rather insistent, "besides, it will only be temporary."

"Well, if you insist." Abigail was happy inside, and grateful. God was answering her prayers.

"Abigail," Ernest called out to her. "Your turn is next."

Abigail stood up and handed Josie to Alice, then she went into the store part to the table that was available for a new game. She was the first one to sit, and Abigail wondered who she was playing against. She began to shuffle the cards when a hand grabbed the back of the chair, pulled it away from the table and sat down. Right there, sitting opposite to her, was the irritating Dr. Parker.

Abigail inhaled deeply at the sight of the young doctor.

"Well, look who is my playmate."

"Hello, there." Abigail continued to shuffle the deck of cards without disclosing how aggravated she really was.

"Don't we need to cut the cards to see who shuffles?"

"My mistake." Abigail set the deck down on the table. Dr. Parker picked up part of the deck and revealed his card. Abigail did the same.

"I guess it's my crib," Dr. Parker grinned.

"Hmm, I guess so." Abigail looked at his two of spades and her ten of diamonds.

He picked up the deck and with a few more shuffles he dealt the cards to each of them. The room quieted downed as he and Abigail picked up their hands and fanned them out to look at them. Not taking much time to place their cards in Dr. Parker's kitty, Abigail cut the cards and he turned up a four of spades.

"Three." Abigail laid down the three of spades.

"Four." Dr. Parker laid down an ace of diamonds.

"Eleven." Abigail laid down a seven of hearts.

"Fifteen two." The doctor's mischievous lips curved slightly as he laid down the four of diamonds, then pegged his points on the crib board.

Abigail didn't pay attention, she had much more in mind. *Let him get his points while he can*, she thought.

"Nineteen for two." She placed a four of hearts down and took her points.

"Look who is on her toes." He looked at his cards and picked one quite quickly. "Twenty-four." He leaned back in his chair, quite anxious to see what she had in mind.

"Thirty for three," she placed a six of diamonds down and took her points.

"Go." Dr. Parker let Abigail take her one point before laying down his last card. He quickly looked in his kitty, took the three points for the run of three he had and tossed the cards on the table.

Abigail grasped the deck and continued to break it.

"What a nice surprise to be playing against you." Dr. Parker smirked once again and taunted her with his words.

"We all have our crosses to bear." Abigail turned her nose up as she dealt six cards to each of them. Both picking up the cards, each of them put down two cards for the kitty for Abigail. Abigail smiled to herself as she admired her hand. Dr. Parker cut the cards and Abigail turned over a king of hearts.

"Nine." Dr. Parker laid down a nine of diamonds.

"Fifteen for two." Abigail put down a six of spades, then pegged her points in the wooden rectangle crib board.

"Twenty-three." The doctor laid down the eight of diamonds.

"Go." Abigail smiled as she shifted in her chair.

"Twenty-eight." He revealed a five of hearts. "Twenty-nine." Placing an ace on top of the five, he sat back in his seat.

Everyone in the room looked at Abigail, waiting to watch her next move.

"Ten," she glanced over at the doctor as she held the remaining cards. "Twenty for two, thirty for six." She placed three kings, one on top of the other consecutively. "And one for last card." Abigail pegged the nine points, the additional twelve for her hand and smiled as she looked in her kitty.

Ooh's and awes filled the room as she took another eight points for a double run of three.

Dr. Parker lost his smirk as he leaned forward, gathered the deck of cards and began to shuffle.

"Well, it's not starting off so good for you lad," Ernest spoke up as the audience laughed along with him.

"Maybe you should quit while you're ahead, Doc!" another shouted out.

"Hey, there is no other 'doc' around here besides Doc Johnson!" someone else added.

"Be nice, fellas." Abigail enjoyed toying with the annoying doctor as she gathered her cards. Playing with Ernest this last winter had paid off, she was getting much better at the game.

People still gathered around them patiently waiting, yet anxious to see what they were going to play. The store door flew open and a man dashed through the doorway.

"Sorry to interrupt your tournament," Claude spoke as he ran toward Abigail sitting at the table. She quickly stood up.

"What is it, Claude?" She met him part way. "What is wrong?"

"It's Jane! She's in labour. Can you come with us?"

"Of course." She looked at her opponent. "I am sorry, I really have to go."

"I will step in for you, if it's permissible," Ernest spoke up.

"The twins will be fine with us." Alice stepped forward, Josie on her hip and Danny's hand in hers beside her.

"I will be here as well." Mrs. Ford added.

"Thank you, Ernest," she nodded as she grabbed her shawl, then her coat. "Thank you, Alice, Mrs. Ford."

"Don't worry, everything will be fine," Ernest reassured as she ran out the door, Claude on her heels.

"She's in the wagon," Claude explained as they hurried. "She insisted you come with us to Doc's. After last time, she didn't want to take any chances." Abigail nodded, as she climbed onto the back of the wagon.

"Hello, Jane," Abigail smiled as she knelt down beside Jane. "You sure know how to get a person's attention."

"Oh, Abigail, there's no time to be funny." She grinned, then grasped her belly, gritted her teeth and drew her knees toward her inner body.

"Try to relax and breathe, Jane." Abigail pushed back her hair from her forehead. As the wagon began to move, Abigail grabbed hold of the edge of the wagon to keep her balance. The vibration and motion made it very uncomfortable for Jane.

"We are here!" Claude yelled to the back of the wagon. He pulled the reins to slow the horses. They stopped and he pulled the brake. He jumped off the front of the wagon and ran to the back.

"Let me help," Doc hurried out of the house and reached up to assist Jane down. Claude stood across from him as Abigail helped from behind. Mrs. Johnson held the door open and they held onto Jane as she walked to the house.

"Come over here, dear," Mrs. Johnson smiled. She nodded at Abigail. Abigail couldn't help but notice that there was sadness in her eyes. Jane stopped. She groaned under her breath and her knees buckled as she grabbed her front with another labour pain. Claude and the Doc helped her stand until the pain subsided. Abigail bent down to Jane's level and grabbed hold of her right hand.

"You can squeeze my hand as tight as you want."

"Let's go into the patient room." Mrs. Johnson directed them to the room at the right separated by the curtain in the one-room house.

Six hours later, Doc was concerned that her labour was lasting longer than he expected. Everyone was nervous. Her condition seemed to stay the same. Since Jane had had a miscarriage, Doc suspected something may be not quite right. Of course he kept this information between himself and his wife.

"How much longer can she be able to handle the pain?" Abigail asked Mrs. Johnson as they made tea in the kitchen.

"I don't really know, Abigail." Mrs. Johnson carried the tray of beverages.

"Well, isn't there something Doc can do?" Abigail followed and kept her voice low.

"He's doing everything he can," Mrs. Johnson turned her head back as she continued to walk forward.

"Abigail," Claude grabbed her arm. "What is happening?"

"Everything is going to be alright," Abigail patted his arm. "She just needs more time and a few prayers."

"Oui, I have been praying." Claude slid his hands over his head, pushed back his hair, took a deep breath and began pacing again.

"God is a good God," Abigail smiled. "Only He knows what is going to happen. God's timing is perfect." Abigail didn't want Claude to know how worried she was as well.

There was a knock at the door. Abigail walked to the front door, reached for the door latch and opened it.

"Ernest." Abigail backed up holding the door wide open. "Is everything alright? The twins? Are they-"

"Oh, Yes, of course. Danny and Josie are in bed sound asleep. Alice is spending the night."

"She is so kind and so good to us," Abigail smiled. Ernest removed his hat as he entered the house. "I came to see how things were here."

Abigail closed the door behind him. "We made tea. Come on in, Claude could use the company." She smiled faintly.

"Claude." Ernest walked over to shake his hand. "How are you doing?"

"I am worried about Jane."

"I am sure everything will be fine," Ernest assured him despite the look Abigail had given him when he came in.

"How was the crib tournament?" Claude asked.

"It raised quite a lot of money for the soldiers," Ernest half smiled. "Abigail will be pleased."

"Good to hear," Claude nodded.

"I will be pleased to hear what?" Abigail had come from Jane's bedside and overheard their conversation.

"About the crib tournament," Ernest added. The last thing Abigail was thinking about was that. Another long hard cry came from Jane.

"I have to go." Abigail ran back to Jane's bedside. "I am here." Abigail wiped Jane's forehead with a cold, wet cloth.

"I can't take this much longer, Abigail." Jane squeezed Abigail's hand and pulled her closer to her.

"Doc!" Abigail called out. Doc didn't take much time to be by her side. "Isn't there something you can do?" Whispered Abigail.

"It's a waiting game at this point, Abigail." Doc patted her shoulder.

Ernest went back to The General Store to see how Alice and the twins were doing. He would come back when he could.

Early morning came with a knock on the door. No one had slept at all. Besides feeling sorry for Jane, they had listened to her cries that came in the night.

"Good morning, Dr. Parker." Mrs. Johnson answered the door. Despite the sleepless night, Doc's wife looked her elegant self.

The door opened as Doc and Dr. Parker came in.

Abigail looked at Dr. Parker as she walked toward the doorway.

"I thought maybe a second opinion would help with Jane's labour." Doc explained.

"Good morning, Abigail." Dr. Parker took his hat off and nodded toward her.

"Morning," she nodded with a faint smile.

Abigail knew something with Jane wasn't quite right, and now that Doc brought in Dr. Parker, it was confirmed.

Dr. Parker and Doc talked privately in the corner of the living room. Abigail did her best to keep Jane comfortable. Claude went outside to chop wood and pile it up by the house to keep busy. Truth was, he couldn't stand to hear Jane's cries of pain.

"Abigail, you're going to have to step out of the patient's room." Doc began gathering medical equipment.

"What do you mean?" Abigail gasped as she followed him around the room. She saw Dr. Parker putting on a white gown over top of his clothes.

"Dr. Parker and I have to do a procedure called a caesarean," Doc talked as he continued to pick up tools. "Mrs. Johnson!"

"A what?" Abigail grabbed his arm.

"We have to cut the baby out."

"What? Are you serious? That could kill Jane!"

"It's our only choice. It's either try and save the baby or lose them both.

"But Doc-" Abigail stood in front of the doctor.

"Abigail! Stop!" Doc said firmly, holding a metal bowl in his hand. "There isn't time for this. Please step aside. Please!"

"What do I tell Claude?" Abigail looked back at Doc.

"Tell him we don't have time for anything else, we have to do something."

Mrs. Johnson walked in, carrying a pail of hot water. She looked at Abigail with sympathy.

"We will take good care of Jane," Mrs. Johnson smiled faintly. Jane groaned again in pain from the bed. Abigail gasped, her heart ached for Jane.

Oh, Jacob, I wish you were here. She told herself. *What am I going to say to Claude? You always have the words.* She took a deep breath and grabbed her shawl off the hook by the door. She unlatched the door and stepped out.

"Has something happened? Jane? The baby?" Claude dropped the axe and ran toward Abigail.

"Doc and Dr. Parker are doing a procedure." Abigail grabbed hold of her shawl and pulled it tighter around her shoulders.

"What do you mean?"

"It's called a caesarean." Abigail's bottom lip began to quiver, partly from the cold, but also she couldn't help but feel sad for Jane. What were the chances she would live?

"Jane won't be able to take the loss of another baby." Claude shook his head. "What will this caesarean do?"

"It's where the doctor cuts the baby out of the mother's stomach." It almost made Abigail sick to say that.

"What!" Claude grabbed Abigail's arm and ran toward the house. As he reached the door latch Abigail called out.

"Claude, stop!" She ran and reached out to him. "She needs you to be strong."

"She needs me in there."

"She needs our prayers, Claude." Abigail led him to sit on the porch chairs in front of the house. Abigail knew how to pray, she did it by herself. She felt awkward to pray out loud in front of someone. She felt ashamed that she had these feelings. She didn't know how Jacob had the strength to pray for people, with them and even with only the two of them. She knew he had to have God's help. She knew she had to muster up the courage to do it. She had to do it for Jane. God wouldn't want her to be ashamed of praying.

"Dear Heavenly Father, we come humbly before You with heavy hearts. We lift up Jane and her baby to You. May You guide the doctor's hand and give him the knowledge and strength to see Jane through this surgery. We pray for both of their lives and give us peace and comfort as we wait. In Jesus' Name, Amen."

"Now we can go in the house and quietly wait." Abigail stood up and headed toward the door. Claude followed. Abigail unlatched the door pushed the door open when they heard the sweet cry of a baby. Abigail turned around and smiled at Claude. He smiled back as he raised his eyebrows with surprise. They quickly closed the door behind them and anxiously waited for someone to come from behind the curtain. They heard talking between the doctors, the baby crying and the sound of metal on metal.

Abigail couldn't help but think, *what about Jane? Just because the baby is crying, doesn't mean...* She stopped the terrible thoughts that came to her mind. *In Jesus Name,* she told herself. Both she and Claude paced back and forth until Mrs. Johnson came out from behind the curtain, holding a bundle of blankets in her arms. Abigail and Claude ran toward her.

"Jane?" Claude looked at the baby, then at Mrs. Johnson's face.

"The doctors are finishing up with her." She handed the baby to Claude. "You have a beautiful baby boy." Claude awkwardly took the baby from Mrs. Johnson and held him with two hands.

"Jane's alright, right?" He asked as he looked down at the wrinkled baby face.

"Let the doctors work," she smiled.

Abigail didn't like the fact that Mrs. Johnson wouldn't say anything about Jane. She touched the top of the baby's head and stroked it gently with her finger.

"He's beautiful, papa," she smiled up at Claude. "Congratulations."

"Thank you." A single tear rolled down his cheek. He lifted up the bundle, bent his head down and kissed his baby boy's forehead. The love he felt was like no other. Becoming a father was a whole new role for him. He wasn't only a farmer, he wasn't only a husband, but he was now a father, one of the most important roles yet.

It felt like hours to Claude and Abigail as they sat on the couch and kept the wee little newborn content, while waiting for news about Jane.

Doc and Dr. Parker both came out from behind the curtain. Abigail searched their faces for answers as she and Claude stood up to meet them.

"Since we have never done this before," Doc rubbed the top of his head, "we won't know how fast Jane will heal."

"But I have high hopes," Dr. Parker intercepted. "In the cities this operation has been done before with much success."

"We are not in the city," Doc continued, "and we didn't have all the proper equipment but you can thank Dr. Parker for being here tonight." Doc was a gruff fellow but he always gave credit where credit was due.

"Merci, Dr. Parker." Claude reached his right hand out to the doctor. "God sent you to us and I will be eternally grateful to you."

"Thank you, both," Abigail smiled. "Can we go and see Jane, now?" Abigail was grateful to both doctors, but didn't want to give Dr. Parker anything he might gloat about.

"Jane is sleeping, and she will need quite a lot of rest during this time. We have to be mindful of infection," Dr. Parker explained

"Continue your prayers," Doc added. "She isn't out of the woods yet."

"Thank you, Jesus." Claude looked up in the air in gratefulness.

chapter fourteen

A month had passed since Jane gave birth to a baby boy. Claude and she named their baby Noah Benjamin, after each of his grandfathers. Jane stayed with Abigail. She and Mrs. Ford's daughter, Elizabeth, cared for her and the baby until she was healed enough and ready to go home. With Elizabeth's help, Abigail was able to continue to help at the hospital. Abigail couldn't believe how having Elizabeth there made it so much easier to get everything done in a day.

Abigail still hadn't received any letters from Jacob. She worried more with each passing week but there was nothing she could do about it. She kept herself as busy as possible, with not much time to sleep. Abigail took the twins along with her to the hospital some days. The patients seemed to love the children. They were walking now and were more curious than ever, visiting each person. Abigail also played the piano on Sundays for the wounded. Just as the children put a smile upon their faces, she put a song in their hearts.

Most of her time was spent at the hospital helping the mystery soldier with his burns. Each day, once Abigail finished changing his bandages, she sat and read to him. She felt he was a lost soul who needed a friend. It was apparent that he didn't have family, or friends for that matter. It did her heart good to reach out to someone in need and felt that if someone was as good to Jacob wherever he was, she would help as many men as she could until he came back to her.

"Abigail, could you help Dr. Parker with that patient, please?" Doc pointed to the doctor across the room.

"Of course." Abigail tried to hide her reluctance as she put down the strips of cotton she was tearing up for bandages. Her hair was neatly up in a bun with a nurse's headdress covering most of her head, and her apron over her pale blue dress was crisply ironed and clean white. She stood up and walked toward the doctor and realized he was with the mystery soldier.

"What can I do to help?" Abigail stood next to her least favourite person and looked down at their patient.

"Hello there, beautiful," Dr. Parker smiled. "Can you hold these?" He handed her a tray.

"Sure." Abigail took the tray as she wondered if there was something wrong with the mystery soldier.

"How are the twins?" She sensed his mocking tone in his voice as he looked at her with a smirk upon his lips." Are they talking yet?" He enjoyed playing with her mind.

"They are hardly talking age, Dr. Parker," Abigail pointed out coldly.

"Oh, I wish you would call me Jonathon."

"I prefer to be formal." Abigail remained firm.

"So, what are they? One? Two?" He continued to gather his tools as he chatted like they were at a tea party.

"Almost two."

"Well, they obviously won't ever know their real father." He stopped staring at Abigail as he held a metal pair of scissors in his hand. Abigail could feel her ears burning.

"Let's just stick to our work, shall we?"

"Oh, Abigail," he laughed, "you are always so serious. Tell me, do you ever have any fun?"

"Of course!" Although she didn't feel the need to explain herself, she still found herself answering the question.

Dr. Parker laughed again as if this was fun for him. Fun to make fun of a young mother with a missing husband, who needed to run her own business, who fought the war as a civilian the only way she knew how.

"What is happening with this young fellow?" Abigail tried to set her feelings aside. She wanted to help soldiers the best she could.

"We are removing his facial bandages," he explained, "and if the healing progressed nicely, we won't have to put them back on.

The mystery soldier was sitting up in the bed where he had spent weeks. He still had bandages covering his upper body. The white cotton wrapped around his arms and chest made him look like a mummy. Dr. Parker began to cut the cotton fabric with the scissors up the side of his face, beginning at the neck. He carefully made sure he didn't cut anything he wasn't supposed to. Once he finished cutting, he carefully tugged at the bandages in case they were stuck to the patient's face. For the most part, the bandage didn't stick, but in the odd place it pulled a little newly grown skin away and left the flesh to bleed a little.

Abigail was anxious as she watched the doctor. The mystery soldier's eyes appeared to be wide and concerned and never left Abigail's face. He appeared to be apprehensive, which was understandable. His face most likely wouldn't be the same as he remembered it and Abigail knew how she would feel if it were she, or even Jacob, for that matter. It would be like looking at a stranger in the mirror.

Dr. Parker completely removed the full bandage and he pulled it away as he revealed the mystery soldier's freshly scarred features. His skin was blotchy scarlet raw flesh with darker skin patches, while around his eyes it looked like they may have been protected as the perimeter around them were in perfect condition. His ears were slightly distorted but still well shaped. Patches of hair were missing but that could possibly grow back after time.

Abigail cocked her head to the side and squinted her eyes as she watched the doctor. The mystery soldier looked very familiar. She had thought that about his eyes the day she met him but didn't really know since she couldn't see his whole face.

"Everything appears to be healing." Dr. Parker was still hovering over the patient as he looked around each side of his head and neck and evaluated his situation. "If your arms and chest look as good as this, you will be able to go home soon."

The man turned his head away.

"Well, that won't be for some time," Abigail intercepted, realizing the young man didn't want to go home. "Isn't that right doctor?"

"He will if he is healing this well." The doctor continued and handed Abigail a jar. "Apply this to the affected area twice a day." Abigail took the jar.

"I will see you later." Dr. Parker left the mess for Abigail to clean up and moved on to the next patient. "And you sir, I will check on you in a couple of days and see how your scars are, as well as your upper body."

Abigail had mixed feelings as she watched Dr. Parker walk away. Yes, he is a good doctor she thought but he was such an arrogant man. It's like he's two different people in one body. Abigail turned to the mystery soldier. She unscrewed the jar of salve and with her fingers she scooped out some of the yellow cream. As she bent over, Abigail smoothed the ointment over the raw wounds on his face. Still he spoke no words to her but watched Abigail's every move. Their eyes met for a second and Abigail knew!

"How are you feeling?" The soldier slightly shrugged his shoulder as Abigail finished with wiping her hands on a towel. She then helped him lay back for bedtime.

She was hoping she could get away without having to see Dr. Parker before she left. With Dr. Parker living at the hospital, it was hard not to have to speak with him while she was there. Abigail didn't want to have another awkward moment. She checked each patient for comfort before she left the room. As she took her coat off the hook by the door and slipped her arm into one sleeve, she heard footsteps walk around upstairs and head toward the stairwell.

"I am leaving now." Abigail hurried, she had her other arm in the other sleeve.

"Alright, good night." Dr. Parker called from above. He appeared to be walking down the stairs by this time. Abigail opened the door and quickly closed it behind her. She began her walk toward The General Store.

As she walked, she thought about the day Jacob and she got married. *It was a beautiful fall day. He carried her over the threshold as if she were the queen of his castle. She loved their home he had built; every detail, every thought he put into it. The upstairs was supposed to be her library where she could spend her time reading and writing at the desk Jacob was going to build her. Now a stranger is living there, a stranger she didn't even like, and up in her special room no less.*

"Lord, give me grace and a whole lot of mercy," Abigail looked up to the sky. "Are You listening Lord?"

chapter fifteen

"Will you dress the twins after breakfast, Elizabeth?" Abigail stirred the pot of oatmeal. Abigail crouched down in front of the cookstove. With a potholder she opened the wood door, stoked the fire and put a couple of logs inside, then closed the door.

"Sure, ma'am." Elizabeth filled two bowls to feed the children.

"I am going into the store now." Abigail kissed the top of Josie and Danny's head as she headed toward the kitchen door.

"Good morning, Abigail." Abigail was sweeping the store floor when Ernest came in the doorway. Ernest was staying there for a week while he waited for a shipment to come in to take back to his farm.

"Good morning to you, too. There is porridge on the stove. Elizabeth is feeding the twins."

"Sounds good, thank you. A letter came for you," Ernest handed her an envelope. He took the broom from her and continued to sweep. He stayed close to her and tried not to be anxious for what she was about to read.

Abigail's stomach began to churn as she stared at the letter in her hand. It was addressed to 'Mrs. Jacob Hudson.' The return address was the War Office. It almost took her breath away. Her hands shook as she tore open the envelope and pulled at the folded paper inside. She unfolded it. Staring at the printed words, her eyes began to well up with tears as she read.

> *...I regret to inform you that your husband Lt. Jacob Hudson 12548 of the 42nd Battalion is missing in action as of 13 July, 1916.*
>
> *At the time, Jacob was in France and involved in the Battle of Somme. While leading his men on an advance on the enemy fortified positions, he was one of thousands of men fighting. The troop was supported by an extensive artillery barrage and heavy machine guns during the advance when they were struck by enemy artillery, wounding 108, killing 54 with 5 missing in action, including your husband. Jacob is one of 5 men missing or presumed dead...*

Abigail felt her knees buckle as she swayed in the spot where she stood.

"Are you alright?" Ernest dropped the broom as he ran over to steady her on her feet. "Come, sit down." Ernest walked her to the chair beside the table that held the crib board.

"He's missing, Ernest, he's missing!" Abigail sat in a daze. It was all she could say as she handed the letter to him. As Ernest read, Abigail began to weep and tears streamed down her cheeks. She brought her hands to her face and sobbed uncontrollably. Ernest drew her close to him and held her head in his arms as he stood next to her. Ernest knew there were no words he could say to make her feel better. He let her cry it out.

"Is everything alright?" Elizabeth stood at the kitchen doorway holding Danny in her arms.

"Go back to the kitchen, Elizabeth," Ernest waved her to go back where she had been. Elizabeth nodded and stepped back into the kitchen.

Abigail felt numb as the morning went by. Elizabeth carried on with the daily chores with the twins. Ernest kept the store going. She was all cried out by mid afternoon, unable to shed another tear. She felt so lost, with a hole in her heart. The letter she hoped she would soon receive, the letter she had been praying for, wasn't from Jacob.

In her room, Abigail moved from her rocking chair, to her bed then to her desk. Something inside her wanted to reach out and write Jacob a letter. Abigail hadn't told him everything she wanted to say. There were certain things she was waiting to tell him when he got back from the war. Things like how she didn't know she could have children; that she found the account of her father's and discovered that Jacob had paid her father's debt plus the rest of his bills until his health was better. Not only did Jacob work at Goldenrod Ranch and work at his store in Abbington Pickets, but he had used all his savings to pay Abigail's father's overdue debt. Abigail's heart had swelled even larger for Jacob when she discovered his unselfish deed. She knew what a sacrifice it was for him, considering he had saved all his money for their wedding and the house he was building. She was proud of the way he put her ma and pa before himself, and to keep this noble deed to himself made her love him even more.

Abigail felt guilty that she hadn't even written to tell him the good news about Jane and Claude's new addition. *He can't be missing. Jacob can't be dead. There are so many things*

I wanted to tell him, to show him, to do with him. Abigail had never felt such helplessness before. Not even when the tornado hit their home, not when he left on that train to the war and not when she gave birth to the twins. But this was almost as much as she felt her heart could bear, the not knowing. If they sent his body home, she felt then she could understand and take the news - but missing? *"Dear God! Where's my beloved Jacob?"* she wanted to scream.

"Abigail?" A woman's voice called softly from the other side of the bedroom door with a gentle knock.

Several minutes went by before the knock sounded again.

"Abigail, it's me," voice persisted. "Alice."

Abigail lifted her head from her pillow and looked toward the doorway.

"Come in, Alice." Abigail sat up and swung her legs down off the edge of the bed. She touched her hair with her hands and felt the state it was in before greeting her company.

The door slowly moved inward, light peered through as Alice's petite frame walked through the doorway and cast a shadow on the floor. She turned around. As she quietly pressed the door shut with her right hand, the light disappeared. The lit lamp on the desk was the only glow in the room.

Alice walked slowly over to Abigail and sat down next to her.

"Ernest told me, Abigail." Alice put her hand on her shoulder. "I am so sorry."

The emptiness rose back up inside her as the tears fell down her cheeks.

"Oh, Alice!" Abigail leaned toward her company. Alice put her arms around her and held her close. Abigail cried out loud, as she never did before. Alice didn't say a word, only held her as she wept.

"Only God knows where Jacob is," Alice consoled her. "You have to trust in Him and have faith. It's hard times for our country, it's a tragedy for our friends and family. You are not alone."

Abigail felt a bit ashamed of the way she was feeling, as she remembered that last week Mrs. Smyth's son was brought home. The funeral was only the other day. The farmer who lived south west of Goldenrod lost his son as well. It was their only son. Jane and Claude's neighbour, Mr. MacDonald's son came back with one leg, not to mention the young lad who was in the hospital right now with burns on 60 percent of this body.

Alice was absolutely correct, she needed to have faith. She needed to be strong for her children, *their* children. Abigail needed to continue doing what she was doing and be here when Jacob came back.

Abigail felt a sense of peace wash over her and she knew deep down in her heart, God was there, and that He had never left her. She knew she did have the strength, all she had to do was ask.

"Oh, Alice," Abigail smiled at her friend. "How did you know I needed you right now?"

Alice smiled and squeezed Abigail's hand. "It was grocery day."

They laughed together.

chapter sixteen

"Good evening, sir." Abigail walked over to the mystery soldier's bedside. "How are you feeling today?" She noticed how well his scars were healing on his face.

Still he didn't say anything, only shrugged his shoulders.

"Your face is looking better each time I see you," Abigail smiled. She looked at the other bandages on his upper body. There didn't appear to be any evidence of weeping on the outside of the bandages, which was a good sign. "I am sure the doctor will be removing those soon as well."

The soldier turned his head away, as if that wasn't good news.

"Won't that be great?" Abigail pulled his covers up to his chest. Again he only shrugged. "Would you like me to fluff your pillow?"

He shook his head.

"Is there anything I can get you for the night?" Abigail felt the loneliness this young man was feeling. She couldn't figure out why he wasn't happy to be alive, why he wasn't happy to be healing well, and why wasn't he pleased that he may be going home soon. She didn't understand, but she wanted to make him comfortable while she was there at least.

Abigail finished up her evening by making more bandages and changing beds. Doc Johnson was at home tonight. There hadn't been any new patients for a couple of days, so there wasn't any needed for close attention. Dr. Parker was out of town, thankfully, and one of the volunteers would spend the night with the patients who were there.

"Alright, I am leaving," she told the lady who was staying the night. "If you need anything, I am not that far away." Abigail took her apron off and hung it up. As she reached back to pull her shawl across her shoulders, she felt a hand touch her.

"Let me help you with that," the deep male voice boomed. Abigail spun around abruptly.

"Oh, my goodness, you scared me." Abigail's fear turned to anger when she saw the face of Dr. Parker.

"Pardon me," Dr. Parker smiled. "I didn't intend to startle you." He touched the hair over her forehead and moved it aside.

"Excuse me, I am going home to my family." Abigail grabbed a hold of her shawl and yanked it tightly with her right hand.

"Going so soon?" He continued to antagonize her. Abigail wanted to wipe that smirk right off his face but didn't want to look at him any longer.

"By the way, I thought you were out of town for the night." Abigail turned back, her gaze met his.

"I guess I had a change of plans," he smiled, "or I wouldn't have run into you this fine evening." He stepped forward and reached his hand out to her.

Abigail stepped backwards.

"I would appreciate it if you would stop speaking this way to me."

"What do you mean?" He walked closer again. "You are very beautiful. I want you to know how I feel."

"I am a married woman," Abigail's voice rose. "Don't you understand that?"

"Be honest," he brushed the hair off her shoulder with one hand, "you know as well as I do, he's not coming back."

"Stop it!" Abigail opened the door and ran out. Tears welled up and trickled down both cheeks. She didn't stop running until she reached The General Store. She stopped at the door and crouched down and wailed loudly. She sounded like a coyote howling in the night. It had only been a few weeks since the letter from Jacob's commander had arrived. It was so fresh in her mind and she did her best to stop thinking about it and put her faith in God, that He was protecting Jacob. She felt that Dr. Parker was doing everything in his power to make her feel weak and helpless.

"Hello?" A voice came from the front of The General Store.

Abigail sniffled, trying to be quiet. She didn't want to talk with anyone right now. She thought maybe whoever it was, would keep moving along. She then heard steps coming toward her, rocks crunching under shoes as they walked.

"Abigail, is that you?" The voice sounded closer.

Abigail wiped her tears swiftly with her fingers and she quickly stood up and grabbed her hat as it was about to fall off her head.

"Oh, hello, Mr. Edwards." Abigail smiled as she greeted him. "I seem to have dropped my hat pin. I was down there looking for it."

"Oh, well, let me help you look for it." Mr. Edwards bent down as he looked close to the wooden step. "But it's a bit too dark."

"No, no, it's alright, Mr. Edwards, I have another."

"Are you sure?"

"Yes," Abigail stopped, her heart began to race and then she looked at Mr. Edwards face clearly. "Is everything alright? Charles?"

"Oh, yes, everything is alright," Mr. Edwards smiled. "Got a letter from Charles today." He looked down at the ground.

"Oh, that's good." Abigail was relieved to hear someone was safe and sound. "Come on in. I am sure Ernest has the tea on." She reached for the door latch when Mr. Edwards touched her arm.

Abigail stopped abruptly and turned around.

"Uh, um," he began, "uh. Well, that is why I am here." He continued to look at the ground, trying not to make eye contact.

"I don't understand." Abigail knit her eyebrows as she looked up at him. Mr. Edwards looked at her as he dug into his pocket.

"This came for you." He handed her three envelopes tied together with a string wrapped around all four sides. Abigail stared down at Mr. Edwards' gloved hand that held the package. Again her heart began to pound. It pounded so loud that she could hear it in her ears.

Abigail reached out slowly, took the envelopes from him and pressed them to her chest tightly.

"Abigail," Mr. Edwards looked sympathetically down at her, "I uh-."

"It's alright, Mr. Edwards," Abigail looked down at her handful, "I know how long the mail can take."

"I am so sorry," he shook his head.

"It's alright, really." Abigail looked up at him. "Now, that tea," she turned around, grasped the latch and opened the door. "I am home," she called out as Mr. Edwards followed her into the store and he took off his hat.

"I really don't need to stay for tea," he assured her.

"We don't mind," Abigail smiled and looked at Ernest as he came out of the kitchen. "Do we Ernest?"

"Of course not, I just filled the tea pot," he smiled. "The twins are still sleeping and Elizabeth is doing her homework."

"You're quite the domestic," laughed Mr. Edwards as he took off his coat. "You will make someone a good husband one day."

Abigail checked on Danny and Josie. She placed the envelopes on her desk in her bedroom, then met the men in the kitchen for tea. The three of them sat at the table.

"Elizabeth made some cookies." Ernest held out the plate of cookies to Mr. Edwards. "They are quite good."

"Thank you." Mr. Edwards took one from the plate.

"Mmm, 'Dad's Cookies'." Abigail glanced at the plate Ernest set down on the table, familiar with the family recipe. She picked up the teapot, tipped it and poured tea in the first teacup.

"Oh, dear, I poured too soon," Abigail looked at the amber coloured liquid in the bottom of the teacup. "Not as strong as you like it, Ernest."

"I will take that one," Mr. Edwards offered, "I like my tea a little weak."

Abigail passed it to him. She set the pot down giving it another few minutes to steep.

"I read in the news about women voting." Mr. Edwards dipped his cookie into his tea. Abigail finished pouring tea for her and Ernest.

"Do you not think women should vote?" Abigail looked at Mr. Edwards.

"Well, uh-," he hesitated looking at Ernest, who looked away, not wanting to get involved, "I don't know. Many are against it."

"Of course! Many men." Abigail argued.

"Possibly." Mr. Edwards wiped his forehead, not wanting to get himself into trouble.

"Men aren't smarter than women, you know," Abigail smiled. "They only want you to think they are."

Both men smiled.

Once the men had finished their tea and were visiting in the store over a game of crib, Elizabeth went to bed. Abigail finished cleaning up the table, filled the cookstove, washed up for bed and retired for the night.

"Good night," she said to Ernest and Mr. Edwards as she left for her room and closed the door behind her. The twins were still fast asleep.

Abigail took the glass chimney off the oil lamp and took out a wooden match from the box she had in her desk drawer. Striking it against the side of the box, the little wooden stick ignited the red sulphur on the end of it. She held it to the wick on the top of the lamp. The wick lit, she placed the clear chimney over top, and turned the adjuster on the side to soften the flame, stopping when the flame quit smoking. Abigail picked up the letters from the desk where she had placed them earlier, grabbed the chair, pulled it close and sat down.

Abigail's heart was thumping inside her chest. Since the moment Mr. Edwards had handed her the letters, she couldn't wait to read them, but in her own time. She looked over each envelope and checked the stamped date. Each one was dated a month apart, but were mailed more than six months ago.

Abigail picked the oldest one first. She slid the letter opener under the flap and slit open the envelope. She pulled out the paper and slowly unfolded it.

My darling Abigail,

Hope this letter finds you and the twins well. Thank you for your last letter, it sure lifted my spirits. I can only imagine what our children look like. We finally had more than two days of sunshine, and made it feel not so grim here in the trenches.

How are Bert and Alice and the children? How is Ernest? I think about Jane and Claude often, praying they are doing well.

Our battalion received a box and each one of us were gifted a package that consisted of a pair of socks, a shirt, a toque and a scarf. There

*were letters from kind ladies who made the items.
It was so wonderful and made us all feel like a
taste of home was with us. It reminded me of my
mama. She would have wanted to make things
to send to the soldiers.*

*I hope and pray that you are doing well with
Jacabig becoming a hospital. I also have been
praying Dr. Parker and you have an understanding and that he doesn't irritate you as much as
you said in your last letter. I trust you will know
how to handle him, Girlie.*

*Missing you like never before. I love you,
Daniel and Josephine and will be home as soon
as I can. May God strengthen you at this time
my darling and keep you safe.*

*Loving you always,
Jacob.*

Abigail sighed as she ran her fingers over the words written
on the page. Anything to make her feel closer to Jacob. She
lifted the paper to her nose and inhaled deeply, closed her
eyes and hoped the aroma of Jacob would still be there. After
a few minutes, she put the letter down on the desk, picked
up the next one, opened it, pulled out the letter, unfolded it
and read....

My dear Girlie,

*How I have missed you. It feels like an eter-
nity since I last saw you, last heard your voice,
touched your hair. The twins must be growing so
fast and I am missing these moments with them.
It's another one of my regrets.*

You know I can't say anything about where I am and what we are doing, but I can reassure you that I love you and I miss you dearly, and I pray to God every day for you and our children to be safe. Germany keeps coming at us and the allies are fighting along with us. I met a nice young lad from France. Reminded me of Claude a little bit. How are Jane and Claude doing? I bet Peter has been working Claude a lot as he likes to be pretty bossy. I am grateful that they were spared having to go to war. I am sorry that I left you. I never dreamed it would be for this long, no one could have known.

Kiss the twins for me, tell them papa loves them and will be home as soon as he can. I love you.

Love and Prayers, Jacob.

After reading the third letter, Abigail felt as though her breath was taken away. Her heart was still pounding as she folded the letters on the same creases they were pressed the first time, slid each one back into their original envelopes. Abigail reached down and grabbed the wooden box from the shelf in her desk. The rectangle chest meant a great deal to her. It was beautifully handmade, constructed of hard maple. The grain had a unique pattern, Jacob called it "birdseye maple", which she had never seen nor heard of before. The top of the lid had "ABIGAIL" carved into it, highlighted by a dark stain to make it stand out. The gold hinges had points where each nail was driven in, with a latch to keep it snuggly closed. Abigail placed it on top of the desk, lifted the lid, then placed the letters on top of the ones she had received before. Even though she would probably take them out each evening and read a few of them, she liked to keep them together. As

Abigail stared down at the box, she remembered the day Jacob had presented her with the gift. Abigail recalled how he had asked her to sit at the table and close her eyes...

"Now wait, and don't open them until I tell you." Jacob had smiled from ear to ear as he left the room to get the present. He walked back to the kitchen table and placed the wooden box in front of her on the table. Jacob was always so sweet with his gifts, wanting them always to be the biggest surprise ever and took delight in watching the happiness on Abigail's face.

"Alright," Jacob stood before her. "You can open them now."

Abigail took her hands away from her face and opened her eyes. She looked down at her name carved in the wood, her eyes grew wide and sparkled as she looked up at Jacob.

"It's beautiful, Jacob." She lifted it up and looked at every side, even the bottom, noticing the different wood.

"It's unique," Jacob knew what she was thinking. "Just as YOU are." His dimpled smile always made her tingle deep inside. Lastly, she lifted the latch and opened it. Inside the box was a folded piece of paper.

"And what's this, Mr. Hudson?" Abigail grinned, raising one eyebrow. She knew exactly what would be written on the note she was about to unfold. Jacob mischievously grinned at her as she opened it.

Abigail began to read:

Smile my love,
For all those years,
That we will spend together,
No matter what our fears,
Smile my love,
For all the loving days,
That we loved together,
In all our loving ways.
Jacob

"Oh, Jacob, you always know just what to say." Abigail slid the chair back as she stood up and walked over to Jacob. She looked up at her husband with a grateful heart. Jacob held out his hands to put his arms around Abigail's back and pulled her close to him.

"And you, my darling," Jacob gently held each side of her face in his tanned callused hands, bent forward and kissed her forehead, "always know how to love me." He cupped her jaw, held her neck softly, his lips reached hers and kissed her slowly.

Abigail quickly shook her head, bringing herself back to the present. What she wouldn't give to have that moment back, to feel Jacob's embrace, kiss his lips and hear his voice. Abigail put the small chest back on the shelf. Knowing that something this beautiful, made by someone as special as Jacob, held his letters of comfort until his safe return.

chapter seventeen

"What do you mean you sent that soldier home?" Abigail raised her voice at Dr. Parker. "Was he even ready?" She scowled at him begrudgingly.

"He was healing fine." Dr. Parker spoke firmly as he looked through papers on the table in the kitchen part of the hospital. Now that the round house was used for the hospital, the kitchen was used for the medical supplies, the doctor's desk and heating the building with the stove. "Besides we need the bed."

"The man didn't even speak!" Abigail shouted. "He wasn't ready."

"He was," the doctor continued on with what he was doing, paying no attention to what Abigail was really saying.

"You are a heartless man!" Abigail stood in front of him with her hands on her hips. Her ears were red and her head began to ache. At that moment the doctor stopped. He leaned over the table, looked up at Abigail and smiled as he removed his glasses from his face to look at her.

Abigail couldn't figure out how a man with all that talent, could be so heartless. She reminded herself every time he angered her of the day he saved Jane and Noah's life, but then he said or did something to make her dislike him even more.

"You sure are beautiful when you're angry."

"Would you please stop it!" Abigail turned away.

"Stop what?" He continued to come closer to her, so close Abigail thought he was going to grab her. She stepped back further and further, she then felt the wall behind her.

"Why do you look scared?" He tried to reach out to her as Abigail quickly put her hands behind her back. "I would never hurt you, love."

"Don't call me that!" She turned away with the worried look still on her face.

"I want to marry you, not hurt you," he grinned. "Jacob is never coming home and let's face it, your bills are beginning to pile up, aren't they?"

"I am sorry to disappoint you but I will NOT marry you, and Jacob IS coming back to us." Abigail could feel her ears burning as the doctor tantalized her. *How does he know how my finances are? Who does he think he is. Oh, how I dislike this man.* She thought to herself. "We are doing just fine."

"Is that why the shelves at The General Store are getting bare?" He stood back and raised his head with his eyes still on her. "And you need to order everything..."

"Excuse me," Abigail adjusted her coat and firmly took her ground. "My store is none of your concern. If you don't need me today, I will be on my way." She turned around and reached for the door latch.

"But I do need you today."

Abigail stopped abruptly, took in a deep breath, let go of the door handle and slowly turned around. She figured he was only saying that to keep her here.

"What can I do for you?" She inquired.

"You can start by changing the bedding of the soldier who just left. I believe there is more laundry to be done, as well," he pointed toward the other room as he spoke. "And the bandages are low."

"Anything else?" She tried to keep her sarcasm to a minimum. Abigail took off her hat, pulled out the pin, placed it back through the hat, hung it on the wall beside the door and hung up her coat. Her apron was there where it always was. After tying it on she headed for the bed that needed to be changed.

The morning continued without another confrontation with Dr. Parker. Abigail had only begun to sit down and rip rags to make more bandages when the door swung open. Abigail dropped the fabric and stood up quickly.

"Hurry!" Doc Johnson yelled as he followed the two men who were carrying the patient through the doorway. "Get Dr. Parker!" He looked at Abigail as he walked past her. The local men lifted the wounded soldier onto the examining table. The small cries from the lips of the young man were hard for Abigail to hear. The men left Jacabig and waited outside in case Doc needed any more help.

"Yes, Doc." She ran to the bottom of the stairs and began to run up the steps, when a shadow cast down the stairwell.

"Coming!" Dr. Parker darted down the stairs and passed Abigail on his way. She turned back around and followed him, moving as fast as her legs would take her.

"Abigail, hot water!" Hollered Doc as he began telling Dr. Parker what had happened.

Abigail was already pouring the water into the biggest pot she had. She opened the door of the oven, stoked the stove and added logs to get the water to boil faster.

"We were picking up soldiers on the train at Pickets,"

Doc's hands moved quickly as he ripped clothes away from the man's leg. "This poor fellow was in so much pain, we moved as fast as we could. Then he started to bleed."

"How much blood has he lost?" Dr. Parker quickly gathered the sterilized tools necessary and placed them on the metal tray.

"Too much, and if we don't get this leg sewn up," Doc looked at his fellow doctor, "we are going to lose him."

The young fellow began to moan as he rolled his head back and forth in discomfort.

"Abigail! We need you!" yelled Doc.

Abigail ran into the exam room.

"We need bandages," Doc pointed, "then come! We need your help."

Abigail swiftly ran back to the kitchen and grabbed the packages of bandages out of the crate into which she had piled them. Abigail could hear the soldier's moans getting louder; her heart broke for him. She wasn't trained in nursing, however common sense and fast learning taught her what was necessary at the time of every crisis, but this was the worst she had seen yet. With an armful, she quickly made her way back to the doctors. She abruptly stopped for a moment and gasped at all the blood. She knew it was bad, but to see someone with missing limbs and oh, there was just so much blood!

"Now, Abigail!" Doc reminded her. She immediately moved forward. Despite Abigail's surprise of what she saw, she was amazed how the doctors knew exactly what to do at every moment and that they were doing it. The patient wouldn't lie still anymore. He was beginning to become more conscious each moment.

"Can you try to console him?" Dr. Parker's pleading eyes almost made Abigail feel sorry for him. She remembered the time he came in and saved the day when Jane was in labour.

Abigail nodded and sprinted toward the soldier's head and tried to avoid the sight that was before her. She bent down close to the young lad, brushed his hair back and cooed at him as though he were a baby. It soothed him somewhat, but every time Doc placed a needle into the wound to suture close the end of the stump of his once full-sized leg, the lad cried out.

Abigail began to pray for this lad. She recited The Lord's Prayer over and over. She wondered if he gave his life to The Lord or whether he knew of God at all.

What appeared to be hours was only forty-five minutes. The doctors did all they could. The blood loss was extreme. Abigail held the soldier's head in her arms as she watched him close his eyes and the life slowly faded right out of his face. Her heart thumped so fast and broke for his family. How was Doc going to tell his mama? She was going to be devastated.

Everyone in the room was sombrely silent as they cleaned up the emergency chaos. Abigail gathered the blood-soaked sheets and placed them in the basket to take home to wash. She set it by the door. As she was walking away, the door pushed opened. Abigail grabbed the door, helping it open further.

"Mr. and Mrs. Smyth," she nodded to the couple standing at the threshold. The tall gentleman was dressed in a grey suit, with a hat; his face filled with sorrow. Mrs. Smyth stood clutching her handbag in front of her. She wore a big brimmed hat with a black velvet ribbon tied around the head piece. Her eyes were red and swollen; her bottom lip quivered. Abigail didn't know what to say. She only backed up to let them in the doorway.

"We are here to see our son." Mr. Smyth stepped forward and removed his hat from his head. He held on to it, as they both stood before Abigail. Doc was still with the fallen soldier. Dr. Parker had left for a house call. Abigail's heart broke as she looked at Mrs. Smyth. Mr. Smyth was being so formal in this sad situation. Although they went to the same church and attended every event in Abbington Pickets together, it was as though they were strangers. Abigail knew she couldn't do anything. She felt awkward as she stepped forward and reached out to Mrs. Smyth and hugged her quickly.

"I am very sorry." Her voice cracked, tears filled her eyes. Not wanting to upset Mrs. Smyth, she wiped them briskly with the back of her hand as she turned her head. She backed up and looked at Mr. Smyth sorrowfully and he nodded and received her unspoken sympathy. "Please, come with me." Both of them followed Abigail as she led them to the room where their son lay.

Mrs. Smyth began to sob as soon as they entered. Abigail stood back to give them privacy. Her heart continued to break as she listened to their cries. Mrs. Smyth wailed louder and her husband grabbed her from throwing herself onto her son's lifeless body. He held her as she called out his name.

Abigail couldn't bear to watch it any longer as tears slowly spilled down her cheeks. She pulled a handkerchief from her pocket and wiped them away quickly. She turned back toward the kitchen and couldn't help herself; her tears turned into air gulping sobs. She covered her mouth to silence her crying and sprinted to reach the outside door. She grabbed the door handle and jerked open the door, but as she went through the doorway, Wham! She looked up as she ran into Dr. Parker.

"Abigail," he pulled her close to him, held her and cupped her head in his hand, "it's alright," he soothed. For several minutes Abigail cried her heart out, standing in the arms of the one person she could hardly tolerate. Quickly she jolted back. He stared at her as she shot him a deadly gaze.

Abigail covered her face with her hands, her tears flowed all the more, and she ran with all her might. She didn't know where she was going, she only ran.

Minutes went by. She sprinted until she was out of breath. She stopped, gasped for air and looked up to see the tall grey steeple. Abigail had gone a great distance by foot in a hurry, but time didn't seem to go by while she ran. She wanted to be anywhere but the place where she was. To be held and touched by *that* man was more than she could tolerate. How could she let that happen? How *did* it happen? Abigail felt so ashamed of herself. Jacob is fighting for our country, possibly wounded, only God knows where, and she is nestled in the arms of another man. What was she thinking?

"Abigail?" A voice sounded from behind her.

Abigail raised her head to look up at Reverend Young through tear filled eyes. Her cheeks were wet with strands of hair stuck to the sides of her face. Embarrassed, she quickly wiped her eyes and face with her hands and pushed her locks back behind her ears with her fingers.

"Reverend, I didn't know you were there."

"Are you alright?" His concerning eyes watched Abigail as she stood up straight to gain her composure.

"Oh, of course," she smiled faintly. "How is Mrs. Young?"

"She is well. But I am a little worried about you."

"I am doing fine." She was about to turn and walk away. "Really."

"Why don't you come in for a minute?" The reverend held out his hand toward the church door.

"Well..." Abigail searched for a reason not to, "I really must... Uh...be..."

"Come."

Abigail stared at the door for a moment, then she walked through it as the reverend held it open for her. She coasted down the church aisle and sat in the third pew from the front. The reverend sat down in the one in front of hers, and turned around to face her.

"Have you heard news of Jacob?"

"No, not since..." Her voice broke.

"Something is troubling you."

"Mr. and Mrs. Smyth's son just passed away." She began to sob as she remembered the ordeal.

"Oh, I am terribly sorry to hear that."

"They are with him now." She breathed in with a gulp of air. "I had to leave, I couldn't stand-." She began to weep harder. The Reverend handed her a handkerchief, she took it and wiped her tears. She couldn't stop sobbing. "It was the first time I held someone and watch him die before my eyes."

"It's something that isn't easy to watch." Reverend consoled her. "I remember my first time visiting someone on his death bed." He recollected. "I was so very young, like yourself. Nothing prepares you for your first death. Nothing."

"I was there when Jacob's brother, Andrew, died," she sniffled, "but not there, there, holding his head in my arms like this-."

"It's much different when you're right before them," he agreed, "not in the next room, or even two feet away. It's more personal when you're sitting next to them."

"I keep thinking of Jacob and wondering, is he hurt? Is he alive? Where is he?" She wiped her eyes again with the already damp hanky.

"Only The Lord knows where he is and when he will return to us, and how. It's up to us to pray and have faith in our God," he smiled. "He will never leave us, nor forsake us."

"I know," Abigail looked down at her feet, "but, it's sometimes difficult to remember."

Abigail began to feel better, and although she didn't want to confess to the Reverend what happened between herself and Dr. Parker, she had peace in her heart. Reverend Young prayed with Abigail for peace, comfort and understanding at this difficult time. He also prayed for the Smyths for the loss of their son, and the safe return of Jacob.

The next day the village of Abbington Pickets prepared yet another funeral for one of their own.

The church yard was full with friends and family of the Smyths. Everyone was gathered around the pine coffin that stood before them. Mr. and Mrs. Smyth stood close together along with their other children.

Reverend Young spoke about how friendly and kind Jack Smyth was, always helpful to his ma and pa and that he had planned to leave for the city for work right before the war broke out.

Mr. and Mrs. Smyth stood strong throughout the service and kindly greeted everyone who came out to honour their son. Each person had a little story or memory of Jack and it seemed to please them to hear each one.

Lunch followed, provided by the church ladies, on a table covered with a white linen tablecloth. It was set up against the south wall of the church. Iced tea was served for a beverage.

The funerals were getting to be such a common thing. Reverend Young hadn't been as busy as he had these past couple of years. Not only was he conducting funeral services but he was also visiting families after a fatality.

Abigail couldn't help but think that one day she would soon get 'the letter.' She shuddered at the thought.

chapter eighteen

"Jacob! You're back!" Abigail stared up at the tall uniformed man who stood in the doorway. Jacob's familiar dimpled smile formed as Abigail ran toward him. He dropped his bag, and jumped forward to grasp the woman he had been dreaming about for years. He wrapped his arms around Abigail's waist, kissed her lips, smelled her hair, and nestled his face in behind her ear. "Girlie, it's so good to feel you again." Jacob couldn't hold her enough, it had been so long. "I never want to be away from you again, my love." He whispered.

"You will never have to be darling." Abigail reassured him as she held on to his neck for dear life. She continued to reach, but he seemed so far from her. She looked down at her belly, it was bulging. Jacob let go of her and touched her stomach.

"I can't wait to meet this little one," he crouched down to her waist level.

"Jacob, we already have the babies." Abigail pulled him up to her.

"No, we don't" he looked at her, "we haven't been blessed yet." He touched her stomach again and smiled down at her.

"We have Josie and Danny," Abigail persisted, "I told you. You know, in all the letters."

"What letters?" Jacob backed away. "What are you talking about?" "Jacob! Jacob!" Abigail reached further for him, but he kept backing away. "Where are you going?"

Jacob only stared at her as Abigail ran after him, but he seemed to get further and further away.

"Jacob!" She shouted louder. "Come back, please don't-

"Abigail," A foreign voice sounded faintly. "Mrs. Abigail."

Abigail could feel her arm being moved, her head felt foggy and she could see light through her eyelids as though the sun was shining on her face.

"Elizabeth." Her eyes sprang open. There stood Elizabeth in her long white nightgown, her blonde hair flowed down the left side of her shoulder as she held a candle with her right hand. "What is it?"

"I heard talking," Elizabeth quietly spoke. "I came to see who it was."

"Oh, my dear, I am so sorry," Abigail patted her arm. "I must have been dreaming. Let me take you back to bed. I will check on the twins while I am up."

"No, I can go by myself," Elizabeth insisted. "The twins are fast asleep. I checked them already." She was as proud as a mama looking after her cubs.

"Thank you," Abigail smiled. "I sure don't know what I would do without you, Elizabeth."

Elizabeth bashfully smiled and turned around to go back to bed.

Abigail laid back down in bed and rested her head against the pillow. A dream? Why did she have to dream such a strange dream? She wished she could really hold Jacob at that moment, as she thought she felt moments ago.

"Jacob, where are you?" Abigail took in a deep breath. "Lord, please keep Jacob safe, wherever he is, and please bring him home to us soon," she prayed. She closed her eyes and thought she better get some sleep. Morning would come soon enough.

The next day Abigail rose with a dull headache. She remembered clearly the vivid dream she had. She wished it were all true, but she knew the truth.

"Good morning, Elizabeth." She kissed Danny and Josie quickly. "I am going to go to the hospital early today." She took a sip of the already perked coffee that Elizabeth had obviously made for her.

"Alright, Mrs. Abigail," Elizabeth smiled. Abigail liked the fact that Elizabeth never said much. She didn't ask questions and never complained. Silently Abigail worried that she would want to go to school instead of home studies like she had been. It was selfish, she knew, but she was so grateful that Mrs. Ford had the idea to let her come help her out.

"I will be back to open The General Store at dinner time." Abigail gulped the rest of her coffee. She quickly cut a slice of the fruit loaf that Elizabeth had made the day before. She took a bite as she scurried around the room and made sure she didn't forget anything.

It had been a couple of weeks since the Smyth funeral, and Abigail was finding it harder and harder to keep up with everything. It was the time of year that Ernest was farming. The store was open most of the time, but not always. She had spread herself too thin in order to manage everything. The store wasn't always busy anyhow, and the folks of Abbington Pickets got used to the note on the door that said the store would be open later that day.

"Ma, ma," Danny smiled and cooed to her as he banged the spoon on his highchair table. Both twins didn't say a whole lot yet, only a few short words like, ma, no, and a bit of babbling only the two of them could understand. But it melted Abigail's heart when they did, and she wished Jacob could be here to witness the miracles of their children. Their first year was the most important. The one year they learned more than any other in their lives. It saddened Abigail that their father missed it all while fighting a senseless war! *Darn you Jacob Hudson,* she thought to herself.

"You're a sweetheart." Abigail went back over to the twins and once again kissed the tops of their heads and rubbed their cheeks with her forefinger. "It's so hard to leave you."

"You go, Mrs. Abigail," Elizabeth stood close to the children. "They will be fine," she smiled.

"You're sweet, Elizabeth," she touched the young girl's long hair. "I don't know what I would do without you."

With that, she picked up her hat on the way out the doorway, placed it on her head, pinned it and walked outside.

Another nice day. As little as she spent outside, she did enjoy her time alone. The walk to the hospital wasn't far but she had enough time to collect her thoughts before having to see the irritating good doctor.

Just as she was about to grab the door latch, a loud rumble sounded from behind her.

Honk! Honk! Honk! The sound scared the daylights out of her. She turned around to see Dr. Parker pulling up in his tin box. *Ugh, and so it begins,* she said to herself. She was hoping to get her work all finished and be gone before he showed up from visiting his village patients. *I wonder if the lady who stays with the patients when she couldn't be there, finds him as arrogant as I do?* Abigail asked herself.

Dr. Parker gracefully exited his car through the side door. She turned back around to go into the hospital and hoped she could get to work before he bothered her.

"Well, good morning to you, Abigail," he called out after her as he sprinted from the car to the building.

"Good morning," Abigail nodded, continuing through the doorway with Dr. Parker right on her heels.

"You are here mighty early today." His mischievous eyes followed Abigail around the room.

"I can only stay until noon," she said bluntly. She took off her hat and put on her apron. Not wanting to mince words, she went in to see the patients.

"Good morning," she smiled as she opened the curtains wider than they were. The patients stirred and weren't quite ready to face the day. "It's a beautiful day out there," she chimed.

"If you want to go for a rest for the morning, I will be here until dinner time," she informed the lady who was there helping. She had been sitting in the rocking chair by one of the beds. It looked like she had spent the night. Possibly Dr. Parker had been out most of the night, which would explain why he was only getting there now.

"I think I will." She was already taking off her apron.

"Good." Abigail smiled lightly at her. She liked her. She was quiet, did the job well and didn't seem to mind staying. She wasn't married and didn't have any children so she had more free time than Abigail, but she couldn't be there all day and all night.

"Will see you in a while then," she nodded and left. Dr. Parker didn't say a word to her as she left. Abigail wondered *why doesn't he tease her as much as he does me?*

"I will be back with breakfast," she informed the men in their beds.

Abigail went back into the kitchen and began making some cooked oatmeal for the patients.

"I put on the coffee already," Dr. Parker said matter-of-factly.

"Thank you." Abigail put the pot on the stove and poured water into it. She grabbed the sack of oatmeal from the cupboard and set it on the table. She took the stack of bowls down from the shelf and set them next to the oatmeal. Abigail felt self-conscious as the doctor watched her every move.

"Have you changed your mind yet?" He held a cup of coffee in his hand as he leaned up against the table close to Abigail.

"Excuse me?" Abigail's eyes narrowed.

"To marry me," he said bluntly.

"I have told you before, and I will tell you again," Abigail turned and looked straight into his eyes. "I am already married!"

Both their eyes were locked, both stubborn, both trying to make their point. It was a stare off, neither was going to even as much as blink.

"I have told you before, and I will tell you again," Dr. Parker copied her. "Jacob is never coming back." He said those five words slowly, as if to mock her.

Abigail broke their gaze, picked up the sack of oatmeal, turned around and measured it into the pot of boiling water on the cookstove. She ignored his words and pretended that it didn't bother her. She wanted to burst out and tell him that if he continued to talk to her this way, she would quit coming to the hospital. But she knew very well that would not happen, she would still come. There was no sense in egging him on. It was best to ignore him and get to work.

Dr. Parker stepped over to the stove, almost in her way. *Boy, he doesn't give up,* Abigail said to herself. She stood there stirring the oatmeal. Now that she had it in the pot, she couldn't leave it unattended until it was almost done.

"You don't know how a war works, Abigail." He began. "Men go fight, men die, men come back in a pine box, that's the way it is."

"Oh, really!" She continued to look into the boiling pot. "Because you have served in so many wars," she blurted out. "And by the way, why didn't you go and serve your country?" She was tired of his arrogance. She wanted to put him in his place.

"I am, by staying here," he said with pride. "I am a better use here than dying over there."

"You could be helping the wounded over there." She argued.

"And die myself. Makes no sense." He crossed his arms as he continued to stand near Abigail.

"Only a coward would stay behind," Abigail whispered. Part of her wanted him to hear and the other part didn't. She would have given anything for Jacob to have stayed behind, knowing it meant dishonour to his country, but at least he would be alive.

"What did you say?" He put his hand on her free arm.

"Nothing," she retorted and pulled her arm back away from him. "I need to get the patients fed." She picked up the pot, took it over to the table and spooned the oatmeal to fill each bowl.

"Excuse me, please." She reached for the tray that was hanging on the wall. She put three bowls on the tray, along with spoons, napkins and a creamer of milk. She would need to do two trips because she needed five bowls to serve the men.

Once Abigail fed the patients, she stripped the bedding that needed to be done and filled the wicker laundry basket. She did the usual chores including the dishes from breakfast.

The doctor finally left Abigail alone and tended to his own work at his desk.

"Thank you for the break." The grateful woman came back right before dinner time to go back to work.

"You're welcome," Abigail gave her a small smile. "I will take the laundry home and wash it."

"Alright," she said.

"You know if you ever need anything," Abigail looked at her, "all you have to do is ask."

"Thank you," was all she said.

"We shall see you soon." Abigail hung up her apron and headed out the doorway.

"Just wait," a voice sounded after her. Abigail didn't have to turn around to know it was the doctor.

"I have to get home," she called over her shoulder.

"It will only take a minute." He grabbed her arm and she spun around to look up at him.

"I am sorry about before." He still had a hold over her arm. *What? The good doctor apologizing? Well this is a first.* She told herself.

"It's alright," she said loosely, "but I really have to go. She pulled her arm away from him.

"Let me give you a ride home," he persisted.

"No, thank you," she turned back around and stepped forward.

"When you're ready," he stood back with his arms crossed once again, "I will be here."

Just when she thought he might be human, he had to blow it.

She only wished he would make this volunteering a little easier. She found it hard enough to juggle the store, pay the bills, mind the children, keep up with the work, and try to help soldiers like Jacob - there weren't enough hours in the day.

As she walked past Hudson's Carpentry Shop, her heart ached. She knew she had to write a letter to Jacob. Even though he probably wasn't getting them, she needed to talk to him.

That evening, when everyone was in bed, Abigail sat at her desk at her bedside. She pulled out the stationary, lifted the pen, and began to write.

My dearest Jacob,

How are you my darling? I can't tell you how much you have been on my mind. In fact you never leave it. They tell me you are missing in action, so you may not ever see this letter, but I am mailing it anyway. I know you are out there somewhere, I know you are out there fighting for us, fighting for both our countries and you are praying selflessly for us. I know this because I know you, Jacob. I know how you are, I know who you are. You have influenced me so much in the time that I have known you, and I am doing my best to uphold your honour by honouring others, just as you do.

I want to be honest with you Jacob, and I know this isn't how it should be said, but I need to say it. Since Dr. Parker has arrived in Abbington Pickets, he has been making advances. At first it was only words, then a touch on the arm. He is bound and determined you aren't coming home and that I am to marry him. "Why, in fact, who else would marry a widow with two children?" he says? I thought I could handle him, but his remarks are inappropriate. This has been weighing on my heart and I needed to tell you. I don't want you to think that I have ever given him any reason to be this way toward me, in fact I have been the opposite. I held my head high and told him straight forward, that I am married. It seems to fuel his intentions all the more. I know there is nothing you can do, but I needed to tell you. Please come home soon, my love.

I know your troubles are far worse than mine, but I just needed to talk to you. Wherever you are tonight, I pray you are safe and will someday be coming home to us.

I love you with all my heart,
Your Girlie

Abigail folded the letter in thirds, slid it into an envelope, licked the flap and closed it. She addressed it and then, as she always did, she kissed it, pressed it close to her heart for a moment and prayed it would arrive in Jacob's hands.

chapter nineteen

"Please get the twins ready for the day, Elizabeth," Abigail instructed, "I have to take the laundry back to the hospital." She took a big sip of her coffee and placed it down on the kitchen table.

"I will," Elizabeth smiled as she held Danny on one hip.

"If anyone needs anything at the store, tell them I'll be back soon." She placed her hat on her head and pinned it in place with the pearl hat pin. She picked up the wicker laundry basket full of folded sheets, hoisted it up on her hip, grabbed the latch and opened the door.

"See you later," she called out as she walked out and closed the door behind her.

It was a beautiful day with only a wisp of a breeze to cool her skin. She swiftly walked toward Jacabig hospital thinking about what the day's chores entailed. She had to get ready for the next A.P.L.G. meeting on the following Tuesday, finish the laundry for the week and order the groceries for the next freight shipment. The list seemed to be longer than she remembered it.

Almost daydreaming as she got closer to the hospital, she saw movement in the corner of her eye. She turned her head quickly to see what it was. She could have sworn she saw someone go into Jacob's shop. No, she must have been mistaken.

Abigail continued on to deliver the laundry, since she needed to get back to the store. She reached the front step, lifted the latch and stepped through the open door.

"Hello," Abigail called out, "I am only here with the clean sheets.

"Well, hello there," stepped out Dr. Parker.

"Yes, hello," Abigail placed the basket down on the table. Dr. Parker watched intently as she pulled out each folded sheet, and put it in the proper drawer. "I am here for only a minute. I can't stay today."

"Well, that's too bad," Dr. Parker smirked. "Any word on your husband?"

"Yes, well, I have a lot to do today." She ignored the question.

Dr. Parker stepped in front of Abigail. She stepped to the side, he moved along with her. She stepped back in the other direction, still looking down at the floor. Irritated for his childish games, she spun around, tucked the empty basket under her arm roughly and headed to the door.

"Aw, don't go away angry," Dr. Parker called after her. Abigail kept on without stopping, through the doorway and down the road. She couldn't help the burning of her ears, or the flushing of her cheeks. *I don't know why I keep going back there, or why I even help at that place!* She thought to herself angrily. Oh, she knew perfectly well why she did it, and that would never change. She wouldn't stop for anything. That was the truth of the matter. Wild horses couldn't keep her from going back. She did it for Jacob. The love of Jacob. Abigail knew darn well that if Jacob were here right now, he would be helping each and every person that he could and wouldn't stop there. Jacob was just that kind of person. She wasn't about to let him down because of an arrogant man like Dr. Parker who didn't have enough sense to come out of the rain. Why did he have to be so presumptuous, yet such a good doctor?

Before she knew it, she was back at the store. Elizabeth had the twins dressed with bonnets and was just about ready to take them for a walk.

"Oh, there are my little angels," Abigail kissed their foreheads. "You have a good walk with Elizabeth," she cooed.

"We will have a good time, Mrs. Abigail," Elizabeth reassured her. "It's such a lovely day."

"Thank you, Elizabeth," Abigail smiled.

Once the door was closed, Abigail began her chores. She pulled out the order forms and began writing down all the stock she needed for the next shipment. She was careful about what she ordered, choosing only what she really needed and knew would sell. As much as she disliked the good doctor, he was right. Bills were adding up and folks weren't buying what they used to before the war broke out.

Folks didn't have the money they once did. Not that it was that plentiful before, but it certainly wasn't now. They held on to everything possible to make things go further. Old clothes that couldn't be patched any more were used to make things like quilts. They used the places that were less used, such as the back of the leg in a pair of britches, or the upper arms of the shirt, or the back of a man's shirt. Quilts were made to keep warm so less wood had to be used.

Fancy things weren't bought for frivolous reasons, only out of necessity. Rubber and steel were goods the war effort needed in order to make guns. Anything made from these items was hard to find, and folks had to make do with what they already had, and hoped it lasted a long time.

Abigail decided it was time for a cup of tea. She headed to the kitchen and grabbed the kettle to fill with water, but when she looked in the pail of water, it was empty. She put the kettle down, picked up the water pail by the handle, and headed out the store door, but not before flipping the sign on the door that read 'Be back in a few minutes.' She stepped down the steps and walked down the path to the street.

Abigail looked up at the blue sky, closed her eyes, and took in a deep breath. She swung the pail back and forth in a rhythm as she headed south toward the water pump. It wasn't far away, only across the street and a bit west of there.

"Good morning, Abigail." Mrs. Johnson was headed east as they crossed paths.

"Good morning," Abigail nodded. "How are you doing? I haven't seen you for a while."

"Doing well. How about you?" she smiled.

"Alright," the last thing she wanted to tell people was that she wasn't doing well. The fact was, she was doing pretty well, considering. But she had her weak moments.

"Aw, that's good," Mrs. Johnson smiled sympathetically. "We are praying for you." She touched her arm as she continued to walk on.

"Thank you," Abigail politely replied as she looked toward her destination.

Abigail reached the water pump. She placed the pail on the knob on the top of the spout, grabbed the handle and began to pump it. It clanged and wobbled with each stroke. After several strokes, the gurgling sound of water began. The pumping got stiffer as the water climbed up the inside of the iron metal pipe and poured out the spout. Water splashed into the bottom of the empty pail. Once the flow began it didn't take many more pumps to fill the pail. Abigail let go of the handle and let the last of the running water fill the container. She waited for the last drop then lifted the pail handle back over the nub of the spout, being careful not to spill too much.

She carried the heavy bucket of water back to The General Store. Her arm was getting a bit tired as she looked toward the store. In the distance past The General Store she saw something. Again, for a brief moment, she thought someone was walking into Jacob's carpentry shop.

My eyes can't be playing tricks on me twice today, could they? She asked herself. Abigail thought and thought. Now who could be going into Jacob's shop? Everyone in Abbington Pickets knew that Jacob was gone, no one would dare go in without at least asking Abigail first.

Abigail reached The General Store and went inside. She placed the pail of water in its spot in the kitchen, went back outside and proceeded to Jacob's shop.

It was a little further jaunt than the water pump but Abigail's mind wasn't thinking about the distance at all. In fact, she wasn't thinking about anything except what she thought she saw.

Abigail's breathing was slightly laboured as she walked faster and faster until she arrived at the front door. She put her right hand on the latch and gently pressed her left hand against the door. She took in a deep breath, closed her eyes and let it out again. Slowly she pressed her thumb down on the latch, pushed with her other and gradually opened the door. A squeaking sound began. Abigail stopped abruptly. She waited a couple of seconds and started again, stepped forward and followed the door as it opened. The stuffy cool air tickled her nostrils as she entered the dusty room. The sun was shining in the window beaming floating dirty air. She left the door open behind her.

"Hello?" She said quietly as she advanced further in. "Hello? Anyone in here?" She listened for an answer. There was none.

Abigail walked over to Jacob's work bench, bent down, looked under it and saw nothing but stacked lumber. She shuffled over to the cupboard, grabbed both door knobs, pulled both doors open only to find shelves with old brushes in tins and old rags folded next to jars with some sort of clear amber liquid. She closed the door, spun around and studied the rest of the room.

"Hello? Is there anyone here?" Abigail persisted and walked to the other side of the room. She bent down and looked behind the wood stove. There was nothing but a fire poker and a small straw broom lying on the floor, but she realized that the stove was warm.

What, how can that be? She never saw smoke come from the chimney, ever, she asked herself. Abigail saw a blanket laid out in the north east corner of the room between the small table and the little washstand. Abigail walked over to the table and noticed the plate and utensils on top, along with a coffee cup. She knew Jacob hadn't left that sitting there. She crouched down and lifted up the edge of the blanket. *This looks like a blanket from the hospital,* she thought to herself.

Abigail heard a noise from behind her and turned around on her toes, still crouched down. She made a quarter turn with her eyes and met another pair staring back at her. She fell back on to her buttocks, her heart felt like it had jumped up into her throat. As fast as her legs could move, she hopped up and headed for the door.

"Wait-" a voice called out. "Please!"

Abigail stopped with her hand on the latch. The pleading voice tugged at her still racing heart. She let go of the door handle and slowly backed up. She turned back around and saw a shadow move from under the table, carefully pushing the chair away. Crawling out from under the table, standing tall, stood a man with a face familiar to Abigail.

"It's you!" Abigail took in a breath and quickly covered her mouth. She stood still for several seconds, watching the wounded mystery soldier walk toward her.

"What are you doing in Jacob's shop?" Abigail gasped.

"I had nowhere else to go," today was the first time Abigail had ever heard him speak. He walked up and stood before her. His scabs had healed, but the skin was left with thick reddened scars.

"Have you-" Abigail hesitated, "have you been here since you left the hospital?

"Yes ma'am." He put his head down.

"What about your home?" Abigail asked. "Where you lived before?"

"I don't have a home anymore." He pulled the collar of his shirt closer together to cover up the burns he had there. Despite the fact that Abigail helped nurse him back to health, he was rather embarrassed about how he looked to her.

"What do you mean? Where are you from?" Abigail was confused. *Why was he here at this hospital if he wasn't from this area?* Abigail wondered.

"My house burnt down while I was in the war." His eyes glanced at the window. "As ironic as it sounds." He shook his head.

"Because of-" Abigail put her hand on her face in the same place as his wounds. He nodded.

"I am so sorry." She looked down at the floor, not wanting to make eye contact.

"Well, Mr. Soldier." Abigail was never told his name, and as he never spoke, she always referred to him as the 'mystery soldier.' "You will need something to eat," she said plainly.

"Uh, what?" he blurted out dumbfounded.

"Come." She opened the door and backed up to allow him to pass through the doorway as she held the door and closed it behind them. "First, we will get you something to eat. Then we will talk about what we are going to do."

Speechless, he followed her to The General Store. As they walked up the wooden sidewalk toward the steps, Abigail saw Elizabeth and the twins coming back from their walk.

"You're back," Abigail smiled. "How was your walk, Elizabeth?"

"Very well," she smiled as she held each of the twins' hands. "We stopped at Mrs. Johnson's and she gave the children each a cookie, then we stopped at the water pump for a drink of water. We saw the school children in the school yard, and we could hear Mrs. Smyth playing the organ in the church."

"This is Mr. Soldier," Abigail introduced her to him. "Mr. Soldier, this is Elizabeth, Josie and Danny." She touched each of the children when she said each name.

"Hello," Elizabeth said shyly.

"He was at the hospital for quite some time, wounded from the war. He will be eating with us today," she explained. She still referred to him as Mr. Soldier, since he didn't seem to want to share his name and Abigail didn't want to pry.

Abigail picked up Danny and Elizabeth picked up Josie. The five of them entered the store.

"Have a seat," Abigail directed the soldier toward the table and chairs as she walked over to the pantry. She retrieved her apron, put the strap over her head and tied it up at the back. "Tea?"

"Yes, thank you," he said as he sat gently on the chair. The tightening of the scaring was painful.

"Elizabeth," Abigail called out, "can you wash up the twins and put them in their highchairs?"

Abigail put the kettle on top of the stove. She opened the stove door, stirred up the coals, put a few sticks of wood inside, closed the door, grabbed the frying pan off the wall and placed it on the stove next to the kettle.

Abigail fried up last night's leftover potatoes and carrots in the pan. She cut four slices of bread, cutting one in half for the twins. She set the cold chicken from the evening before on the table. It was a treat that one of her neighbours had brought her a freshly butchered chicken.

After saying grace, everyone began to eat. The twins were hungry after their stroll. Abigail put them down to nap as soon as they were finished and washed up. Elizabeth started the dishes as Mr. Soldier finished another cup of tea.

"Well, I am pretty sure they will be down for a while," Abigail marched back into the kitchen. "I hardly got out of the room and they both were sleeping." She pulled the chair back from the table and sat down across from the mystery soldier.

"Now, let's talk about what we're going to do." Abigail looked straight at the gentleman before her.

"Aaa-lll-rrright?" He tilted his head slightly, not sure what she was going to say.

"You can stay at Jacob's carpentry shop as long as you need to," she began as she linked her hands in front of her on the table. He raised his eyebrows and opened his mouth to say something but Abigail continued. "You can help me around the yard, keep the woodbox full, make deliveries when necessary and keep the water pail full."

"Are you sure?" He sat up straight and his eyes seemed to brighten somewhat. "I can do anything."

"I am sure you need a place to lie your head and I need the help," Abigail nodded. "You can eat every meal here with us. Breakfast at seven, dinner at twelve, lunch at three and supper at six." She said it as if she was reading off an itinerary.

"I will start right away." Mr. Soldier stood up from the table.

"Wait." Abigail stood up as well. "There are a few things we need to get you, if you're going to continue to stay in the shop."

"What else?" The soldier looked confused, obviously content with what he had.

"A bed for starters," she smiled.

"Thank you, ma'am."

"There is a cot in the storage shed behind the store. It isn't much but better than the floor." She pointed toward the north. "I will get you some sheets and a proper pillow."

He nodded and headed toward the doorway. "And thank you for dinner, Mrs. Abigail."

"You're welcome," she nodded. She watched as he left the room, already thinking of much needed chores he could do.

Mr. Soldier chopped wood, hauled water, pulled weeds and set up his bed the same afternoon Abigail had found him. He shyly came back to The General Store for supper that evening. Abigail had made a list of daily chores and gave it to him, along with clean bedding for his new bed.

The next morning, Abigail greeted Charles' father in The General Store. "Good morning, Mr. Edwards, how are you?"

"Alright," he said lowly as he took off his hat. "How are you doing?" He was looking sympathetically.

"Good." She stopped dusting the shelf of canned goods. Elizabeth was playing with the twins in the bedroom upstairs. When Ernest wasn't helping at The General Store, she spent less time at the hospital. Today she was working most of the day at the store and planned to go to the Jacabig Hospital in the early afternoon. "Any word from Charles lately?"

He nodded. Abigail knew he was sparing her feelings by not telling her they had received letters from Charles unless she asked.

"Good to hear," she smiled. Abigail truly was happy for them.

"What can I do for you today, sir?" Abigail asked, as she stood with her dust cloth in one hand, her hand on her hip.

"Well, uh, Abigail," he shifted from leg to leg, "I have a favour to ask of you."

"Of course." Abigail's eyes met his.

"You know I wouldn't be asking," he fidgeted with his hat with his hands, "if it weren't important."

"I know." Abigail smiled slightly. She would be happy to help him out but she had so much to do and think about. She secretly hoped it wasn't too much for her to handle.

"Could you write to Charles?" He blurted it out as if he was asking for the moon.

Abigail lifted one eyebrow. Mr. Edwards saw her curiosity. He cleared his throat and shifted again where he stood.

"I mean, I am sure you're wondering why I am asking." He continued to play with his hat.

"Well-" she looked at him.

"From the last few letters from him, the missis and I have been worried about him."

"Oh?"

"He sounds so down. I can't imagine fighting for your country and feeling so alone. We wondered if you could send him a word of encouragement." His voice was low and steady. "Since you are the closest thing to his best friend, I thought-"

"I would be happy to do it," Abigail smiled. "I will do that tonight and mail it tomorrow."

"Thank you." He smiled.

"It's nothing, really." Abigail was indeed relieved that was all he wanted for a favour.

"To us, it's not nothing." He smiled, nodded as he put his hat back on and left the store.

After Mr. Edwards left, Abigail picked up the latest news-paper that had come in. The headline read 'BULGARIA DECLARES WAR ON ROMANIA!'. Abigail tossed the paper back down. *When is this war going to be over?* she said to herself. *When the whole world enters the war and destroys it?* Abigail was fed up with the war when it just began but now she was ready to throw in the towel. No end was in sight if more countries were now joining the war.

"I finished cutting more wood, Mrs. Abigail." In walked Mr. Soldier. "I know winter will be here before we know it."

"Surely you're right," she nodded. "How about some din-ner?" Abigail headed toward the kitchen. "Elizabeth has some sandwiches made up for us."

"Alright, ma'am," he nodded as he walked past her to wash up at the washstand.

"Mr. Ford brought us some fresh milk, said they had extra," Abigail explained as the two of them reached the table. "Would you mind looking for the wooden butter churn in the storage shed out back?" She looked at him. "Remember the one your bed was in?"

"Sure, I can do that right after dinner."

"Elizabeth! Danny! Josie! Come and eat," Abigail called out to them.

"Coming," Elizabeth answered, carefully walking the twins down each step.

After dinner, Abigail showed Elizabeth how to make butter.

"Mama always did it and wanted everyone out of the way," Elizabeth explained as she watched Abigail pour the cream in the freshly washed butter churn.

"I only learned since I came to Canada," Abigail explained as she put on the lid. "Would you like to churn it?"

"Sure," Elizabeth beamed as she began to turn the handle.

"It will take a little while," Abigail smiled. "If your arm gets tired, I will do it."

Quite a while went by as Abigail put more water on the stove to boil for washing the churn when they were done. She also had two pitchers of cold water ready to wash the butter. Abigail placed the big round wooden bowl on the table along with the butter paddle. She had another bowl ready to pour the buttermilk into.

"I can hardly turn it." Elizabeth slowly moved her hand, then she stopped and looked up at Abigail.

"Let me see." Abigail lifted the lid and peeked inside. "Looks like it's almost done!" she grinned at the young girl. Abigail churned it for a few more minutes until she could see big lumps of butter inside.

There was a small hole with a wooden plug near the bottom of the wooden churn. Abigail brought the churn to the edge of the table, then held a bowl right below the plug and asked Elizabeth to pull out the plug.

The butter milk splashed as it landed in the bottom of the bowl, but then it streamed at a constant speed until the churn was emptied of the liquid. Abigail tipped the churn forward to empty all the buttermilk out. She tried to get every last drop.

"Now we can put the butter in the big bowl." Abigail explained as she dumped the churn upside down and the clumps of butter fell into the wooden bowl with a splat. Some buttermilk came out as well.

"We have to wash it." Abigail poured some cold water over the butter and with the butter paddle then squished and moved the butter around to remove the buttermilk from the butter. She then drained the milky water and repeated the procedure several more times.

"If you don't get the buttermilk out of the butter," Abigail looked at Elizabeth, "the butter will go bad faster."

"Here, you try it." She handed the paddle to Elizabeth. "Keep squishing it and pressing it against the bowl." Abigail poured more cold water over the butter. The more cold water she poured on it, the stiffer the butter got. They continued until the water was fairly clear. She drained the last of the water.

"Now we add some salt for taste." Abigail put some salt in her hand for measuring and then tossed it into the butter. "Mix that up with the paddle," she directed Elizabeth.

Abigail and Elizabeth made four-inch butter balls, wrapped them in butter paper, then put them in the ice box.

"Well, that's a good job done." Abigail wiped her hands on her apron. "Time to clean up. We will make biscuits with the buttermilk tomorrow."

The twins were still happily playing on the floor as Abigail and Elizabeth washed the butter churn and butter making tools. It was greasy and needed hot water to get the oil out of the wood so it wouldn't go rancid in storage.

"There! We will leave it to dry in the sun." Abigail set everything outside by the door to air dry.

"I guess we should get supper going." Abigail was so grateful for Elizabeth's help. Just to have someone to chat with made it less lonely.

chapter twenty

Summer was almost over and the weather was warmer than usual. Abigail's A.P.L.G meetings were still held every Tuesday. Abigail was able to spend a little more time with Danny and Josie because of Mr. Soldier helping out. Going to Jacabig hospital was still the same. Meeting up with Dr. Parker remained a challenge. There were the odd days that Doc Johnson was there instead, which brought more enjoyment to the day than usual.

Elizabeth went home to spend some time with her family. Abigail's mama came to stay while Elizabeth was away. Abigail realized how much Elizabeth helped her with the twins, but having her mama was nice. They didn't get to spend much time together since Aunt Gladys had passed away.

Mama and Abigail were sitting down at the table drinking a cup of tea, when the bell above the store door rang. Abigail stood up and headed out to help the customer.

"Good morning." Abigail entered the room to find familiar faces smiling at her.

"Good morning to you, too," Alice beamed. There stood Alice, Bert, Ernest, Grace and Annie.

"Oh, my," Abigail rushed over to greet her good friends and called over her shoulder as she walked, "mama, mama come see who's here!" She stretched her arms out to Alice and hugged her tightly.

"Hello?" Mrs. Rodgers stood in the doorway of the kitchen. Her confused look turned to a big smile when she spied their guests. "What a wonderful surprise!" She quickly stepped toward them and hugged Alice and the girls.

"Ernest," Abigail walked over and gave him a little hug, "it's so good to see you. We sure miss you around here and the twins miss your horse rides."

"It's good to be here, Abigail." Ernest grinned. "I must say I miss all of you too."

"And look at you two!" Abigail touched the cheeks of Grace and Annie. "You have grown so much!" Grace was six years old now. She was very petite like her mama, with fair, fine hair, pushed behind her ears with tiny facial features. Annie was four years old and looked more like her father; darker hair and a little stockier build with a natural scowl over her green eyes. The two stood side by side and were almost the same height, with their matching dresses made by their mother.

"Would you two like to go play with Josie and Danny?" She crouched down to their level.

Both of them nodded shyly.

"Well, they are in the kitchen, playing," she directed them toward the kitchen. The girls hadn't visited there very often. They both hesitantly walked hand in hand to play with the twins.

"Come on in, come in," Abigail held out her hand and directed their company to the kitchen table. "Let's have some tea."

Alice and Mrs. Rodgers moved forward. Bert and Ernest were right behind them and Abigail followed.

"Have a seat," Mrs. Rodgers told everyone. She took the tea cups and saucers out of the cupboard and placed them on the table as everyone sat down. Abigail put more water in the kettle to boil on the cookstove. Since her mama and she had just made tea before everyone had come, she began filling cups for Alice, Bert and Ernest. Abigail took out some cookies from a square, gold tin box. The box had a faded picture of an English house with flowers in the garden. It was Abigail's favourite tin, brought back from England. She spread the cookies out on a plate.

"Here are some ginger cookies mama made." Abigail placed the plate down in front of everyone.

"Well, tell me all the news." Abigail sat down beside Alice. "What have you all been doing?"

"Well, getting ready for winter," Ernest piped up. "Moved the cattle to the north pasture, and played crib the other night with the Hills." He smiled at Abigail.

"Oh, Ernest." Alice shook her head. "You know that's not what she means."

"Well, she asked." Ernest took a sip of tea with a mischievous smile. "And I beat them too!" He added quickly, then took a bite out of a cookie.

Ignoring Ernest's last comment, Alice shifted in her chair and looked at Abigail. "Bert and I celebrated our sixth wedding anniversary."

"That's wonderful," Abigail smiled at Alice. "Did you do anything fancy?"

"We did." Alice beamed. "The Rileys had us over for supper and Mrs. Riley made us a delicious fruit cake with almond paste and icing.

"How nice of them!"

"The Rileys have been the kindest neighbours," Alice took another sip of tea.

The bell over the store door rang again. Abigail stood up, but before she could leave the table, Mr. Soldier came in.

"You're just in time for tea." Abigail smiled, and was about to introduce everyone to her new helper, but he shied away.

"Just a minute," Abigail followed after him. "Come in and have a break and meet everyone."

"No, thank you, Mrs. Abigail." He quickly looked down after seeing the room full of people. "I only came in to tell you that I finished the deliveries."

"Thank you," Abigail smiled, "but are you sure you don't want some tea?"

"I will see you at supper," he grinned lightly. "I have to clean out the stable and then haul water to the hospital."

"Alright." Abigail watched him walk out the door, wondering why he didn't want to join them. Perhaps he is self-conscious of his burns, or maybe only shy around people he didn't know. Confused, she joined the others.

When she sat back down she glanced at Ernest who was giving her a concerned look. Abigail narrowed her eyes in question.

The afternoon went by so quickly. Catching up with the Hibberts was medicine no doctor could give and Abigail truly needed it. It felt like old times. Not that it had been many, many years, but since the war started, the life she had before was like another lifetime, a different world.

Alice did her shopping while Bert went to the Blacksmith's shop and a couple of other stops. The children played contentedly most of the afternoon until Danny fell down the last two steps of the stairs and banged his head. Danny cried until his sister cried, and the poor Hibbert sisters stood back watching as if they were in trouble.

"It's alright, my boy." Abigail picked up her son and rubbed his head where it was red. "You're alright." Josie stood at Abigail's feet, tugged on her dress and sympathetically cried "mama, mama, mama," as she tugged harder.

"It's alright, little one." Abigail crouched down to Josie's level pulled her on her other knee and hugged both twins at the same time.

"I don't know how you do it, Abigail." Alice shook her head. "Two babies the same age. I can't believe you stay sane."

"I couldn't do it without the help of mama and Elizabeth," she confessed. "It's not easy, but it's worth it." She beamed as she held her children tighter to her body and kissed the top of their heads.

"Danny sure looks like Jacob." Alice's kind face met Abigail's. "The undeniable dimple, that curly blonde hair." She smiled and touched his cheek, as he finished crying, sniffling a little.

"He sure does." Abigail played with the top curl on his head.

Abigail saw the sympathy behind Alice's eyes. She was like all the other people in Abbington Pickets. Say they think of her, give her that pathetic look and then pat her on the back or give her a hug. Not that she didn't appreciate the sentiment. She knew folks cared for her and the twins, and would do most anything to help, if they could. It's only she was tired of being looked at that way.

"Are you ready to go?" Bert walked through the store doorway and took off his hat when he got inside.

"We are, my dear," Alice looked at Bert like she was seeing him for the first time. They too, had a love like no other. They knew what sacrifice was. It was a long year for Bert when he came to Canada from England before Alice. He had left his whole family behind. Oh, they knew what it was like to miss someone dearly.

"Well, we better get going," he encouraged, "we want to be home before dark." He picked up Annie and swung her up on his hip.

"You're right." Alice took Grace's hand. "It was so good to see you, Abigail, and the twins." She reached over to give Abigail a hug with her free arm. "If there is anything you need."

"I know," smiled Abigail. "I know, thank you. We are fine, Alice. We will be just fine." She was still holding Danny and Mrs. Rodgers was holding Josie.

"Safe journey home." Mrs. Rodgers smiled. "Don't let it be too long before we see you again."

"Hopefully not," Alice said.

Ernest was already outside and stood by the wagon. He had taken the horses for a drink and some hay at the livery. Abigail left Danny and Josie inside with her mama and walked Alice, Bert and the girls outside.

"Now, you take care of yourself," Abigail touched Alice's arm.

"I will, don't worry, Bert is good to me," she reassured her.

"Don't be a stranger." Abigail walked over to Ernest as Bert helped the girls and Alice onto the wagon.

"Abigail," Ernest's once friendly face turned sober. "Do you know what are you doing?"

"What do you mean?" Abigail lifted her eyebrows.

"You know exactly what I am talking about," Ernest gruffly whispered as he stepped closer to her.

"I am afraid I don't," she said lowly, "what are you talking about?"

"That man,"

"What man?"

"The one who came in while we were having tea."

"Mr. Soldier?"

"He is no 'Mister.'" Ernest said frankly, "and no good soldier, either."

"He is now, Ernest," Abigail insisted. "You're worrying for nothing, Ernest." Abigail looked back toward The General Store and saw her mama looking out the window. She couldn't let her mama know what they were talking about.

"Are you coming, Ern?" Bert called out from the other side of the wagon.

"Coming!" Ernest replied over his shoulder, turned back to Abigail and his face changed back to concern. "I don't feel right leaving you here, alone, near that drunk."

"I am not alone," Abigail whispered. "Mama is here, and besides, he's been here for a couple months."

"What?" Ernest scowled. "You mean-" his voice got louder.

"Shhh, keep it down," Abigail put her finger to her mouth. "He's been helping around the store since-"

"Are you really serious? Are you mad? After he shot you? Brought on early labour? You could have died, the twins may not be alive because of him."

"But I didn't," Abigail looked at him. "The twins are fine, and besides, it was an accident."

"Abigail-" he whisper-shouted as he glanced around. "He has to pay for what he did to you, Abigail." Ernest's eyes narrowed.

"No, Ernest," Abigail disputed, "I don't want that."

"He shouldn't get away with it," Ernest retorted.

"He has changed, and for what he's been through," Abigail looked down, "I think that's enough."

Ernest had no words, he just shook his head.

"He has really changed."

"Oh, really?" Ernest put his hand on his hip.

"Yes, really, and I don't want anyone else to know." Abigail looked back up at Ernest.

"But, Abigail-"

"Promise me, Ernest, you will keep it our secret," Abigail pleaded.

Ernest reluctantly nodded.

"I will be fine. He doesn't drink anymore and he has really been a great help to us," Abigail explained. "Besides, he doesn't know that I know who he is."

Ernest's eyes narrowed.

"I will be back to check on you," Ernest promised. "Jacob will never forgive me if anything happens to you."

"I appreciate that, Ernest," Abigail smiled. "Really I do, but please don't worry. Everything is fine."

"I don't feel good about this, but I have no choice." Ernest shook his head again. "I have to start harvest right away."

"It's alright. I promise." Abigail gave him a quick hug.

"I am not happy, but right now there's nothing I can do about it." Ernest took off his hat, scratched his head with the same hand then put his hat back on his head.

"Goodbye, Ernest."

Abigail stepped back and walked closer to the wagon where Alice and the girls were sitting behind the front seat. Ernest pulled himself up onto the wagon seat, next to Bert.

Alice and the girls waved with smiles on their faces. Bert tipped his hat and started the horses. Ernest frowned at Abigail as he nodded goodbye.

Abigail watched for several minutes until the wagon was out of sight. She thought about what Ernest had said. She recognized his concern but knew in her heart he had nothing to worry about. Mr. Soldier had changed, the accident changed him, the war transformed him, he is far from dangerous Abigail believed. She wanted to help him in any way she could.

Abigail turned back toward The General Store. Her mama still looked out the window, but over to the left she saw Mr. Soldier as he stood beyond the back of the store, leaned against the rake he had in his hand and stared at the Empire Hotel. Abigail wondered what he was doing.

"Mr. Soldier," Abigail waved as she sprinted toward him. "Are you ready for that tea?"

The young man looked at Abigail coming toward him and gave a half-hearted smile.

"Alright, Mrs. Abigail." He set the rake against the building and he followed Abigail into the store.

chapter twenty-one

Today was an emotional day for Abigail. It was September 9, 1916. It was Jacob and her fifth wedding anniversary. Abigail had imagined celebrating this special day a little differently. A romantic moment of a husband and wife exchanging intimate words toward one another, possibly a special meal together, maybe a picnic like they used to do, in their special place under the tree at 'Appleton's Haven.' But this time it would be a family picnic. Abigail imagined how Jacob would be with the twins. Chasing them as Danny and Josie giggled, looked behind them and squealed with laughter when each realized their father had caught up to them. Abigail imagined Jacob throwing Danny up in the air, catching him as his dimpled smile beamed back at him. He would hold Josie close, as she nodded off to sleep in the crook of his arm. Jacob would rest his chin on the top of her head as he cradled her. Then Jacob would hold Abigail as she sat in front of him and leaned against his chest, sitting on a homemade pieced quilt under the tree while the twins slept peacefully beside them. They would stay at Appleton's Haven for hours while listening to the stillness of the day. The grass softly stirring, cicadas harmonizing in the distance while butterflies floated above Indian Paintbrushes.

"Elizabeth," Abigail was standing at the table making sandwiches. "Can you get the twins' sweaters on them? It may be a chilly breeze."

"Yes, Mrs. Abigail." Elizabeth began putting one sleeve on Josie, as the toddler squirmed away from her grasp and giggled as she tried to run from the girl.

"Come- on- Josie-," Elizabeth struggled with her, when finally she got the sweater on her. She then ran to tackle Danny.

"Well, Mrs. Abigail," Elizabeth seemed to be exhausted over wrestling with the children. Abigail gave her a second look.

"Are you alright?" She touched Elizabeth's forehead with the back of her hand, then she felt her hands. She appeared to feel the right temperature.

"Why don't you have a rest while we are gone?" Abigail suggested.

"I have those dishes to do and..." She looked a little pale.

"The dishes can wait," Abigail looked at her sternly. "You go lie down."

"Yes, Mrs. Abigail." She nodded as she began to take off her apron.

"We won't be very long," Abigail took the twins' hands, carried the basket over her arm and headed out the doorway.

"Hello, Mrs. Abigail," Mr. Soldier called out to her. "Do you need some help?" He had been splitting wood behind the house. His brow was beaded with sweat and his shirt was damp under his arms and down his chest. His scars glistened bright red in the sunshine as he took off his hat and wiped his forehead with the back of his hand.

"Actually," Abigail stopped to get a better grip on Danny's hand, "would you mind pulling out the wagon from the shed back of the house, please?" Mr. Soldier knew where she meant as he had gotten many things from the shed before. It was still full of Mr. and Mrs. Adair's possessions. Jacob found most of them to be rather useful and said to leave it all in there, as they may come in handy some day. And he was right, as always.

"Sure, of course." Mr. Soldier seemed happier than usual, Abigail thought. He walked away and left Abigail to struggle with the children as she waited for him to return. When he came back, he was pulling a small rectangular wooden wagon with metal wheels. The wood was old and a grey worn-out colour. The metal was rusted but overall in good shape.

"Here, can you take the twins?" Abigail gave Mr. Soldier their hands. "I forgot the quilt for the picnic." Abigail sprinted back into The General Store.

Abigail returned with a quilt over her arm as she moved swiftly toward Mr. Soldier and the twins. She bent down to put the quilt in the bottom of the wooden wagon. She then picked up Josie and placed her on top of the quilt, then Danny. When she stood up to take the wagon handle, Abigail thought she could smell alcohol near Mr. Soldier. *That couldn't be,* Abigail said to herself. *She had never seen him go there, besides where would he get the money? She must have been mistaken,* she told herself.

"Have a great picnic, Mrs. Abigail." Mr. Soldier tipped his hat at her.

"We will. Thanks for getting the wagon for me." She smiled, pulled the handle, and the twins jerked forward with the surprised movement.

"My pleasure," he added as he watched Abigail walk away with the children.

"Oh," Abigail turned around to look at Mr. Soldier, "I almost forgot. Can you help in the store if someone comes? Elizabeth isn't feeling well and is lying down."

"Of course," Mr. Soldier smiled, "I would be happy to help."

The walk was longer than Abigail remembered, since she and Jacob had ridden their horses instead or taken the wagon team to spend time under the great tree. It was a beautiful fall day, just as it was the day Jacob and Abigail were married. The birds glided down low and sang melodies of happiness. The autumn flowers had bloomed and waved in the gentle breeze.

Abigail reminisced along the path as she pulled the twins through the matted fall-coloured blades of grass. She saw the same landmark that had been there since she had been coming here. Jacob said it was there as long as he could remember. The abandoned, decrepit old wagon sat slightly tilted on one corner as the wooden wheels were rotting away where it was slowly falling down, piece by piece. Abigail remembered when Jacob gave her the wedding gift, the eight day Sessions clock and the beautiful poem. He had surprised her by taking her on a picnic under the big tree. She also remembered racing Jacob on horseback to their favourite spot and she couldn't forget the time she fell from a branch and broke her leg. Jacob revealed then how devoted he was already to her, while only just friends.

As they neared the tree, Abigail spotted the familiar sign Jacob had made. 'Appleton's Haven' hung on the tree. The twins were happy for the ride they received but also glad to get out and toddle around the tall grass that surrounded the unique willow tree. Both squealed as they chased each other around and around.

Abigail took the quilt out of the wagon and spread it out beside the trunk of the tree, right under the branches full of green-turned-yellow leaves, which were beginning to fall. She lifted the basket and placed it on the quilt.

"Josie, Danny, come here." Abigail called out to them. "Time to eat."

"Mama, mama. Yum, yum." Josie headed toward Abigail and Danny followed. Josie reached out in front of her as she waddled carefully.

"Come, sit down." Abigail patted the quilt on which she was sitting.

Abigail took out the sandwiches and the jar of iced tea. Both twins sat quietly and nibbled on their sandwiches. They both enjoyed it when it was time to eat. Abigail leaned back against the tree and took a bite herself. She stared out into the prairies as she thought of how she should have been spending this day with Jacob and their children.

It wasn't long before Josie and Danny wanted to get off the quilt and explore again. Abigail thought she would let them have a little fun before packing up and heading back to Abbington Pickets.

"Lord, wherever Jacob is," Abigail looked up to the sky and closed her eyes as she spoke out loud, "let him know I am thinking of him at this moment." She took in a deep breath as she looked back down and saw her precious boy and girl wobble as they walked. Their fair hair blew back off their faces and their eyes shone half moons while laughing in the moment. *Oh, Jacob, if only you were here,* she said to herself. *I think it's time Josephine and Daniel heard more about their papa.*

"Children, children, come here," she called out to them. "Mama wants to see you," she cooed. Just as before, they made their way to the quilt where their mama was. Abigail scooped both of them toward her and placed them on her lap.

"Mama wants to tell you a story," Abigail began, "about your papa." Her eyes welled up as she said those words.

"P-aaapa." Danny repeated, then Josie duplicated.

"Yes, your papa." The twins sat still as Abigail put her arms around them, they leaned back against her and intently listened.

"Your papa's name is Jacob Hudson," she said. "He was born a farmer's son." Danny lifted his head up toward his mama and Abigail grinned at him.

"He grew up to be a great carpenter," she continued, "and fell in love with an English girl." Abigail smiled, recalling the day they met and also the day Jacob came to live at Goldenrod Ranch.

"Gurl?" Josie repeated with a curious look.

"Yes, girl," Abigail corrected as she looked at her. "That was me."

Abigail knew the twins really wouldn't know what she was talking about but it gave her satisfaction and thought that if she told the same story to them enough times, they would get to know their father. They would know him when they saw him for the first time, *if they do get to see him for the first time,* Abigail's little voice in the back of her mind added.

"They fell in love and got married." Abigail remembered that day, the day she knew she loved Jacob, the day she knew he really loved her. It was actually the night before she left for England. She had gotten into the wine, oh, too much wine. Jacob had helped her sober up before her parents found out. When she said goodbye at the train station the next day, she knew then that she was leaving her love behind.

"Papa?" Danny repeated again only saying it more correctly this time than the first.

Yes, it was time, time to start telling them about Jacob.

Abigail began putting everything back into the basket when she heard something in the distance. She looked toward the south, vaguely seeing something coming her way. She stood up and put her hand over her brow to block the sunlight. She realized it was Dr. Parker's car. After a few minutes, he began honking, almost scaring the children out of their wits.

"What's the matter with you!" Abigail called out as he neared her.

"Come quick!" It wasn't Dr. Parker at all; it was Mr. Soldier. "It's Elizabeth."

"What's wrong? What's the matter?" She grabbed the quilt and shoved it into the car. Mr. Soldier picked up one twin, Abigail the other, and got into the car while he explained.

"I went into the store to help a customer and she was lying on the floor in the kitchen," he gasped for air as he spoke while driving.

"What?" Abigail was almost screaming.

"Dr. Parker is with her now, at the hospital." He continued, "I carried her there. She was burning up bad."

"Oh my-" was all Abigail could say, as she held onto the twins, each of them bouncing up and down with the springing of the car as Mr. Soldier did his best to navigate around all the holes in the ground.

"Dr. Parker told me to take his car to fetch you."

"You know how to drive this- uh this- car?" She looked at him with caution.

"The army," he stated as he continued looking straight ahead.

"Did Dr. Parker say what was wrong with Elizabeth?"

"No, he didn't." Mr. Soldier looked scared as he turned to look at Abigail, then back to the road ahead of them, as they moved up and down with the motion of the car.

"Once Dr. Parker looked her over," he kept talking, "he sent for you."

The roar of the car engine, with the creaking and cracking of the bouncing from the seats, was all Abigail and Mr. Soldier could hear for the rest of the ride to Jacabig.

Mr. Soldier pulled the car right up to the door. Abigail reached for the door handle and pulled it hard to open the door. She reached for Danny as Mr. Soldier took Josie and followed Abigail into the hospital.

Abigail pushed open the door and walked briskly toward the patients' beds. Her eyes scanned the room but nowhere did she see Elizabeth.

"In here." Dr. Parker stepped out of the operating room. "Thought it would be more private for her in here," he explained.

Abigail brushed past the doctor and walked over to Elizabeth's bedside. Elizabeth lay under the white sheets on the bed, her forehead damp along her hairline and sweat-beaded, her cheeks flushed. Her eyes were slightly open and she half grinned when she saw the twins. Abigail reached for her hand and squeezed lightly. She looked back at Dr. Parker.

"What's wrong with her?" she questioned.

"I am not exactly sure." He walked closer to Abigail. "Her fever is our big concern right now. We may have to use ice."

"Mr. Soldier," Abigail looked in the doorway where he stood holding Josie. "I think you better go fetch Elizabeth's mama."

"You can take the car," Dr. Parker added. "It will be faster."

"But-" Abigail shook her head. "I think- " Abigail held her tongue, realizing Mr. Soldier wasn't a child and could do what he wished. "If you're comfortable with that," she finished.

"Yes, Mrs. Abigail." Mr. Soldier set Josie down and headed back toward the door.

"What shall I do to help?" Abigail looked at the doctor with concerned eyes.

"Take the twins home," he abruptly ordered.

"I can-"

"I said take them home!" His voice rose. "If it's what I think it is, you don't need them getting sick, too."

"What do you think it is, Dr. Parker?" Abigail pressed.

"I don't want to get everyone stirred up." He looked over at a worried Abigail. "Please, just go."

Abigail didn't comment again. She took Josie by the hand and, still carrying Daniel on her hip, walked toward the door.

She followed the path back to The General Store. Abigail's mind was racing with what she should do now. Poor Elizabeth. She hoped her mama would get there quickly. Elizabeth needed someone to be with her. It broke Abigail's heart not to be able to help her as she had so many other patients at the hospital, but her twins needed her as well. She looked up at the sky in desperation. "Lord, we need You."

Abigail stepped up to the store, unlatched the door and walked through the doorway. As she turned to close the door behind her, she heard a loud bang from the front of the store. She felt her heart jump and spun around to see a shadow move.

"Sorry," a male voice sounded as a person had bent down quickly to pick up something. "I didn't mean to startle you, but I dropped the hammer." He walked toward her and carried the hammer in his right hand.

Abigail stood still, her heart still beating quickly.

"Oh, my, you scared me," she gasped as she held her children tight. The man walked into the light and Abigail let out the breath she was holding.

"Peter! What are you doing here?" She was so relieved to find it was her brother-in-law. She knew that Mr. Soldier was still fetching Elizabeth's mama and papa and she wasn't expecting Ernest any time soon.

"I came to town for some supplies," Peter stood before her explaining. "There was no one around here," he looked around the store. "I was going to leave you a note-"

"Sorry about that, Peter," Abigail let go of Josie's hand and bent to set down Danny. "It's Elizabeth. She's very ill."

"What's wrong?" His eyes searched Abigail's face.

"I don't know," she began. "The twins and I were at Appleton's Haven, Elizabeth was looking after the store, and Mr. Soldier was outside working..." Peter listened intently while Abigail told him the whole situation.

"I sure wish I could help, Abigail." Peter rubbed the top of his head as he looked down. "But we are starting to harvest tomorrow."

"Don't worry, Peter," Abigail shook her head. "You have enough to worry about. I know how busy you are." She looked away.

"It breaks my heart that I can't help my only brother's wife and children while he is away." His eyes looked worn and tired, but Abigail noticed the sadness on his face.

"Peter, we are doing alright." Abigail wasn't about to tell him that money was her biggest worry, that she felt like giving up every day not to mention that it was a chore to get out of bed every morning. The not knowing whether her husband was dead or alive tore her up inside, and she screamed silently every day.

"It's only that-" Peter persisted.

"You have your own worries, Peter." Abigail continued. "I have everything under control. Mr. Soldier is a great help and Ernest will soon be here." She reached out to him and touched his arm.

Abigail had never seen Peter act like this before. He always was in a hurry, always had things he had to do. The truth was, Abigail hardly ever saw Peter. With farming Andrew's and his land, along with helping the neighbours and his growing family, there never seemed much time for extra visiting.

As Abigail tucked the twins into bed that evening she noticed Danny's warm forehead and red cheeks. Maybe he is teething, she told herself. He didn't seem out of sorts and went to bed with no fuss. Kissing their foreheads, she took the oil lamp with her to the kitchen.

Mr. Soldier had come back for supper after returning from the Fords with the news of their daughter. Mrs. Ford rode back with him to the hospital and Mr. Ford followed later in horse and wagon. Abigail prayed for Elizabeth's complete healing, still not knowing what was wrong with her. She was beginning to feel the burden of Elizabeth's illness, and her financial dilemma was sinking in, not to mention the fact that she felt utterly alone. Abigail decided to do the one thing she always did when she felt this way. She took the lamp to her bedroom and set it down on top of the desk. She reached for the writing paper and fountain pen. She sat down at the desk, touched the tip of the pen to the paper...

My dearest Jacob,

I hope this letter finds its way to you. I haven't heard from you for months but I am trusting in The Lord that you are safe and are coming back to us soon.

Today was our special day and I wonder if you are remembering it as well. It was a difficult day here, mostly because I miss you so desperately and that you and I should be spending this day together with our two children. But I must say I made the most of it and I packed a lunch and walked the twins to our favourite place. The children played under the big tree as I spread the quilt out and I told them our love story. I told them how we love this place, and how you and I fell in love. I know they aren't old enough to understand but it made me feel closer to you, as if you were almost there with us.

Our picnic was short lived, as Elizabeth suddenly fell ill. Jacob, I am so worried about her. Dr. Parker sent me home, saying I couldn't help in any way, and he wanted me to take the children home and stay here while he tended to Elizabeth. He scared me so much. He is a rude, obnoxious man, but there was fear in his eyes and for once I believed he wasn't fooling around. We sent for Elizabeth's parents and I brought the children back to The General Store. I fear something is really wrong with her and I don't know what to do.

Oh, my love, if you were here, you would know what to do. You would take care of everything. I feel so helpless Jacob. Not only do I feel sadness from you being away from me this long, but I feel hopeless. You are the head of this family, the rock, our foundation. I feel like my prayers aren't like your prayers, my faith isn't as faithful as yours and my strength isn't strong like yours. I know, if you were here, you would have the perfect thing to say. You would lift me up and I would be encouraged. I miss you so much, I feel my heart can't take much more of your absence.

Peter stopped by today, I thought you would like to know that I saw him. He looks sad and tired. This war has taken a toll on everyone. Not only the soldiers who have gone to war but also their families they have left behind. The shortage of men to work the fields and the lack of young men to do the hard work is leaving the older men exhausted and even sick. I can't imagine what it's like for you, when I am here complaining about such trivial things compared to what you and thousands of young men have been through, and are going through.

I do hope and pray for the day your letter will find me and give me peace of mind that you are indeed coming home to your family.

I must sign off my love. I love you until forever comes.

Your loving wife,
Girlie

A tear fell from Abigail's cheek onto the letter. The tear fell on the ink and blurred the words 'forever'. Abigail reached in her apron pocket for her hankie and dabbed the coloured liquid lightly to not smudge it any more than it was. She blew on it, drying it quickly. Waiting for the ink to dry, she filled out the outside of the envelope, then folded the letter. She slid it inside, licked the flap, closed it, and kissed the back of it. She placed it back on the desk to be mailed tomorrow.

chapter twenty-two

Abigail woke with a start and her heart pounded as she heard the blood curdling scream. In a dazed consciousness she swung her legs over the bed, her feet reached the floor as she stood up and felt for her housecoat. It was still dark out which made it hard to find it. The screaming seemed to be louder and Abigail rushed to find a wooden match to light the lamp. Fumbling to get the matches out of the box, she dropped the first one she had a hold of. Still her heart was pounding. She took out a second match and struck it against the box, lifted the chimney of the lamp and instantly ignited the wick. She didn't even take the time to adjust the flame and put the chimney back on when she darted out her bedroom doorway to find the twins in their room, both wailing. She first saw Josie who stood up in her crib, cried hard and reached out for her mama to pick her up. To Abigail's surprise, Danny was still lying down, his face as red as a ripe tomato. With tears streaming down, he sobbed uncontrollably. Abigail passed by Josie as she bent down to scoop up Danny. As she touched him, her hands felt as though she had touched a hot frying pan. Her heart jumped into her throat and her ears rang as the crying continued. She rocked Danny back and forth and tried to soothe him. She reached out to Josie.

"It's alright, little one," she rubbed the top of her head. "Don't cry, it will be alright." Abigail felt like crying herself.

"Is everything alright, Mrs. Abigail?" The voice sounded from the hallway.

"Oh, my goodness Mr. Soldier," as if Abigail's heart couldn't get further into her throat, she almost felt like she was choking on it. "You scared me to death."

"I am sorry, ma'am." Mr. Soldier stood there, in his undershirt and she could tell he had just pulled on his britches and threw on his boots. "I could hear the screaming from the carpenter's shop."

"I am glad you are here." Abigail felt a sigh of relief.

"Can you go fetch Doc?" Abigail asked. "And go fast!"

"Yes, Mrs. Abigail." He didn't waste time. He spun around on his heels and he was back out the doorway.

It felt like forever before he returned, but to Abigail's surprise he brought Dr. Parker instead of Doc. Both children were still crying. Abigail was in the rocking chair, still trying to console Danny. She had taken Josie out of the crib, and she stood next to her mama, whimpering. She didn't have a fever like Danny did, but she seemed out of sorts, almost like she felt sorry for her brother.

"Doc was on a house call already, Mrs. Abigail." Mr. Soldier looked at Abigail as he came in.

"I woke up to the twins crying," Abigail explained as Dr. Parker put his black leather bag down beside her rocking chair. He knelt down to Danny's level. Dr. Parker touched Danny's forehead with his hand.

"He definitely is burning up."

"I thought as much." The sarcasm slipped out of Abigail's mouth.

The doctor pulled down the skin below Danny's eyes with his thumb as he looked at the redness inside.

"Can you hold him still?" Dr. Parker ordered Abigail as he opened his bag and dug inside it to find a tongue depressor. "He isn't going to like this."

Abigail held Danny tight, tried to hold his forehead back against her chest with one hand and hold his legs down with the other.

"Hold the lamp close to his mouth." Dr. Parker directed Mr. Soldier toward the lamp sitting on the dresser. Mr. Soldier walked over, picked it up and stood as close as he could without being in the way. He held the lamp steady.

As Danny wailed even harder because of being restrained, his mouth opened wider. Dr. Parker quickly stuck the tongue depressor into his mouth, pressed his tongue down, and Danny choked. The doctor brought his head closer to see into his mouth. As fast as he stuck the wooden stick in, he was already pulling it back out. He had apparently seen what he was looking for.

"We need to take him to the hospital." Dr. Parker put on his stethoscope as he spoke, placed the ear pieces into his ears and the chest piece onto Danny's chest. Then he tried to listen while Danny was still crying.

"Can't I look after him here?" Abigail's eyes pleaded.

"You live in a public building, Abigail." Dr. Parker took his stethoscope off. "He shouldn't be exposed to every person who walks through that doorway," the doctor said firmly as he pointed toward the door to The General Store.

Abigail felt like a child being yelled at by her teacher. The blood left her face as her heart sank.

"He needs to be where I can look after him, and if he is contagious, he should be in the hospital," Dr. Parker said calmly as he put the stethoscope back into his bag and closed it. He could see the look on Abigail's face.

"Well, then, I am coming with him." Abigail sat up straight and sniffed while wiping her nose with her hankie.

It was at that moment she felt a different strength from within herself. She wasn't going to let the doctor intimidate her, especially not Dr. Parker. When it came to her children, she wouldn't back down.

"Mr. Soldier." She spun around to see him standing behind her, holding on to Josie. "Can you hitch up the horses and go to Goldenrod?"

"Yes, Mrs. Abigail," Mr. Soldier nodded as he set Josie down onto the floor and was about to dart out the doorway without further instruction.

"When you get there, ask mama to come straight away," she finished.

"I will." He threw on his hat and was out the door with a bang as the door slapped the door frame.

Abigail turned back to Dr. Parker.

"I may not be a formal nurse, but I am the best one you've got at that hospital and I am not leaving my child there alone." Abigail's face reddened as she stood her ground and held Daniel tightly as Josie stood at her feet.

"You're right." Dr. Parker smiled lightly, "you are the best I have had help me."

Finally he has taken me seriously Abigail said to herself. *Maybe he will leave me alone and when this wretched war is over he will go back to where he came from.*

"Once my mama gets here, I will bring Danny to the hospital." She gave him a slight glare.

"If you insist," he shook his head, "I can't stop you. But you are risking everyone who isn't sick."

"What kind of illness are you talking about?" Abigail's eyes narrowed as she glared at the doctor.

"I suspect," he took in a deep breath, letting it out slowly before he answered, "scarlet fever."

Abigail stared at him. She had heard about scarlet fever, but she hadn't known anyone who had it. She knew it was a scary disease, with high fever, rash and that it could result in permanent damage to certain organs.

"Are you certain?" She didn't doubt him, but Danny wasn't sick before this. It seemed to happen so fast.

"Quite." Dr. Parker nodded. "I want to speak more to Doc about it."

"But Danny wasn't sick before now."

"Well, he is young, and may not show the signs of a sore throat besides not eating much and being fussy."

"I guess he hasn't been eating much." Abigail thought about how last night for supper his plate was still quite full. It had been so busy that she hadn't thought much about it.

"I will pack a bag, feed the twins," Abigail said, while still rocking Danny to soothe him as she spoke," and as soon as mama gets here we will be at the hospital."

"I will have the bed ready." Dr. Parker looked over at Josie. "Maybe I should have a look at this one, too, before I go."

"That's maybe a good idea." Abigail for once felt like she could agree with Dr. Parker.

Dr. Parker crouched down to Josie's level and touched her forehead. She stepped closer to her mama and turned her head to the side, revealing her shyness.

"It's alright, Josie," Abigail prompted her to look at the doctor. "Dr. Parker only wants to have a look at you."

Dr. Parker took the stethoscope back out of his bag, put it on again and reached out to place it on Josie's chest. Josie backed away from him.

"Josie," Dr. Parker softly spoke as he pulled her toward him. "Can I put this on your chest like this?" He showed her by placing it on his own chest. When he slowly reached out to her, she stood still as he listened to her chest.

Several seconds passed as Dr. Parker moved the stethoscope from one place to another on her chest as well as her back. The doctor cleared his throat, took the stethoscope off, placed it back into his bag, and then searched for the tongue depressor. Josie cooperated better than little Daniel.

Abigail impatiently waited to hear what Dr. Parker had to say and held her tongue as long as she could.

"Well?" Abigail searched his sober face.

"Josie," he hesitated, taking in a deep breath, "doesn't appear to have any visible symptoms."

"But why do you look like there is something wrong?" Abigail persisted.

"I can't believe it," he looked up at Abigail. "The two sleep in the same room, as close as they are to one another, and she doesn't appear to be sick."

"Praise God," Abigail smiled, "but that's a good thing," Abigail stated as she noticed the sober look on his face.

"Yes, of course," he nodded. "This is why you need to get Danny to the hospital. They should be separated so she doesn't get sick. Chances are, she still could."

Dr. Parker bent down, picked up his bag and then stood up straight.

"How is Elizabeth?" Abigail looked up at the doctor. "Is she better?"

"She is about the same. Extremely high fever, sore throat and rash. Come as soon as you can." He grabbed his hat and placed it on his head. "For now, wipe his forehead down with a cold, wet cloth, and give him a lot of liquids to keep him hydrated." He nodded at Abigail and headed out the doorway.

Danny began to cry. His voice was hoarse and his cheeks redder than before the doctor came. Abigail began to worry all the more since the doctor had put a fear in her that wasn't there before. The fact that Josie could get the illness and that it could be scarlet fever began to sink in. She shook her head. No! This wasn't going to happen. God is faithful. Jacob has told her that over and over and Josie will not get sick and Danny will get better. She needed to have Jacob's faith and she needed to pray now.

"Dear Jesus," Abigail bowed her head and began to speak to God. "I lift up my children, Danny and Josie, to You. That You will heal Danny's body from this illness and keep Josie from getting it. I pray You will also heal Elizabeth from this sickness and keep her from getting worse and only get better from here on in. May the blood of the Lamb be upon them and Your angels surround them, in Jesus' name, Amen."

Abigail lifted her head, looked at both her children with a half-hearted smiled. Tears welled up in her eyes and rolled down her cheeks. She missed Jacob terribly and wondered how far her faith would take her. Would her faith be enough? Abigail took in a deep breath, wiped her cheeks with the tips of her fingers, stood up as she carried Danny in her arms, took Josie by the hand and they went into the kitchen.

Abigail began to prepare for the hospital as she waited for her mama to get there. She fed the twins boiled eggs and milk. Danny didn't eat very much, he mostly drank. Abigail continued to wipe him down with a cold, wet cloth and changed him into clean night clothes.

Josie was asleep in her bed when mama and Mr. Soldier arrived. Abigail was waiting in the kitchen with Danny, packed and ready to leave.

"Oh, Abigail," her mama hugged her when she came into the kitchen. "Mr. Soldier told me." Her sympathetic face was a sight for sore eyes, Abigail thought.

"Thank you for coming, mama," she gave a slight smile. "Don't come near Danny," she quickly backed away. "He could be contagious, and we don't need you sick."

"Of course," her mama agreed.

"Josie is sleeping, the kettle is on," Abigail pointed toward the cookstove. "I have to go, and will be gone until Danny is better."

"Everything will be fine," Mama reassured her. "Isn't that right, Mr. Soldier?" She looked at him for concurrence.

"You bet, Mrs. Rodgers." Mr. Soldier nodded.

"I know it will be." Abigail held Danny on her right hip. "Send Mr. Soldier for me if you need anything."

"Don't worry," her mama urged.

"Mr. Soldier, can you take us to Jacabig please?"

Mr. Soldier gave Abigail a quick nod as he put his hat back on and followed her and Danny out of the door.

There was a crib bed prepared for Danny in Elizabeth's room when they got to the hospital. Since no one else shared the same symptoms, it was safe to keep the two together to prevent the spread of the disease.

"Abigail," Mrs. Ford got up from the chair beside Elizabeth's bedside. She gave Abigail a half hug, not getting too close to her, as if to avoid contamination. "I heard about Danny." She looked worn out and tired but her face still had compassion despite her own suffering.

Abigail nodded as she held Danny on her hip.

"How is Elizabeth?" Abigail glanced past Mrs. Ford and saw Elizabeth's face reddened with a rash, which looked more scarlet in colour against the white sheets.

"The same," Mrs. Ford shook her head.

"She's in my prayers," Abigail smiled.

"And you as well," Mrs. Ford nodded toward Danny. "I best let you get him to bed. I don't like to leave her for very long."

"Thank you." Abigail tried to look more up beat than she was really feeling, but feared her face betrayed her.

She put little Danny into the metal white-painted crib. She laid him on the white sheets and then covered him up with the top sheet. He didn't seem to mind to be put down. His cheeks were as rosy as Elizabeth's and the rash was beginning to spread to his arms, hands and legs. It was most prominent in the creases of his skin, behind the knees and under his arms. He watched his mama as she looked down on him but he didn't have the strength to fuss. He just watched.

Abigail set down his basket near the crib, pulled out his favourite toy, and placed it beside him in his bed.

She walked over to the hook on the wall by the door and reached for the apron she always wore when volunteering.

"Glad you got here," a voice sounded from behind her.

Abigail turned around to find Dr. Parker standing there.

"Yes, Danny is in the crib you prepared for him. Thank you." Abigail tied the apron on at the back as she spoke.

"Well, you can thank my volunteers," he seemed to boast.

"Of course," Abigail nodded as she passed by the doctor to retrieve a cloth from the cupboard and cool water from the pail in the corner on the floor. She poured some of the water into a smaller bowl and took it to Danny's room. The doctor followed Abigail as she soaked the cloth in the water, then wiped the fevered child down with it.

"That will feel good to him," Dr. Parker watched her from the edge of the crib, "but we really need to get the fever down."

"Won't this help with that as well?" Abigail looked up at him, confused.

"The only thing that may take down the fever is lying him in cold water, possibly with ice."

"What?" Abigail gasped. "He will freeze."

"I know, but at this point, it may be our only option," he continued.

"What about Elizabeth?" Abigail pressed.

"Her, too," he glanced at the sick little girl. "We can do it at the same time. I will wait until morning and see if there is any change."

Abigail nodded. Fearing the worst, Abigail couldn't stop thinking of what could happen if his fever didn't break, although she didn't want to put poor Danny into a bath of water and ice. She could imagine the screaming he would do. It would break her heart, but on the other hand, they needed to get his fever down or it could be very serious. Dr. Parker had said a fever can cause a seizure. Abigail had heard what that was but never knew anyone who had a seizure. It terrified her to no end.

Even though her thoughts were here with Daniel, she wondered how little Josie was doing. But she had faith in her mama. She would take care of things, and also, no news is good news. No one had come to say otherwise. She had to quit thinking about what was happening at home and worry about the situation at hand. She had to stop worrying about Jacob. At one point it was almost driving her mad as she wondered if he was safe, dead or alive. She had to concentrate on her babies, keep the income coming in and the home fires burning.

The night was a restless one for both Danny and Abigail. He tossed and turned, fevered, with the rash worse than it was before. Abigail spent most of the night wiping him down, changing his clothes and trying to persuade him to drink more water.

Elizabeth's mama was in the same position. She didn't sleep well and Elizabeth's fever didn't seem to falter. Abigail knew what would be happening early next morning.

Abigail dozed off right before sunrise. In her sleepy state she vaguely heard Doc Johnson and Dr. Parker as they talked in the other room.

"I sent Mr. Soldier to fetch some ice from the ice house," said Dr. Parker.

"Good idea," Doc agreed.

In that moment, Abigail jumped from the scream that completely widened her eyes.

"Nooooo!" Cried out Mrs. Ford. "No, Elizabeth, stay with me..." Abigail jumped to her feet and spun around to find Mrs. Ford hovering over her daughter, holding her shoulders down as the little girl thrashed around in her bed. Her arms were twitching and her legs tossing about uncontrollably.

Dr. Parker and Doc ran into the room as fast as they could get there.

"Take Mrs. Ford!" Dr. Parker shouted at Abigail and he pushed passed the mother to move Elizabeth onto her side. Within seconds Abigail glanced at her own baby to make sure he was alright before darting away. She noticed he was sleeping soundly, with his red cheeks glowing in the pale light.

"Mrs. Ford," Abigail leaped as she reached out to her, grabbed both arms with her hands and pulled her away from Elizabeth's bedside. "Let the doctors help her."

"Buuuuut-" Mrs. Ford wailed. "I can't lose another child." She sobbed into Abigail's shoulder.

"It's in God's hands, now," Abigail soothed.

"I wish my husband was here." She continued to sob. Abigail tried to keep her eye on what the doctors were doing, and see if Elizabeth was still moving.

What was only minutes, felt like hours to Abigail, but Elizabeth stopped moving around. With a few twitches, she completely stopped as the doctors, one on either side of the bed, began to look into her eyes, check her pulse and listen to her heart.

Abigail noticed the look that Dr. Parker gave Doc as she quickly glanced back at Danny again. Feeling rather paranoid, she wanted to make sure he was alright.

"What's wrong?" Mrs. Ford shouted as she freed herself from Abigail's grasp and darted toward Dr. Parker. Lunging to the bed, she grabbed a hold of Elizabeth's hand and pulled it up to her chest. She leaned over her, placed her head on her daughter's chest and wept.

Doc looked over at a wide-eyed Abigail and shook his head slowly. Dr. Parker stepped back further to allow Mrs. Ford her time with Elizabeth.

Abigail gasped, as she covered her mouth whispering, "No." She then dashed over to Danny and scooped him up in her arms. He woke up crying, as he felt his mother's sudden tight hugging as she held him close to her chest. He wiggled to be released from her tight hold. He cried out. Abigail plopped down on the chair next to his crib and felt like the wind had been knocked out of her. She let him sit up on her lap and held him. Abigail couldn't lie to herself but she was grateful Danny was still alive and that it wasn't her child who had died. She felt terribly guilty that the thought even crossed her mind. She couldn't possibly imagine what Mrs. Ford was going through. She had never lost a child or even someone that close to her. The guilt of having Elizabeth stay with her and the twins this past year, knowing that her mama missed that precious time with her youngest daughter, made her feel sick.

Abigail burst into tears as she bowed her head and sobbed into little Danny's head of curly blonde hair, knowing at this moment that she couldn't even console Mrs. Ford because she didn't have the strength to stand up. Abigail truly felt at her most helpless moment. She told Mrs. Ford that it was in God's hands, and then God took her child away without warning. What kind of advice was that? What right did she have to say such a thing?

Abigail felt a warm hand on her shoulder. She looked up to see Dr. Parker looking down at her. His face was emotionless, but yet had a little softness to it. She noticed that Doc was standing behind Mrs. Ford, muttering consoling words to her.

"Are you alright?" Dr. Parker rubbed her shoulder slightly as he looked at her.

"No." Abigail said bluntly and tears streamed down both cheeks as she looked at him. She wanted to scream at him. Of course she wasn't alright. How did he think she would feel? Why would she feel alright when her friend lost her daughter and Abigail didn't know if Danny was going to get over the sickness, her husband was missing and her other child could possibly have the illness. Of course she wasn't alright!

"I think we better see if we can get his fever down." He spoke as if he hadn't even seen her face, heard her speak or even witnessed the death of her good friend.

"Already?" Abigail stared at him as her eyes narrowed and whispered. "But Mrs. Ford has just lost her daughter-"

"Yes, now." Dr. Parker cut her off firmly as Mr. Soldier came through the doorway with a block of ice over his shoulder.

"She is gone, yes, but Danny is still alive and we need to keep it that way." He pointed for Mr. Soldier to set the ice in the big pail that was beside Danny's crib.

Abigail gasped at his candour.

"Shhh." She glared at him. "Mrs. Ford is right over there."

"There isn't time for being nice, only time to get it done."

Dr. Parker directed Mr. Soldier to chip the ice with a hammer and ice pick and to put the chunks into an oval metal tub. Dr. Parker grabbed the pitcher of water and began adding water.

"Strip him down to his diaper." He ordered Abigail.

Abigail was so apprehensive, her emotions were swirling around in her head. She wanted desperately to help console Mrs. Ford, but Danny was her first priority. Listening to the low sobbing of Mrs. Ford, Abigail tried to ignore it and began taking Daniel's clothes off. Tears still welled up in her eyes and ran down her face. He didn't fight her undressing him. He was listless and sleepy. Danny was red from head to toe. The rash had completely covered his body.

"Alright, set him in the tub, and begin to pour water on his upper body where it doesn't reach," Dr. Parker instructed.

Abigail dreaded the thought of putting him in the tub of ice chilling water. Her heart pounded and she silently prayed for mercy as she set Danny's bottom in first. His body clenched as he tried to grab on to his mother's arms for safety. He began to cry hoarsely, as Abigail took a cloth and wiped his shoulders and back with the cold water. Her hands hurt in the water and she couldn't imagine what the little boy was feeling. Abigail also wiped his forehead and his head, praying it would release the heat in his body and cool his body temperature down.

The low moaning of Danny's cry kept Abigail from hearing Mrs. Ford. Abigail continued to hold him in the little tub and wipe him down. Mr. Ford burst through the doorway and he raced to Elizabeth's bedside. He grasped Mrs. Ford from behind as she was still laying on Elizabeth's chest. His arms reached to his daughter and, hugging both of them at the same time, he too began to sob into Mrs. Ford's back.

Abigail watched over her shoulder as the family cried together, and she wished she was anywhere but there at that moment. It was the hardest thing to watch, parents losing a child. She continued with Danny as Dr. Parker watched her.

"How much longer?" She looked up at him.

"A little while." He began to write on a piece of paper and put it in a clipboard above the crib.

Abigail took in a deep breath. Her arms were beginning to ache holding Danny in the same position, even though he didn't make much movement. Even with no strength to fight, he was heavy and slippery. *Heaven forbid the good doctor to help,* Abigail thought. *He can't even console a grieving mother,* she told herself.

She watched as Mr. and Mrs. Ford left the room, with arms wrapped around each other. Abigail's heart broke, especially with the fact that she couldn't go over and speak to them or hug them or do anything. She was helpless. "Oh, Jacob, where are you when I need you so desperately?" She whispered to herself.

Finally Dr. Parker let Abigail take Danny out of the cold water and lay him in his bed. She continued placing the cold cloth on his forehead and wiping him down under his arm pits and behind his knees to keep him cool.

The day went by as Abigail tried to give water to Danny, but he wasn't much interested. He cried in his sleep and moaned as she watched him from the chair. The rash was still there and Abigail didn't really think that the ice water had worked. Dr. Parker came to see him periodically, checked his heart, looked into his eyes and monitored the fever. He never said too much and then would leave.

Evening came with no change. Abigail worried all the more. She didn't know what to think, her prayers hadn't been answered. Danny seemed no better and she felt weak, helpless and more alone than ever.

"How are you doing, my dear?" A familiar voice sounded near her.

Abigail looked up and saw Mrs. Johnson holding a tray.

"I brought you something to eat and a cup of tea," she smiled sympathetically.

Abigail was relieved to see a friendly face. She couldn't remember the last time she ate, or even drank for that matter.

"Thank you, Mrs. Johnson." Abigail stood up to greet her guest as Doc's wife set the tray down on the table closest to Abigail. She handed her the cup of tea first which Abigail took from her with a half smile. Little hairs flew around Abigail's head from not brushing it, and the bun was half way down her head. Strands of hair tousled onto her forehead. She took a sip of the tea and took in a deep breath.

"That tastes good," Abigail looked at her friend as she held the cup with both hands.

"Here. You better eat while little Danny is still sleeping," she ordered.

"Thank you, but-" Abigail shook her head.

"No buts," Mrs. Johnson scolded. "You need your strength or you will be no good to this little guy." She walked over to the crib and looked down at Daniel sleeping.

"That's the problem," Abigail walked over beside her. "He hardly wakes up."

"Sleep is good, it helps the body heal," she comforted.

"I am so worried." Abigail began to cry and brought her hands to her face.

"There now," Mrs. Johnson rubbed her hand on Abigail's back. "It's in God's hands now."

"Don't you say that!" Abigail snapped, cried harder and remembered those were the exact words that Abigail had said to Mrs. Ford.

"I understand how you feel," she soothed.

"I am sorry, I didn't mean-"

"Don't you worry about it." Mrs. Johnson put her arm around Abigail and held her close. Abigail leaned to the side and put her head on Mrs. Johnson's shoulder and sobbed.

"A good cry always helps."

It was several minutes before Abigail stood up straight and wiped her tears with the hankie from her pocket. She sniffed, wiped her nose, walked over to the tray of food, picked up the plate and sat down. She took a bite of the chicken sandwich Mrs. Johnson had prepared for her.

Mrs. Johnson pulled a chair up beside her. Both sat in silence while Abigail finished eating.

"I checked in at The General Store," Mrs. Johnson began. "Everyone is doing well."

"Thank you." Abigail felt so grateful to know. "Josie?"

"Doesn't appear to have any signs of the illness," she grinned. "Your mama is managing well, and Mr. Soldier is a big help from what I can tell."

"I am so happy to hear this." Abigail was relieved for one thing but still panicked over another. "Thank you for checking for me."

"I knew how worried you would be."

Abigail nodded in agreement.

"I heard about Elizabeth," Mrs. Johnson put her head down. "I am so sorry, I know what she meant to you."

"I can't stop feeling guilty." Abigail shook her head.

"Guilty? What for?" She looked confused.

"Well, for many reasons," Abigail started, "one being that if she hadn't been with us, she may not have gotten sick."

"You can't know that," Mrs. Johnson frowned. "It could have been anyone."

"But Danny has it, too," she argued. "And besides, had she not been helping me all these months, Elizabeth wouldn't have missed all that time with her family."

"Stop that," Mrs. Johnson firmly said. "This isn't your fault."

"I can't help but think otherwise." Abigail looked at little Danny, still restlessly sleeping in the crib.

"Only God knows the reasons," Mrs. Johnson whispered, "and it's up to us to have faith in Him."

Another tear welled up in Abigail's eye and spilled down to the floor.

"I know it's so hard sometimes. You have been through so much since..." She cleared her throat, "since Jacob left."

"No more than anyone else in this village," Abigail shook her head.

Mrs. Johnson, grabbed her hand and looked into her eyes. "Yes, you have."

Abigail knew she was right, but she hadn't lost a child, and that had to be the worst thing that could ever happen.

"Hold on to your faith, keep believing God is in control and everything happens for a reason. Jacob is living proof of that."

"It's really hard to do that," Abigail admitted.

"I know, it's not easy. Continue praying and keep doing what you're doing."

Abigail's mind felt more at ease after Mrs. Johnson left. She prayed for Danny, the Ford family and her own family, especially Jacob.

Danny stirred, moved his head from side to side and cried. His eyes were still shut. His cheeks were redder than before. He burned with fever and still seemed so restless. Abigail sat him up, and coaxed him to drink some water. She wiped his head with a cold, wet cloth. Maybe another cold bath was in order.

This time she bathed him without the ice, hoping that would be of some help as well. She hadn't seen Dr. Parker for quite some time, so she took it upon herself to do it without his opinion. At this point, Danny didn't seem better. Abigail tried not to worry and have the faith she told herself she had, but it wasn't easy. She imagined herself in the shoes of Mrs. Ford. How would she feel if she woke up tomorrow morning and her child was dead? What would she do? Abigail didn't want to imagine and didn't want to think about it anymore.

The cold bath seemed to soothe Danny. Abigail had him back in the crib and she sat in the chair and leaned against the side rail. She began to sing him a lullaby.

> *Bye, oh baby bunting,*
> *Daddy's gone a hunting,*
> *To catch a little rabbit skin,*
> *To wrap my baby, Danny, in.*

Abigail sang it over and over. The same song her mama had sung to her, and her grandma sang to her mama. Danny dozed off again. Abigail watched him and continued to hum the song until she, too, fell asleep.

chapter twenty-three

Abigail awoke and reached for her neck as she felt the pain radiate down her shoulder from having her head turned to the side too long. She felt as though someone was watching her. She looked up as she rubbed the back of her neck with her hand and saw Dr. Parker standing on the other side of the crib, watching her with a smile on his face.

What could he possibly be happy about? He never ceased to amaze her with his arrogance and unmannered, candour disposition.

"Glad you're awake," Dr. Parker smiled wider at her. "I think you will be happy to see your lad this morning." He nodded toward Danny lying in his crib.

Abigail stood up as she looked at Danny, who was awake and sat and looked up at her. The first thing she noticed was that his cheeks were almost back to their normal colour.

"My Danny!" Abigail reached down and scooped him up in her arms and hugged him closely to her. "Praise Jesus!"

"His fever has broken and it appears that he is on the road to recovery," the doctor informed her.

Abigail smiled widely as she held her son. Moving from side to side, she was so grateful.

"When will we be able to go home?" She asked.

"A few more days to make sure." He seemed pleased with himself, for at least an unselfish reason this time. "I stopped by to check on Josie, and it appears that she is fine."

"Thank God!" was all Abigail could say.

Danny got better each day. Abigail noticed a change in him almost every hour. He began to eat, drink more and started chattering away the way he used to.

The funeral for Elizabeth was on the afternoon that Abigail and Danny were able to go home. Mama and Josie were very happy to see both of them. Even Mr. Soldier was pleased and wanted to do everything he could to make it easier for Abigail. Josie and Danny were inseparable once they were together. Abigail attended the funeral while her mama looked after the children. It was a sad funeral. Most of the village filled the churchyard for a graveside funeral. Abigail was able to speak with Mrs. Ford and to say she was sorry. She knew it wasn't going to do her any good, but she wanted to tell Mrs. Ford all the same. She saw other women who had lost their children and husbands in the war. She knew it was tough on everyone, not only her. It was a struggle which the whole community bore together but were there for one another as well. Abigail was grateful that Danny was well again and that her children are both home, safe and sound.

Abigail returned to The General Store to find Mr. Soldier unloading the delivery that had arrived from Regina. Abigail felt dread while she watched him, thinking about the bills she had to pay and the items she needed to order for which she didn't have the money. Everyone was in the same boat. Folks could not afford to buy extra things that they needed, and some did without even the bare necessities because they couldn't afford them. Some families traded her milk, cream and eggs for the items they desperately needed. It didn't pay the bills for Abigail but it did help feed them, which was good.

"Thank you, Mr. Soldier," Abigail smiled as she walked by him. "For all you do," she added.

"It is I who should be thanking you." Mr. Soldier stopped while holding a wooden crate, smiled at Abigail and nodded.

"I don't know about that," she added as she walked through the store doorway.

At least she had free help in exchange for his lodging and food. Lord only knows how she would be able to do everything without him, and she no longer had Elizabeth. She was ashamed that the very thought crossed her mind, but it was the truth. She couldn't have helped at the hospital if it hadn't been for Elizabeth. She wouldn't have gotten to know Mr. Soldier and he wouldn't be helping her right now. A lot of things wouldn't be possible if it hadn't been for Elizabeth. Abigail would never forget that, and would always hold her memory and her family in high regard.

"I am back, mama," Abigail hollered as she walked through the store toward the kitchen.

The twins were sitting at the table with cookies in front of them.

"Hello, dear," her mama greeted her. "You're just in time. We are having tea and cookies. The children helped me bake them this afternoon."

"Aw yummy." Abigail kissed each of the twins on top of her heads as she walked past, pulled out the chair and sat down. Mama poured her a cup of tea and handed her the plate of cookies.

"Thank you, very much." She grabbed a cookie and took a bite. "Mmmm. These are good." They dipped the cookies into their tea while Danny and Josie chatted to one another.

"I better ask Mr. Soldier in for these wonderful cookies." Abigail began to stand up.

"Oh, I already asked and he declined." Her mama took a sip of her tea.

"Oh, that's odd." Abigail knew Mr. Soldier always stopped for tea time. "Well, he is only unloading the freight. He could take time for tea." Abigail insisted. "I will go ask him again."

Abigail headed back out the store doorway, but Mr. Soldier was gone. She looked around and then back inside the store. The freight was inside but he wasn't there.

Abigail went back into the kitchen.

"I guess he had other things to do." Abigail sat back down and took a sip of her tea.

"I have some book work to do today, mama," Abigail added. "Can you take care of these little ones?"

"Of course," Mama smiled. "We can make supper, can't we?" She spoke to the twins as they banged on the table.

"Gamma, gamma, gamma!" they chanted happily.

"Thank you, mama." Abigail smiled at her mama.

After the tea Abigail sat down at the desk in the office. She set out all the bills to be paid, the received on accounts, and accounts payable. After adding up each one, it was a fact that Abigail didn't have enough money to pay all the bills. She added it up again to make sure she was correct the first time. She took in a deep breath and let it out slowly. What was she going to do? How could she make extra money?

A couple of hours had gone by but Abigail hadn't come up with any ideas. There wasn't anything she could sell because people weren't in the market to buy anything. She couldn't do anything for anyone because she barely had the time do what she needed here. Her head began to ache as she added up more numbers and tried to decide what to do.

"Excuse, Mrs. Abigail." Mr. Soldier stood in the doorway of the office.

"Yes?" Abigail looked up from her papers.

"Is there anything you need done before supper?" He held his hat in his hand and waited for her reply.

"Uh," she couldn't concentrate on what he was asking, all she could think about was that she didn't have the money she needed at this moment. "I can't think of anything." She hesitated as she ran her hands over her head.

"Well, see you at supper then," he nodded, putting his hat back on. "I have to fetch some water for the hospital."

"Alright, see you then." Abigail looked down at the stack of papers barely remembering that he was chatting with her, but once he left she thought she could smell something in the air. *Hmm,* she thought to herself, *I think it smelled like alcohol.* She shook her head and went back to her paper work.

Abigail decided that since she couldn't pay all the bills in full she would divide what she had and pay a little of each. She thought it was better than not paying one at all and then paying full on the others. She wrote letters of apologies to each one. She wrote the cheques, stuffed the envelopes, licked the flaps and stacked them on top of one another. She looked at the time and hoped to get to the post office before it closed.

She grabbed her shawl off the hook by the door, along with her hat, and pinned it in place.

"I will be right back!" she hollered to her mother.

"Alright, dear." Her mama poked her head out of the doorway of the kitchen.

Abigail walked and clutched the letters in her hand. She was on a mission. She felt sick about the whole situation but this was the only solution. She prayed that the companies would continue to sell to her despite the incomplete payment.

"Well, fancy meeting you here."

Abigail reached for the door that was already opened by Dr. Parker.

"Yes, I guess it is." She tried to brush past him but he stood in her way. "I am in a hurry. Excuse me please," she frowned at him.

"Of course." He lifted his arm above her head and continued to hold the door for her. Abigail ducked a little and stepped over the threshold.

She walked straight up to the counter and laid the envelopes down in front of the postmaster.

"I would like to mail these, please." Abigail smiled.

"Certainly." The postmaster took the envelopes and stamped each one. "That will be ten cents please," she said.

Abigail reached in her little hand bag that hung from her wrist, then pulled out a dime and handed it to her.

"Thank you." The postmaster took the dime and placed it in her cash register.

"By the way," the middle aged lady smiled oddly at her, "you have a letter." She turned around, grabbed the envelope and passed it to Abigail.

"Really? I am not expecting anything-" Before Abigail finished her sentence, it was in her hand.

She looked at the return address, then her name typed on the envelope.

'Mrs. Jacob Hudson. Abbington Pickets, Saskatchewan.'

She began to turn around and slowly walk toward the door. Her heart leapt, then began to race rapidly in her chest.

"Have a nice day." The postmaster called out after her.

Abigail turned her head back toward her but only a mumble came out of her mouth.

"Thanks," she replied with as much effort as she could.

In a daze she opened the door, stood on the step, stared at the envelope and gripped it with both hands.

"You look like you have seen a ghost." Dr. Parker was waiting for her outside. "Can I give you a ride to the store?"

"No...thanks." She barely looked up to see him stare at her with a raised eyebrow.

"Did you reconsider my offer, then?" he pressed, uninterested in the fact that she looked like she could faint right there and then.

"Excuse me?" She didn't look up at him as she slowly walked past him.

"To marry me," he smirked. "You know he is not coming back."

Abigail snapped back to reality. She turned around and glared at the doctor who was smiling at her angry face.

"How dare you!" she pointed her finger at him and lunged toward him. "You have no tact whatsoever. All you think about is yourself!"

"You're so beautiful when you are mad like that." He began to laugh at her. "I am thinking of you."

"Really? How so?" She looked up at him, only inches from his face as he looked down at her.

"You are going to need a man sooner or later. How about sooner? You know as well as I do, that Jacob is dead and not coming home to you and your children."

"My business is none of yours!" she retorted, then spun around on her heal, still clutching the letter, almost crushing it.

"You need someone to take care of you." He raised his voice as she walked away from him. "When you change your mind, I will be waiting." His voice got louder the further away she got.

Abigail's ears were burning, her cheeks were flushed and her head was beginning to ache. What an impertinent man! Why couldn't he leave her alone! She stomped quickly back to The General Store. Anger took over her whole body. She didn't even hear the doctor start his noisy car and drive past her honking his horn. She fumed as she swung the door open, ran into her bedroom and slammed the door behind her.

Moments later, she heard a knock at the door.

"Is everything alright, dear?" her mama asked softly.

"Yes, mama," Abigail wiped her face with her hands. "I just need a moment."

"Are you sure?" she persisted on the other side.

"Yes, I am sure." She cleared her throat. "I will be out in a few minutes." She leaned against the door and pressed the letter to her chest.

"Well, I am here if you need me." Her mama's voice was kind and gentle but worried.

"Thank you, mama." Abigail closed her eyes, and then looked back down at the words on the envelope. The return address was the War Office.

She took a deep breath as she tore open the envelope. As she unfolded the letter, another paper fell from within it. Abigail bent over to scoop it up as it hit the floor. Tears welled in her eyes as she straightened up and read the words. Her heart sank as she skipped the formalities and her eyes followed the sentences...

...With a heavy heart I regret to inform you
that *Lt. Jacob Hudson, who has been assumed*

missing in action, has now been declared deceased.
Please accept our deepest condolences.

He was an honourable officer and leader who
was well trusted and respected by his superiors
and his men. He was a courageous Officer and
will be missed by those under his command
who were close to him.

You will also find the enclosed...

Abigail's vision began to blur and she couldn't see the words anymore. She backed up against the door, and slowly slid down until she reached the floor. Still holding the letter tightly to her chest, she sobbed uncontrollably. She gulped hard with every breath, crying harder each moment. It was as if she had no control over her emotions; the flood gate had opened with no mercy or regret. Jacob's face flashed before her eyes as she tightly closed them with tears seeping through the corners. Abigail's sobs became loud bellows from deep inside her heart.

"God, no!" Abigail threw her head back and yelled. "Please don't take my Jacob away from me!" She could barely catch a breath when her throat let out another cry. She gulped more air as if she had been swept under water in a rapid current in the ocean. It was several minutes before Abigail got control of herself. She had never felt so hysterical and out of control as she did at that moment.

The sobbing slowed down to a double breath, her nose ran, and tears still fell. All Abigail could think about was life without Jacob. She really never considered it before. She knew deep down in her heart that he would walk through that doorway and they would pick up where they left off. Receiving the letter from Jacob's Commander was like a final say, that his life was over and to move on.

Perhaps Dr. Parker was right, maybe Jacob wasn't coming home, and she would need a husband, a father for her children. What would Jacob want her to do? She would like to say he would tell her to run as far as she could and never look back. But Abigail knew Jacob. Jacob the selfless, hard-working, thinking about everyone else first, kind of man. If he were really dead and could tell Abigail to do anything in the world, he would say, "let him look after you, deep down he's a great person. You will never need to worry about working or money again."

Would Jacob really tell her that? Would he say marry Dr. Parker as he wished? Abigail's head began to ache and her face was hot and red with wet tears staining her cheeks. Her lips felt swollen and her eyes were gritty as if she had rubbed sand into them. Taking her hankie out of her pocket she blew her nose and wiped her face dry.

Still grasping the letter, she looked at the extra paper that came with it. It was a cheque for Jacob's remaining pay that he hadn't sent home to her. The devastation she felt was too deep for her to feel the slightest bit happy that her debts could be paid with that money. There would even be some left over to make her next order. Abigail had to admit God did work in mysterious ways but her heart was too heavy to rejoice just yet.

Abigail wanted to get herself together before talking with her mama and she didn't want to be a mess in front of the children. She sat there for quite a few minutes while she prayed quietly. She asked God for forgiveness for her doubting Him. She asked God to provide for their every need, and for comfort and peace of mind.

Abigail placed her hand on the floor and pushed herself up. She stood up, fluffed her dress and then smoothed it down with her hands. She felt her hair, realized it was a bit of a mess, walked over to the mirror, brushed her hair and then re-pinned it into place. She took one more look at herself, picked up the letter, opened the door and headed to the kitchen.

"Are you alright, my dear?" Mama asked with concern.

"Yes, I am fine." Abigail tried to put on the biggest smile she could muster. She didn't want her mama more worried about her than she already was.

"I received this in the mail today." Abigail set down the letter on the table.

"Who's it from?" Mama's eyes narrowed as she looked at the table, then at Abigail.

"You can read it," Abigail encouraged. She walked over to where Danny and Josie played on the floor with the wooden blocks that Mr. Edwards had brought them.

"What are you two doing?" she asked the twins. They each held up a block to show her and in their secret language gibbered something to the other. Abigail didn't want to watch her mama read the letter. She didn't want to get upset again.

Her mama walked over to her and put her arm around her.

"I am so sorry, Abigail," she whispered. "I honestly don't know what else to say." She didn't need to tell Abigail how wonderful Jacob was, and that he was an honourable man serving their country. It didn't need to be discussed. All Abigail needed right now was her comfort and her support.

Abigail tried not to cry as she put her head on her mama's shoulder, but a single tear still fell to the floor. Abigail didn't want to speak. She knew if she did, she would burst into tears.

"I will stay with you as long as you need me," Mrs. Rodgers said as she rubbed her back with her hand. "Your pa can handle things without me, especially with his new field hand. He's pretty handy in the kitchen, too." She gave a half smile.

"It's alright, mama." Abigail said softly, "I am alright, we are alright. When Ernest comes back for the winter, things will be better."

"Well, without Eliza-" mama stopped herself. She knew how hard that was for Abigail, how much she meant to her and not only just for looking after the twins.

"I know, mama," Abigail lifted her head. "We truly miss Elizabeth, and it will be hard to get used to being without her."

"I didn't mean to bring it up."

"She was gone most of the summer and we did quite well," Abigail added. "I feel so terrible for her mama right now and all she missed with her while she was here."

"Don't be feeling guilty about that," her mama scowled. "It's no one's fault."

Abigail slowly nodded. She knew her ma was right but she still had that gut-wrenching feeling. Now another sick feeling came on top, with the news of Jacob. Will she ever know peace and happiness again? Will Jacob ever come home or is Dr. Parker right? What if the twins took ill again? Would she be able to handle that all over again? Would she be able to keep up with the incoming bills? What was she going to do next?

chapter twenty-four

Winter came quickly that year. By the middle of November there was plenty of snow. Ernest returned to Abbington Pickets at the end of October. Between his brother-in-law Bert and his neighbours, the Hills, his cattle were looked after until spring calving.

Abigail's mama went home when Ernest came back, despite the fact that she said she wanted to stay and help more. Abigail knew her mama missed her pa. Abigail insisted that she go and make sure her pa was being fed properly and that she and the twins would be alright now that Ernest was here.

Abigail could tell that Ernest was keeping his distance from Mr. Soldier. Every day, Mr. Soldier politely talked to Ernest, but he didn't respond very much; only a yes or a no, hello or goodbye was all he managed. Abigail had faith that sooner or later he would come around.

It was good to have both men around The General Store. There was a huge amount of snow to be shovelled every day for the incoming freight and customers. The horses were eating more hay, hence more needed to be brought in. The wood needed to be chopped more frequently and hauled into the store. There was always something that needed done more often than not.

Abigail didn't spend nearly as much time at the hospital as she used to. She continued to be helpful by making the bandages at home, and she also did the laundry and sent it to and from the hospital with Mr. Soldier. She began to make meals for the hospital as well and send them there as much as she could. Abigail wanted to do as much for the hospital as she was able since she couldn't actually be there. She did miss the patients she met but her children came first. With Daniel's scare and the death of Elizabeth, Abigail knew what was important. She had an obligation to them even though she felt she also had an obligation to the soldiers because of Jacob.

The A.P.L.G. continued to take place every Tuesday afternoon at The General Store. Wooden crates of more crocheted sweaters, knitted socks, shirts and blankets were constantly sent overseas. Even encouraging letters from the ladies were packed in those crates, hoping to keep up the soldiers' spirits. It brought bittersweet joy to Abigail, knowing on one hand she was helping Jacob in some way but it pained her to know why this needed to be done. This war should be over and the soldiers should be coming back home to their families.

Christmas had come and gone and the rest of the winter dragged on as it seemed to snow every day and never let up. Some days it was only a little, but other days huge flakes fell from the sky. Abigail was used to taking the twins on the sleigh that she and Jacob used to use. She used it to go to the hospital or to get the mail. The children loved the rides and thought they were fun. Abigail was grateful to have it but it wasn't always easy trudging through the snow, pulling it behind her.

The Leader's headline 'PRIME MINISTER BORDEN VISITS THE FRONT' made Abigail wonder where Jacob was and if the Prime Minister really cared who was in this awful war. According to the article, he was pictured inspecting a Canadian Battalion of which his cousin was the commanding officer. *He must care somewhat,* Abigail told herself, *or he wouldn't be there looking things over.* Abigail dreaded the newspaper when it came in as it was always headlined with terrible war news.

When spring came, Ernest left because calving season had begun. He and Mr. Soldier had come to a better understanding. Abigail witnessed a true miracle of forgiveness while watching them over the winter. The two of them even enjoyed playing crib before winter's end. Abigail never thought she would see that day but she did know Ernest had a great heart and that he would eventually come around. After all, he only was trying to protect Abigail and the twins, and she appreciated his cautiousness.

Today was a sunny day and a nice breeze blew. It was near the end of June. Today was a special day, especially for Abigail. Today, on the twenty-sixth of June, she and every other woman in Saskatchewan were able to vote in the provincial election being held this year. Abigail wasn't going to miss that for the world! The polls were set up in certain districts in every rural municipality. Abbington Pickets had a poll set up at the Town Hall.

"I am going to be one of the first people there," Abigail said loudly, as she looked in the mirror above the washstand and pinned the flowered hat on top of her head.

"I am sure there will be other early birds," laughed Mr. Soldier.

"Well, then, I will be the first woman to vote, possibly," she smiled as she took the twins by the hand. Mr. Soldier shook his head at her eagerness.

"Shall we go?" Abigail looked at Mr. Soldier as he put the sign on the outside of the door that read 'Closed momentarily, gone to vote.'

Abigail walked the twins to the wooden wagon which sat outside on the wooden sidewalk. She picked up the children and set them in the wagon.

"I will pull them." Mr. Soldier picked up the wagon handle and began to pull them along as they walked. The Town Hall wasn't too far away, just on the east side of the church. A nice walk, but the children would have tired before getting there and Abigail and Mr. Soldier would end up carrying them anyway.

The grass was a rich green from all the moisture. The lilac trees were almost done blooming and the flowerbeds had started to get a little colour in them.

"Good morning."

"Good morning," Abigail nodded, and Mr. Soldier lifted his hat to Reverend Young and his wife. They were standing in the church yard, probably headed to do the same thing.

"Well, look who it is." Abigail beamed at the sight of her friend in front of the Town Hall while her husband helped her down off the wagon.

"Abigail," Alice called out.

"Alice, Bert." Abigail's stride quickened to reach her friend. "So good to see you two." She held out her hands to hug Alice as she walked closer to her.

Abigail stood back and look at Alice. She had felt a little bump in the front of her when they hugged. She tilted her head and raised an eyebrow with a half grin. Alice knew what she was suggesting and touched her stomach with a bigger smile than before.

"When?" Abigail asked.

"Sometime around December." Alice looked at Bert as she spoke. He was beaming as much as she was.

"Congratulations!" She took both Bert's and Alice's hands in hers and looked at one, then the other.

"Well, this is a happy day." Abigail turned around to Mr. Soldier. "Alice is having a baby."

"Congratulations." He looked at both Alice and Bert shyly.

"Where are the children? And Ernest?" Abigail looked around and noticed the other wagons sat empty, and more pulled up.

"We left them with the Rileys," Alice smiled. "It's such a long trip."

"I understand, but Ernest?" She repeated, always happy to see his smiling face.

"He's already inside, voting," Bert piped up. "I am quite sure there's only so much room in that little building."

"You're quite right," Abigail grinned.

"You go in first, Mrs. Abigail." Mr. Soldier offered. "I will stay here with the twins."

"Are you sure? Because you can go first," Mr. Soldier shook his head, "ladies first."

"You are a dear," Abigail smiled at him. "Now, you children be good." She touched the tops of their heads.

Abigail reached the door just as Ernest was coming out.

"Ernest!" Abigail hugged him quickly. "Good to see you."

"You, as well," Ernest smiled back.

"You're coming for dinner, right?" Abigail gave him a look that he couldn't refuse.

"Well, uh-" he looked at Bert and Alice behind Abigail, both of them smiling. "I guess we are."

"Of course we are," Alice added. "We can't come to Abbington Pickets without a visit."

"Well, I will meet you at The General Store," Abigail nodded as she went inside.

Folks did not talk much about for whom they were going to vote. Most were respectful of others not asking. They went inside, did their duty and carried on. However, all knew for which party their friends were voting by the way they spoke.

Abigail proudly checked off her ballot and handed it to the man across the table. He placed it in the ballot box. She smiled and left. Mr. Soldier went in to vote as well and it wasn't long before they were on their way back to the store.

Abigail and Mr. Soldier walked in silence as they hurried to meet their company. Abigail thought about Jacob. He would be here to vote with her had he not been at war. For whom would he have wanted her to vote for? Did she vote for the right person? There were so many questions going through her mind. The longing to want to discuss it with Jacob tore at her heart. Every important decision she had to make she yearned to hear what he had to say about it. They talked about everything, big or small. She would do anything for a letter from Jacob right now. One that said he was alright, that he was coming home soon, that she did the right thing and that everything was going to be wonderful again.

Bert, Alice and Ernest were waiting for Abigail, Mr. Soldier and the twins when they walked up the sidewalk.

"Come on in," Abigail greeted her guests. She knew they would also be shopping for goods before they left for home.

Mr. Soldier took the sign off the door and held the door open for everyone to walk through.

"You men visit and watch the twins," Abigail looked at them as if she were their mother. "We will get the dinner on the table." Alice followed her into the kitchen and the men watched them leave. Ernest took Danny by the hand and Mr. Soldier took Josie.

"I will put the kettle on." Abigail had the water pitcher already in her hand and poured water into the kettle.

"What would you like me to do?" Alice stood at the table.

"If you like, you could set the table," Abigail pointed toward the dishes in the cupboard. Alice began to count the plates and bowls.

"I made soup this morning," Abigail talked as she put the pot on the stove to heat it up. She also cut some slices of bread and made chicken sandwiches to go with the meal.

The twins were seated in their highchairs. Bert and Alice sat on one side of the table, Mr. Soldier on the opposite side, and Ernest and Abigail at each end.

"Do you think Prime Minister Borden will make conscription law?" Ernest asked Bert as he passed the plate of sandwiches.

"Where'd you hear that?" Abigail piped up before Bert could answer.

"It's been in the papers all spring," Ernest turned to Abigail.

Abigail cleared her throat, "I try to avoid reading the paper."

"Well, I don't know," Bert intercepted, "he seems pretty insistent, but the French are pretty upset."

"Well, I am with the French," Abigail stated gruffly. "What's the sense sending men off to war if they don't want to go?"

"It's honouring our country, Abigail," Ernest said flatly. "And the French aren't being very honourable by refusing," he added.

"Let's not forget," Bert spoke up, "Jacob joined to honour ours and his country. For that he is a true hero - to me, anyway."

"Maybe we should talk about something else," Alice smiled as she noticed the anger on Abigail's face and the sadness in her eyes.

"Right, love," Bert agreed. "I need to pick up a few things from The General Store from the fine lady who owns it." He looked over at Abigail. She couldn't help but laugh a little at his silly humour.

"I can help you, sir." She pretended to be formal as well.

Mr. Soldier helped Bert find what he needed as Abigail and Alice did the dishes and put away the dinner. Mr. Soldier then went outside to do his deliveries and finish the chores.

Abigail stood outside and waved to Bert, Alice and Ernest as they rode away heading east. It was so good to see them. She wished they lived closer.

On August twenty-eighth, conscription became law. Quebec was unhappy about it and many riots broke out in Montreal the day the bill was passed. Abigail understood their feelings but there was no honour to Canada, it appeared. French-Canadians didn't feel they had any obligation to Britain or France. Abigail only wanted this war to be over and felt for the mothers of the ones being forced to go. Her children weren't that old, but she sure knew how she would feel if they were pulled from her grasp and forced to do something she didn't want them to do. Knowing Jacob's personality, and being his children, she knew it would be their honour to serve this country.

Mr. Soldier brought in the freight from the wagon outside, wheeled the heavy crates with the wooden framed wheeler, and piled them up behind the counter to be unpacked. The ones that needed to be delivered or picked up, he left close to the back door. It was now early December and the snow outside was blowing against the building. Lastly, he carried in the bundle of The Leader newspapers and set them on the counter.

Abigail snipped the string that held them together, picked up the first copy and read the headline. 'HALIFAX EXPLOSION - 2000 DEAD!' She quickly skimmed the article in disbelief.

"Did you see this?" she held the paper up as she looked at Mr. Soldier. He set down the crow bar he was using to open the crates, walked over to her and looked at the paper as she held it.

"Wow, that's terrible." Mr. Soldier shook his head. "I wonder what happened?"

"Well, it said that the SS Imo collided with the SS Mont-Blanc, causing an explosion." Abigail pointed out. "It also caused damage to the harbour at Dartmouth." She continued to read, "and the explosion caused huge waves that even wiped out a community."

"Well, there is something to be said about living on the prairies." Mr. Soldier took off his hat and wiped his brow with the back of his hand. "It may be hot in the summer and cold in the winter, but no water is going to drown us."

"Well, that is true," Abigail shook her head in disbelief. *Wasn't the war enough to kill people, that there had to be carelessness like this to ruin people's lives? How terrible the whole situation was.*

Abigail looked below the Halifax Explosion article and saw the title: 'GENERAL ELECTION ON DECEMBER 17.' It was the upcoming federal election to determine the next Prime Minister. Would Sir Robert Borden continue or would Wilfred Laurier win again? Borden was all in favour of conscription and was why many of eastern Canada wanted Laurier to be Prime Minister. It was a concern that divided Canada - the English Canadians and the French Canadians.

"Don't forget, we have to vote next week," Abigail reminded Mr. Soldier as he continued to put away the freight that had come in.

"You bet," he looked up at Abigail. "Wouldn't miss it."

"Me, either." Abigail smiled as she placed the coffee on the shelf.

chapter twenty-five

It was almost Christmas day. Abigail was hosting it this year with the help of Ernest and Mr. Soldier. She hadn't made a meal for this many people since Jacob had left. It was a little tricky baking and cooking to replicate the usual Christmas dinner. Now, during the war with the rationing of sugar, flour and such, folks needed to get creative with their recipes. At least now it wasn't as hard as it was at the beginning.

Thankfully, Christmas cake and pudding didn't take a lot of flour. Abigail improvised eggs by using baking powder. Alice had sent potatoes and carrots from her garden. Raisins weren't too hard to come by and spices were already in the cupboard. Abigail had made both Christmas cake and pudding early so it could season. She then kept it in the ice house until Christmas day.

"Good morning, Abigail." Abigail looked up from the counter to see Doc Johnson walk through the doorway. The wind gusted as he closed the door behind him.

"Good to see you, Doc," Abigail smiled as she put the wooden box of customer accounts back on the shelf behind her. "Come on in out of that nasty weather."

Doc took off his hat and pounded his feet to the floor to get rid of the sticky snow. Flakes of snow fell from his shoulders as he moved. Abigail walked closer to him.

"Where are the twins?" He looked around as he spoke.

"Taking their well overdue nap," Abigail smiled.

"Ah, I see. It sure is toasty in here compared to out there," Doc observed.

"Well, thanks to these great men around here," Abigail boasted and pointed to the stack of wood in the woodbox.

"Yes, they are good to have around," Doc laughed.

Abigail nodded.

"By the way, where are they?" Doc wondered.

"Ernest is over helping Mr. Edwards with something and Mr. Soldier is out doing deliveries."

"Oh, good. That will keep them out of trouble."

Abigail grinned. *It's nice sometimes to not to have to think about this terrible war and have a little fun,* Abigail thought.

"How is Mrs. Johnson?"

"She is good," he smiled. "You got the tea on?"

"Of course! Where are my manners?" Abigail put her hand on her forehead. "Please come to the kitchen. I think I even have a mud cookie or two."

Doc smiled as he followed Abigail to the kitchen table, pulled out the chair and sat down. She took out two tea cups and set them on the table. Taking the kettle off the stove, she poured the boiling water in the tea pot and added the tea leaves. She set it in the middle of the table as she pulled out the tin of cookies and placed a few on a small plate, which she placed in front of Doc. Abigail sat down across from Doc sensing this was more than a social visit.

"I wanted to ask you a favour, Abigail." Doc took a cookie and had a bite.

"Of course." Her eyes narrowed as she poured the tea into his tea cup. "Anything you need."

"Well, you may not say that once I ask," he chuckled.

"Oh?" She lifted her eyebrow.

"The wife and I are going to be away for Christmas."

"How nice!" Abigail grinned at the doctor. "Where are you going?"

"We are going to see her sister." Doc took a sip of his tea. "We haven't seen her in a very long time, you see, and I thought it would be a nice little reunion for them."

"Aw, that will be nice." Abigail sipped her tea. "How long are you gone for?"

"If all goes well, a couple of weeks." He finished the last of the cookie he had in his hand.

"What is your favour, then?" Abigail was curious about what this had to do with her.

"Well, the past couple of years we have had Dr. Parker over for Christmas dinner," he looked away from Abigail as he spoke, not really wanting to see her facial expression. "Well, I heard you were hosting Christmas this year..."

"Yes, I am." Abigail knew where this conversation was headed.

"Well, no one should ever have to spend Christmas alone," he continued.

"Of course, I will invite him." Abigail wasn't about to let Doc down and she sure didn't want him to think she was that terrible a person. She could put aside her differences for one day of the year. She would do anything for Doc and Mrs. Johnson. She was more mature than that.

"Well, I know you have some issues with him," Doc stated.

"Oh, you're right about that," Abigail gave him a slight grin. "I think it's more the fact that we don't see eye to eye," Abigail graciously laughed, but she meant it. Dr. Parker liked her. She just didn't care too much for him and any of his ideas or attitudes.

"Well, that is good of you, my dear." Doc smiled happily as if she had given him a hundred dollars.

"It will be good. Mr. Edwards is coming along with Reverend Young and his wife, mama and papa and, if the weather permits, Peter, Missy and their family and Alice and Bert."

"Isn't Alice due to have a baby soon?" Doc perked up.

"Yes. The end of the month or beginning of January." Abigail agreed. "Maybe it will be a Christmas baby."

"Well, let's hope not between their place and here."

"I am sure Alice knows what she's doing," Abigail smiled. "After all, this is her third child."

"One can't predict anything with childbirth," Doc said seriously. "I am glad Dr. Parker will be here for that day."

"I am sure that if Alice feels she shouldn't come, then they wouldn't," Abigail said matter-of-factly.

"I hope you're right." Doc finished the last of his tea and set the cup down. "Well, I better go." He slid the chair back and stood up. "We have to get going if we are going to get there before Christmas," he grinned.

"It was nice of you to stop by. Say hello to Mrs. Johnson for me," Abigail smiled. "I hope you have a wonderful Christmas."

Doc headed toward The General Store door.

"Thank you, I am sure we will." He put on his coat and hat.

"I will send the invitation to Dr. Parker." Abigail knew that would set the Doc's mind at ease.

"Thank you, Abigail." He grabbed the door latch and pulled it open. A gust of wind brought in the snow again. Then the door banged shut and he was gone.

Abigail didn't look forward to asking Dr. Parker to Christmas dinner, as she didn't really want to see him. It wasn't very polite to send a note or send Mr. Soldier for that matter. Maybe by chance he will be stopping in really soon.

No sooner did Abigail think it, when another big gust of wind burst through the doorway and in walked Dr. Parker, dressed in his citified long black wool coat with fur collar and black gloves.

"Good day, beautiful." Dr. Parker's smile and twinkle in his eye irritated Abigail to no end. He took off his gloves and hat, and not bothering to worry about how much snow was on his boots, he proceeded to walk into the store.

Abigail pretended she didn't hear the remark.

"Hello, Dr. Parker. What can I do for you?" She asked in her business-like manner as she walked behind the counter to feel more comfortable by having something between them.

He smiled and leaned his elbow against the counter top as he swooned in close to Abigail's face.

"Oh, the usual." He put his hand into his breast pocket and pulled out his list. It was always in the same handwriting, on the same paper with the same fountain pen and mostly the same stuff. He held the list out but more closely to him than her.

Abigail reluctantly reached out for it. When she had a hold of the paper and was ready to draw back, he grabbed her hand and held it firmly.

"You have such soft hands." He smiled at her face then looked down at her fingers that he held in his big hands. Hers looked so small compared to his. She pulled back with a start and almost ripped the paper.

"Would you mind!" Abigail scowled at him.

"I am sorry if I offended you," he continued to grin at her. "I find you so very attractive," he cooed. "I can't help but want to touch you."

"Excuse me?" Abigail glared at him. "I find that very inappropriate. I am a married woman." She took the list and began looking for the items that were written down.

"You know as well as I do, your husband is gone," he said as he walked over to the potbelly stove and held his hands only inches away to warm them. "And never coming back."

Ignoring his comment once again, Abigail continued to pick out the items on his list. She was certain she had everything he wanted and that it wouldn't take her long. Then she realized that before she could let him leave, she had to ask him to come for Christmas. She dreaded the thought, knowing he would get the wrong impression.

Several minutes went by as Dr. Parker walked about the store with his hands behind his back, as though he were a teacher, pacing the school room floor around his pupils.

"There you are, Dr. Parker." Abigail set a full paper bag down on the counter she stood behind, hoping he wouldn't charge it to his account and that he would actually pay with money.

"How much do I owe you?" He reached into his other breast pocket and pulled out his money clip.

"Five dollars and seventy-five cents," she stated quickly.

"You know," he paused, "if you marry me," counting his money as he spoke, digging into the pocket of his trousers for three quarters, "you wouldn't have to worry about money again."

"What makes you-" Abigail stopped, "I am doing fine. WE are doing just fine." She looked away from him as she took the money and put it into the cash register.

"We both know the truth to that." His eyebrow lifted slightly as he began to put on his gloves, then his hat and picked up the bag.

Abigail had to bite her tongue. Not only did she want to tell him what she thought of him, but she sure didn't want to invite him for Christmas dinner. She didn't want to spend another moment with that man.

"Thank you, Mrs. Hudson." Dr. Parker nodded as he headed toward the door.

Remembering her promise to Doc, she knew she had to ask him now, but her words just wouldn't come out of her mouth. *Come on, say it,* she told herself.

Dr. Parker reached for the door latch. Abigail watched as she followed toward the entry way.

"You're welcome to spend Christmas dinner with us," she blurted out all at once, then held her breath to hear what he had to say. She knew what he would be thinking. He would be smiling to himself, thinking what he said had worked and that he knew she would come around. She hated the thought of giving him the satisfaction.

"Well, Mrs. Hudson." He turned around and grinned from ear to ear. "What a nice offer."

"Well, only if you like," she added quickly and hoped he had somewhere else to be that day.

"That would be lovely." He was still smiling. "I will be happy to accept your kind offer. Is there anything I can bring?"

"That's great." She clenched her teeth. "No, I believe we have everything here." Abigail hated how syrupy polite he could be one minute and then arrogant the next and wished he would leave.

"Wonderful. See you Christmas Day, if not before." He tipped his hat, opened the door and was gone.

"I hope not," Abigail whispered to herself. Then she heard a cry from the twins' room. She turned around and called out. "Coming!" as she went to go get her little ones up from their naps.

As Abigail was bringing the children into the kitchen for a snack, she heard the door open again.

"Merry Christmas!" sounded the voice. Abigail scooted toward the kitchen doorway to see who it was and there was Ernest, still in his coat and hat covered with snow, with a big smile on his face and a little four foot pine tree he held up next to him.

"Well, of all things!" Abigail was delightfully surprised. She didn't expect to put up a tree since Jacob wasn't here, plus there wasn't much room for one here at The General Store.

"You weren't out helping Mr. Edwards at all," she teased. Ernest smiled and blushed. His secret was out.

"What a wonderful surprise! Look, children!" She turned around to get the twins from the kitchen. "See what Ernest has brought us for Christmas," she pointed. "A Christmas tree."

"Tee, tee," Danny tried to repeat it.

"Tee," Josie repeated what Danny said. Both of them smiled and clapped their hands, not really even aware of what the excitement was all about.

"Well, we will have to figure out some decorations," Abigail decided.

"I found some in the shed out back," Ernest piped up. "I will go bring them in."

Abigail clapped her hands together. Christmas wouldn't be the same without Jacob but it sure would be the best since the war started.

Ernest brought in the wooden crate with dusty old Christmas decorations that had belonged to the Adairs. Abigail washed off the dust and the four of them spent the rest of the afternoon decorating the tree. Ernest had made a stand for it that could hold water so they could keep it moist.

Ernest and Abigail stood back and looked at their masterpiece. It wasn't really big and it wasn't at all fancy. Some of the decorations were even broken, but it was the most incredible thing Abigail had ever seen because it was made out of love. Ernest was so good to her and the children. He was like the brother she never had.

chapter twenty-six

It was a beautiful day on Christmas Eve. The snow was like perfectly smooth white icing on a cake due to the wind that blew the day before. The sky was a glorious blue without a cloud in sight. The sun shone bright and brought extra heat in through the windows.

Abigail was expecting Bert and Alice and the girls to be there any minute. Peter and Missy and family wouldn't be there until the following morning, but since Ernest and Alice came from much further away, they thought it a good idea to come a day sooner once the chores were done.

Abigail began her day at six that morning. Ernest had both stoves full of wood already which took the chill out of the air. The cookstove needed to be hot to prepare breakfast and a few other treats for Christmas day. The twins were very helpful this morning; first getting into the water pail which forced Mr. Soldier to fetch some more, then knocking down the extra stack of wood Ernest had brought in.

"What am I going to do with you two?" Abigail scolded. "You are into so much mischief today. I don't have time for this." She stood up both of them from the floor and picked up the bowl of oatmeal that had gotten spilled. "Now, go play in your room for a while," Abigail ordered.

"You sure are bossy, Mrs. Hudson." A voice came from the doorway. Abigail stood up and looked at the face smiling at her.

"Alice!" Abigail darted toward her friend. "You're here!" She reached out and hugged her. Alice's stomach stuck out so far that Abigail could hardly reach all the way around her.

"It's good to be done with the ride here." Alice smiled and rubbed her back.

"You look so radiant," Abigail gushed as she stood back looking at her very pregnant friend, thinking maybe Doc was right and she shouldn't have travelled all this way.

"Where are the girls?" Abigail looked behind her and didn't see anyone else.

"They are coming. Ernest is helping Bert bring in the luggage and food. The girls are with them."

"Well, I didn't think you would leave them behind," Abigail chuckled. "Here, let me take your coat and come sit down. I will put the kettle on."

"I have been sitting," Alice laughed as Abigail helped her off with her long, tan-coloured coat. "Look at you two little ones." She looked down at the twins who stood there.

"Go see Alice," Abigail gave them each a little push toward Alice. "She doesn't bite."

Both of them toddled toward Alice, who was still standing, not wanting to crouch down to their level. She carefully sat in the chair next to the table.

"Look at that little dimple," she touched Danny's cheek, "and that curly hair." Danny smiled even more, which revealed the dimples on either side of his cheeks all the more.

"And you, little miss," she felt the top of Josie's hair, "are so grown up. Your hair is getting so long." Josie's hair wasn't as light as Danny's or as curly, but it was longer.

"I know. I have had to cut Danny's hair twice so far." Abigail smiled.

"Really?" Alice was in awe. "My girls' hair took forever to grow."

"Hello!" Bert and the girls came through the kitchen doorway. Each of them wore a long winter coat and a bonnet to match. "Boy, don't you two look smart." He looked at Danny and Josie standing side by side. "Look girls, haven't the twins grown?" he asked of Grace and Annie.

"Yes, pa," they both said shyly.

"Take off your coats, girls," Alice instructed them. They did so and took their bonnets off as well and shoved them into the sleeves of their coats.

"The coat hook is by the door," Abigail pointed to the four hook hanger next to the kitchen door. Ernest had installed the hangers when the twins needed a place to hang their coats. He also put two at their level.

"Would you girls like a cookie?" Abigail asked them. Their faces lit up and each of them nodded.

"What do you say?" Alice looked at them sternly.

"Yes, please." Again, simultaneously.

Abigail held out the plate of cookies for them to take one, and gave the twins one each as well.

"Now, what do you say?" Alice asked looking at them, as though they should know better.

"Thank you," they both said together.

"Why don't you take Danny and Josie to play in their room?" Abigail suggested. "There are some toys you can find there."

The two girls each took one of the twins by the hand and headed for their room.

"I have the kettle on, Bert," Abigail smiled, knowing that would be the first thing he would want.

"Good," he smiled. "We have to go get a few more things out of the wagon."

"Tell Ernest and Mr. Soldier to come in, too," Abigail called after him as he was already headed into the store.

"Grace and Annie are like having twins, too," Abigail observed.

"They sure are. They were born close together and Grace wasn't very big, but Annie sure was," Alice explained. Abigail remembered all too well the night Grace was born. "They do everything together."

"Well, they are sisters," Abigail smiled. "I wish I would have had a sister, or a brother for that matter." Abigail never knew why her ma and pa didn't have more children. She never asked and they never told her. This made Abigail a little curious, now that she thought about it.

"I am blessed to have both," Alice said. "that's why I want a big family."

"Jacob has a big family," Abigail looked off as she thought about his siblings and the losses they have had to endure. Maybe her simple upbringing was alright after all.

The men came in for tea and cookies and visited for a bit, but the women shooed them out of the kitchen so they could begin to prepare for Christmas dinner.

Bert and Ernest went out to The General Store and played crib for the rest of the afternoon. Mr. Soldier left to do his work.

It was a nice day of visiting and catching up for the two women. Abigail had enough flour to make a batch of buns for Christmas dinner.

As Abigail punched dough, the two laughed and told stories and even cried when Abigail shared her story about receiving the devastating letter in the mail. Abigail confided in her friend, told her all about Dr. Parker and how he wants to marry her and that he wants her to move on, because Jacob was never coming home.

"Pray to God," Alice encouraged. "Listen, really listen to what He is telling you."

"I have tried," Abigail sighed. "I can't hear anything anymore. I feel I am losing my faith. Faith that Jacob is coming back, faith in God, and faith in myself."

"It's alright to have doubt, Abigail," Alice comforted her. "We are human, we are not perfect. Only God is perfect."

"I don't know anymore." Abigail shook her head.

"Let's pray right now." Alice took Abigail's hands in hers. They both bowed their heads.

"Dear Jesus, I lift up to You my friend, Abigail. She needs You right now. Please give her strength, peace and comfort at this time, and also direction in what she should do next. We ask this in Jesus' name. Amen."

"Thank you, Alice." Abigail knew peace would find her eventually but it would be a daily struggle.

By the end of the day, the turkey was prepared for the oven for the next day and was waiting in the cold room. The buns were ready and the plates were stacked, along with the cutlery. Abigail made her mama's recipe for onion salad with the onions from Bert and Alice's garden. It would taste better left to sit for a day to give it more flavour.

After the children were asleep, Alice and Abigail got out the children's presents. Abigail had made each twin a little quilt. She had worked each night on them ever since Danny came home from the hospital and was feeling better. She had pieced blocks with the fabric that Josephine Adair had upstairs in the spare room. Abigail created matching quilts with different colours; pink and burgundy for Josie and red and brown for Danny. She didn't have time to hand quilt them, so she used the treadle sewing machine to finish them.

Alice brought a sack of things to the table for filling the children's socks from Saint Nicholas. It was a tradition that her ma and pa always had done.

"What do you have there?" Abigail watched Alice as she took out what appeared to be little tiny pies.

"Mincemeat pie," Alice smiled. "My mama always put it in our socks and an orange. And one piece of candy."

"I don't have any oranges," Abigail shook her head. "Or candy."

"It's alright, the girls will be happy anyway," Alice smiled. "I have two here for Josie and Danny as well."

"Thank you, Alice." She got up from her chair. "We can put in one of these," she held up the tin of oatmeal cookies.

"I will wrap them in paper," Alice said, since she was already wrapping the little pies in brown paper to keep them from getting messy in the sock. Abigail took out four cookies.

"Just a minute! I have something for the stockings," Ernest piped up. He handed his sister four nickels.

"Oh, Ernest, you can't be spoiling those girls, again." Alice shook her head as she wrapped the cookies.

"It's my money and I will do what I like with it," he grinned and looked at Abigail.

"Thank you, Ernest. You're too kind," Abigail smiled. She knew the big heart that Ernest had.

"We always put our stockings at the end of the bed when we were kids, so I starting doing that with the girls," Alice explained.

"We had ours at the fireplace. We always had a fireplace." Abigail looked away, thinking of her home in England, then Goldenrod Ranch, and the round house Jacob had built her. All of them had fireplaces. She hadn't really thought about it before. "Well, until now." Abigail was grateful and quite honoured that Mr. and Mrs. Adair left The General Store to Jacob and her to continue on their legacy, but never did she dream she would be living there. Abigail watched Alice put the items into the stockings.

"Jacob built you a fine house, Abigail," Alice smiled. "You will be back in it before you know it." Her words of encouragement meant a lot to Abigail.

"I guess I better get a couple of socks." Abigail left the kitchen to look in her room. She had to really search but she finally found a pair of Jacob's socks.

Abigail put the little pie, cookie and nickel into each sock. She knew they were too little to understand what they were receiving and why, but she thought traditions had to begin somewhere. She placed the socks at the end of each twin's crib on the floor, leaning against a leg of each crib.

Morning came quickly, so it seemed to Abigail. Everyone was up earlier than usual. Grace and Annie were old enough to know Santa made a visit. Both of them made sure they were up long before the sun to see what kind of present they might find under the Christmas tree.

"Look dad," Grace held out to Bert the little doll that sat on a doll quilt. The doll was made with fabric, with a little bonnet and an embroidered face. It wore a tiny dress of calico print and had on a white pinafore; all designed and homemade by Alice. Annie stood behind her sister and held the same thing in a different colour.

"Well, aren't you lucky girls?" Bert grinned and patted both girls on the head. "And what was in your stockings?"

"We haven't looked yet," they both said at the same time.

"You haven't?" Bert exclaimed jumping up with fun. "I can't believe it! Santa came all this way to fill your stockings and you didn't even look!" He scooted after them and pretended to tickle their tummies but the girls squealed and ran off.

"Bert!" Alice raised her voice. "Do you have to get them riled up this early in the morning?" She shook her head.

"Of course! It's Christmas!" He smiled and walked over to Alice to give her a kiss on the cheek. "It's the best day of the year. Jesus was born." He beamed at his wife.

"Yes, I know, but we could start off a little quieter, don't you think?" She looked at him sternly. "I am sure God won't mind a little peace and quiet, either."

"Yes, my dear," Bert grinned and wanted to tease her but thought maybe it wasn't such a good idea. "Would you like me to pour you a cup of coffee, love?"

"The coffee isn't quite ready," Alice informed him.

"Alright, then. I am going to help Ern with the chores." Ern was always the family nickname for Ernest.

"What did you get under the tree?" Bert asked the twins on his way toward the door.

Danny and Josie stood tightly gripping their stockings with their tiny fingers.

"They haven't looked inside yet." Abigail stood there with them. "They aren't sure what it's all about, yet."

Abigail sat them down in front of the Christmas tree and showed them what was inside their socks. They were both curious about the nickel, not ever having had their own money before. Danny tore the paper from the cookie and began to eat it. When Josie saw Danny begin to eat his cookie, she wanted it. She reached over to grab it out of his hand and Danny yelled.

"Here, Josie," Abigail unwrapped her cookie and handed it to her. "You have one of your own." She happily took the cookie and began to eat it.

He would have had his hands in the mincemeat pie as well, if Abigail hadn't picked it up, and Josie's too, and put them on the table for later. She also put both nickels in a safe place, so they could start a piggy bank one day.

Abigail sat down with them and gave them the gifts she had made. Of course the twins didn't get very excited about the quilts, but they were happy to have the company to play with and they toddled around with Grace and Annie.

The morning went by quickly as the men finished their chores and played crib in the store by the potbelly stove. They were supposedly keeping an eye on the children as Abigail and Alice prepared for dinner.

Abigail had the turkey in the cookstove as soon as Ernest had it warmed up for her. She sat at the kitchen table and peeled potatoes. Bert had grown these the summer before. Alice sat across from her and scrubbed carrots for her famous candied carrots. Instead of using sugar to make them sweet she would use molasses.

Her mama was bringing a crustless pumpkin pie for another dessert to go with the Christmas pudding. Abigail was able to make a sauce for the pudding with the small amount of sugar she had.

Company began coming. First it was Reverend and Mrs. Young. The reverend sat with the men, and Mrs. Young came into the kitchen to help in any way she could. She brought fruit cookies for dessert and beet pickles to go with the main meal.

Dr. Parker came in the doorway next, and right behind him was Peter and Missy and their children. It wasn't long before Claude, Jane and Benjamin were there as well.

"Merry Christmas, Jane, Claude," Abigail reached out to hug them and little Benjamin. "It's so good to see you." She stood back and patted the little one on the head. "Come in, give me your coats," she held out her hand as they passed them to her.

The children were excited to have so many others to play with. The last time Abigail checked on them in the twins' room, Annie had them all sitting on the floor playing with their dolls. She smiled as she walked away from the doorway and remembered when she was a child. She didn't have cousins to play with, let alone siblings. One friend that she could really remember visited on her birthday and Easter, but she had to make her own fun at Christmas. It did her heart good to see them playing so happily.

"Merry Christmas!" A loud voice came from the doorway.

"Merry Christmas to you, too!" Abigail darted to the doorway to greet her ma and pa and hugged them both at the same time.

"Where are our little twins?" Mama looked around the room.

"They are playing with all the children in their room," she pointed as she took their coats and put them in the office.

"I will have to go say hello." Mama headed toward the bedroom and pa joined the men. By this time there were two games of crib going with Ernest and Bert winning in each game.

Dinner was almost ready when she realized that Mr. Soldier hadn't come. She did remember inviting him to spend the day with them, didn't she? Of course she did. *I wonder why he hasn't come. I hope nothing happened to him?*

"I have to go check on Mr. Soldier," Abigail whispered to Alice. "I will be right back."

"Everything alright, dear?" Alice looked at her with concern.

"Oh, of course, but I thought he was coming for dinner." Abigail didn't want to tell her guests that she was leaving, so she slipped her coat on quickly at the door, and pulled it open as quietly as she could and closed it behind her.

It was another beautiful sunshiny day, just like the day before. The white snow crunched beneath her boots as she took each step, and made a rhythmic noise in time with her paces. She saw there was smoke coming out of Jacob's carpentry shop where Mr. Soldier stayed. Once she reached the front step, she knocked on the door with three raps. She waited.

She didn't hear anything inside.

"Hello." She called out and then knocked again.

Abigail then heard footsteps, then the cling of the door being unlatched and opened.

"Merry Christmas." Abigail smiled at Mr. Soldier standing before her.

"Merry Christmas, Mrs. Abigail." He gave a half smile as he dropped his head. Abigail noticed he looked rather pale and his eyes were red and puffy.

"Are you alright?" Abigail looked at him with concern.

"Yes, Mrs. Abigail." He looked away from her as he answered.

"Are you sure? You look-" Abigail began as her lips quivered from the cold.

"Come in." Mr. Soldier stepped back to let her through the doorway. Abigail walked in and closed the door behind her. She held her hands together and brought them up to her lips as she blew her warm breath into her palms.

"Didn't you know you were supposed to come for dinner?" Abigail looked up from her hands. "Don't you want to come?"

"Of course," he looked down, "but you don't need me there."

"Don't be silly," Abigail argued, "of course we do. You can't spend Christmas alone."

"I don't mind, really," he insisted.

"But I mind!" Abigail said firmly. "I invited you to spend Christmas with us."

"Yes, I know, thank you." He spoke quietly, "You have a lot of family and friends there."

"Yes, and you are one of them." Abigail's eyes narrowed.

"No, I am not." He shook his head. "I don't belong there."

"What do you mean?" Abigail pressed. "Of course you do!"

"I don't." He raised his hands and put them behind his head. He stepped backwards then turned around.

"You have done so much for us," Abigail stepped toward him. "Don't you realize that?"

Mr. Soldier stepped further away from her and shook his head.

"Now, stop being silly! Get your coat and come with me," Abigail gently coaxed.

"I owe you so much." He began to pace back and forth.

"You owe me nothing." Abigail stared at him. "I helped many soldiers."

"I know." He continued to pace. "That isn't what I mean."

"What do you mean then?"

Tears filled his eyes, he ran his fingers through his hair, still pacing in the same circle.

"You have been so kind to me," he began and quickly wiped his tears before they were noticed. "I didn't deserve it."

"Of course you did, Thomas." Abigail said softly.

He looked at Abigail, his widened eyes pleading.

"You knew who I was," he sniffed, "yet, you still treated me as if I were anyone else?" He began to quietly weep. Abigail's heart broke as she watched him.

"I could have killed you!" he cried. "I could have killed your babies." He fell down to his knees at her feet, hunched over and cried into his hands. Abigail quickly crouched down beside him and put her hand on his shoulder.

"Everyone deserves a second chance," she whispered.

"No," he shook his head. "I don't deserve anything," he sobbed. "I have been such a terrible person. I was the one who deserved to die in the battlefield, not Willie," he sniffed. "And I have had a few drinks since I got out of the hospital. You would have thought I had learned my lesson."

"We are all human, Thomas." Abigail continued to rub his shoulder. "We are not perfect, yet our God forgives us without question."

"God won't forgive me." He looked up at Abigail. "How could He?"

"All you have to do is ask," Abigail soothed.

"It can't be that easy." Thomas took in a deep breath and shook his head. "It just can't." He put his head back in his hands.

"It is, I promise." Abigail lowered her head to his, touched his head and pushed back his hair. "If you want forgiveness and you want to give your life to The Lord, I can help you."

"You can help?" He looked up again and he wiped his eyes with his hands. "How?"

"Do you believe that Jesus died on the cross for your sins?" She asked him.

"Y-es," he nodded. Abigail took a hankie out of her pocket and handed it to him. Thomas took it and blew his nose.

"Bow your head and say: 'Dear Jesus, please forgive me for my sins.'"

"Dear Jesus, please forgive me for my sins," he repeated after Abigail.

"Come into my heart, make me whole again. In Jesus' name, Amen," Abigail continued.

"Come into my heart, make me whole again. In Jesus' name. Amen," Thomas said after her.

Abigail hugged Thomas, still on his knees on the floor.

"Praise The Lord!" Abigail smiled. "Don't you feel like a new person?"

Thomas slowly sat up straight. His face wasn't as pale as it had been.

"I feel peace," he said to Abigail. "A peace I never felt before."

"You can move forward with your life now, Thomas." Abigail smiled as Thomas stood up, reached for Abigail's hands and helped her up. "Don't look back, only look ahead."

"Not as easy as it sounds," Thomas admitted. "But I have witnessed your forgiveness and your kindness when you could have turned me away."

"We have no right to condemn anyone, Thomas," Abigail smiled. "We make mistakes and we can learn from them. We can ask God to forgive us. By giving our mistakes to Him, it frees us."

"I am sorry, Abigail." Thomas stood still, looking down at Abigail. "For everything. Please forgive me."

"You are already forgiven." Abigail grabbed his hand and gave it a squeeze. "Now, get your coat; everyone is waiting."

"Alright," Thomas's face lit up as he grabbed his coat from the hook on the door and they both headed out the doorway together.

chapter twenty-seven

"Where have you been?" Dr. Parker raised his eyebrow as he was the first to greet Abigail and Thomas near the doorway.

"Well, Dr. Parker," Abigail took off her coat as she spoke. "Good to see you." She did not want to be rude, but she was not going to address his question either. Abigail walked past the doctor and headed to the kitchen. Thomas followed but stopped where the crib game was in full swing.

"Abigail," her mama rushed to her side. "Is everything alright?"

"Of course," Abigail could see all the ladies were waiting in the kitchen to get the dinner served.

"Alright, everyone," Abigail clasped her hands together. "Ready to eat. Reverend Young, will you please say grace."

"Of course." Reverend stepped into the doorway of the kitchen. Just as every man, when he heard the word eat, he didn't need to be told twice. "Shall we all bow our heads for grace." He raised his deep voice so all could hear from every room.

"Thank you, Dear Lord, for this glorious day, the day Your son was born to save us. Please bless those who could be here with us. Bless this food, bless the ones who have prepared it, in Jesus' name, Amen."

Everyone said 'Amen' out loud. The men lined up at the kitchen door as they each filled their plates at the table full of food, then sat back on the chairs they had been sitting in, as there wasn't a table big enough to hold everyone at the same time. Abigail set a table for the children in the sitting room so they could all be together. The whole building buzzed with chatter and dishes clanged together as they ate.

Abigail walked from the store room, to the sitting room, then kitchen to make sure everyone had a plate full of food. She knew this was different from any other special meal they had shared together. It reminded Abigail of the time they were all gathered together at Jacabig Place right after Andrew had died. The house wasn't finished yet and they all had to sit on the floor as they reminisced about their dear brother. Jacob was so strong, Abigail remembered fondly. She looked about the store room and the kitchen, and saw all their friends' faces as they talked to one another, smiled and ate in harmony. These friends had been there for them in happy times and in dark ones as well. Good, faithful friends whom Abigail and Jacob considered as family.

Abigail felt warm inside to know that each and every one there meant something to both her and Jacob, except of course Dr. Parker whom Abigail couldn't stand and didn't want to get to know. Jacob would be proud to be here in this moment. He would be the one to greet them at the door, help them with their horses, and of course be the first to win the crib game. Abigail's heart ached for him. It brought tears to her eyes to think he was somewhere freezing, with not enough to cover up, no food to eat and possibly sick or worse, wounded. Her warm feeling began to leave the more she thought about it, and although she was home, she suddenly felt so very homesick.

"Come eat, Abigail." Alice was sitting at the end of the kitchen table. She had pushed the bowls of vegetables closer together to make room for two plates. Abigail sat down beside her.

"I know it's hard for you," Alice smiled. "We are here together, warm, with food to eat and friends to spend Christmas time together. We are blessed but I know you're thinking of Jacob."

Abigail nodded. She began to fill her plate and tried not to show her friend her tears but Alice knew.

"I can't say it will be alright," Alice continued, "but I will say, we are all here for you."

"Thank you, Alice," Abigail smiled back at her. "I know."

"I need to make the plates to send to the hospital," Abigail reminded herself out loud.

"Let me help you." Alice stood up and reached for more clean plates.

"I am sure Mr. Soldier and Dr. Parker will take it over to the patients." Abigail began to fill the plates with potatoes, turkey, dressing and gravy.

"Why don't we all take them over," Alice stopped and looked at Abigail, "and then maybe sing them some Christmas Carols and you could play the piano."

"Why, Alice, what a great idea," Abigail beamed.

The doctor, Mr. Soldier and Ernest took the plates over to give to the patients at the hospital. It was a great treat for them. Most of them didn't have family close by to spend their Christmas with and they couldn't leave the hospital. While Abigail and Alice got the children ready, everyone from The General Store walked over toward Jacabig Hospital.

The soldiers smiled from ear to ear while the group of them sang songs like Silent Night, Good King Wenceslas, Away in a Manger, Deck the Halls, God Rest Ye Merry Gentleman and ended with We Wish You a Merry Christmas. It was a highlight to the day for everyone. The soldier patients had a little taste of home brought to them. As for everyone else, they felt peace and love in that room, and if they couldn't do anything else for this bloody war, at least they could make it easier on the ones who came back.

Some of the men stayed a while longer and played cards with the young lads who were able. The women and children went back to The General Store to do the dishes. The ladies then gathered around the kitchen to do their embroidery, knitting or quilting; whatever they were working on to send overseas. The children played, napped, then played again. The men continued to gather around the potbelly stove and played crib. Ernest and Thomas kept the woodbox full and the stoves stoked so there was plenty of warmth throughout the store. Later on Bert, Peter, Dr. Parker and Claude came back to the store to finish their game of crib.

Abigail came into the store from the kitchen, checked on the children, then stopped by to see who was winning. Thomas even beat Ernest at one game of crib.

"Well, well, well," Abigail smiled at Ernest. "Have you met your match?"

Ernest wasn't amused by her statement, but shrugged it off.

"Caught me at a weak moment," Ernest sniffed.

"More like caught you with a bad hand," Bert slapped him on the back as the men all laughed.

"Well, when you need someone to sort it all out, "Abigail raised her eyebrow, "give me a holler." She turned to walk away with her mischievous grin. "By the way, tea is ready." She got to the kitchen doorway.

"I will give you a run for your money." Dr. Parker stood up.

The room got quiet. Abigail stopped in her tracks and slowly turned around.

Oh, not you again, Abigail thought to herself. *Another game with Dr. Smarty. I couldn't turn him down and have the men laugh at me, but then, again, what if I lose? I didn't mean to play against Dr. Parker. I thought I would play against Thomas, or Ernest or anyone else but him. Crumb! How am I supposed to get out of this?* She pondered quickly.

"Unless you're worried that you won't win," he smiled wide and gave her a wink.

"Of course not!" Abigail raised her chin up slightly, not to be intimidated by him.

"Well, then, you're on!" Dr. Parker slid his chair closer to the small square table. "If you win, I will take you for a ride in my car. If I win, you take me up on my offer."

"Not a fair prize for my winning," Abigail narrowed her eyes at him. "I don't even like your car."

"Alright, you pick." He picked up the cards and began to shuffle. Then he laid them down.

She didn't want to say in front of everyone that what she would really like, was for him to leave her alone, possibly go back to the big city and never come back. But that wasn't realistic nor fair to Doc. Abigail wasn't that selfish but she sure would like him to leave her alone. *How can I say that without saying it?* She rapidly thought.

"If I win you will oblige me with my request from the other day." She stood in front of the chair Ernest held out for her to sit down. He pushed it forward as she sat down.

"Good enough," he nodded. "Pick a card."

She lifted part of the deck, showed the card on the bottom and revealed a queen of hearts. He then did the same and showed a seven of diamonds.

"I guess it's my crib," he grinned.

"Well, we don't know what your code words mean but it will make for an interesting game," Mr. Edwards broke the silence.

"I will go get the tea pot," Bert suggested.

Ernest looked at Abigail with concerned eyes, not because of the game itself, but wondered what she was bargaining? He knew Abigail was a pretty good crib player since they had played many games at the store.

Abigail shot him a quick smile. Inside she was worried to death. She was a person of her word, she couldn't let him win and have to marry him. *But is he a man of his word? Would he leave her alone if she won?* She wondered as she picked up her cards and spread them out in her hands.

Not a bad hand, she thought to herself, *but it could be better.*

"Well, from the look on your face," Dr. Parker jeered, "your hand isn't that great."

"On the contrary," Abigail said. "Quite the opposite." Her face was still sober.

Dr. Parker laid down his first card and then Abigail played. Abigail's hand was definitely better than his, and she ended up pegging more points by the end of the first hand.

They both were getting close to the skunk line. Abigail was ahead of Dr. Parker and everyone watched with anticipation.

"Eight." Abigail laid down her first card, since it was her crib.

"Fourteen." Dr. Parker laid down a six.

"Twenty-one for three." Abigail kept a straight face as she pegged her points and smiled to herself as she had a very good hand. The card that was on the top of the deck was a seven, which went great with her two sevens, an eight and a nine.

"Twenty-two." Dr. Parker put down an ace.

"Thirty-one for two." She said and took her points.

"One." He set down another ace.

"Eight." She set her last seven down.

"Ten." He put down his two and pegged his last point.

Abigail added up twenty-two points in her hand and pegged well beyond the skunk line, which left Dr. Parker a good ways behind her.

Adding up her kitty she had eight more points. Abigail was feeling pretty confident that she was going to win this game.

"Abigail," her mama stood behind her with a grim look on her face. "I hate to cut into your card game but Alice needs your help."

"Alright, mama." Abigail turned around. "I will be right there."

Dr. Parker began to shuffle the cards as Abigail stood up and pushed her chair away from the table. Part of her was relieved that she couldn't finish; the other part wanted to whoop him.

"Can you finish, Ernest?" She looked at him.

"It would give me great pleasure." Ernest loved playing crib. He was sure to win this game and that pleased Abigail.

"Wait a minute!" Dr. Parker stopped mixing the cards. "Hardly fair, don't you think?"

"Not really," Abigail glanced at him, "unless you're worried you won't win." She smirked as she remembered his exact words to her. She headed toward the kitchen and left the men to finish the game.

"What's the matter?" She looked at her mama, then to the other ladies doing their handiwork. "Where is Alice?"

"She's in the backroom." Her mama led the way, looking over her shoulder. "She is not feeling well."

"The baby?" Abigail began to feel unsteady.

"I don't know, she feels sick to her stomach and is weak."

"Alice," Abigail walked to the side of the bed. Alice was lying on top of the bed with a quilt covering her. She was on her side with a metal pail on the floor below her. "Are you alright?"

"Oh, don't make a fuss," Alice shook her head. "Your mama was worried. I feel better now."

"But, maybe it's time?" Abigail insisted.

"No," Alice looked down at her stomach, as she held it with her hands. "Doesn't feel the same. I don't want to get Bert all worked up. I'll only have a rest."

"We did a lot of work today." Abigail felt Alice's forehead. "Rest is a good idea. I will bring you some tea." Abigail headed back into the kitchen.

"Maybe Dr. Parker should have a look at you," Mama said.

"I am fine," Alice lifted her head a little as she lifted the pillow and attempted to fluff it.

"Here, let me help you," mama adjusted the pillow, as Alice propped herself up and leaned against it.

"What's the matter, my dear Alice?" Bert barged in the room as Mrs. Rodgers was helping her. Mrs. Rodgers backed away to let Bert in beside his wife.

"Oh, it's nothing, Bert." Alice smiled at him at her bedside. "I just need a little rest, that's all."

"Are you sure?" Bert held her hand, "I'll go get Dr. Parker."

"That's what I suggested." Mrs. Rodgers frowned at Alice's decision to decline seeing the doctor.

"He's not too far away if you change your mind," Bert persisted.

"I will have a rest and see later," Alice decided.

"Tea will make it all better." Abigail entered the room with a tray holding a hot cup of tea and a bun with butter and honey on it. "Eating may help as well."

"Abigail, tell my girl to let the doctor look at her," Bert looked up at Abigail, pleading for her to change her mind.

"It's up to Alice," Abigail sided with her friend, but only for the time being. "Dr. Parker is only a hop, skip and a jump away if we need him."

"See. Abigail is right." Alice sipped her tea and took a few bites of her bun.

"What's the matter, mum?" Grace and Annie stood at the doorway.

"Your mum is fine," Bert picked up Annie, and threw her onto one hip and took Grace's hand. "She needs a rest."

"Is she going to have the baby?" Grace asked quietly.

"Oh, not yet." Bert assured her.

"Maybe she will have the baby on my birthday," piped up Annie. "It's in four days!" she held up her hand and with her thumb held in her palm, revealed four fingers.

"I don't know about that," Bert smiled. "Your mum has a little bit more time left before she has the baby," Bert added.

"It's alright, darlings," Alice smiled at her children. "I am fine."

"Let's go see who won the crib game," Bert smiled at Alice and blew her a kiss as he led the girls out of the room. Everyone else left as well.

It was late afternoon when most of the company left. Peter and Missy and their children had a distance to go, as well as Claude and Jane and Mr. and Mrs. Rodgers.

"Maybe we should stay and help you out," Mama worried as she put her scarf around her neck.

"We will be fine, mama." I have Ernest, and of course Mr. Soldier. They are a big help."

"Well, if you're sure." She put on her hat.

"I am, mama." Abigail kissed her cheek and hugged her. "And I have Grace and Annie, they are a big help." She winked at both of them. They were standing not too far away. Both of them shyly smiled.

"Goodbye, dear," Mrs. Rodgers said.

"Goodbye, Abigail," Mr. Rodgers added as he hugged his daughter. He was doing so well since he had recovered from his stroke. He was like a new person. Abigail so hoped Jacob could see how his hard work and many prayers had been answered. He fought so much for Mr. Rodgers to get better and wouldn't accept anything less.

"Goodbye, papa." Abigail kissed his cheek as well.

Just like that almost everyone was gone. Of course, the Reverend and his wife didn't have far to go, nor did Dr. Parker, so they stayed for leftovers from the turkey dinner.

Abigail said goodbye to her guests at the door. Dr. Parker was the last to go out the door. He held his hat in his hand. As he went to grab the latch he turned around to her.

"We will have to finish our crib game another time," Dr. Parker pointed out.

"Well, I believe we already have," Abigail quickly responded "I won, remember?"

"I remember you leaving in the middle of a game," he looked at her firmly.

"It was not the middle, it was close to being done, and I was skunking you as I recall."

"It still wasn't the end."

"Ernest beat you fair and square," she said matter-of-factly.

"You were the one who was supposed to be playing," he continued to argue.

"It was almost over," Abigail wasn't going to let it go either. "I was winning. It would have taken a miracle hand to make you win at that point."

"You don't know what I had," he kept it up.

"Oh, stop it please!" Abigail shook her head, but as she was about to turn around, she turned back. "Face it, I won, you have to give me what I demanded, and that's it!" She then spun around. Dr. Parker grabbed her hand and pulled her back.

"What are you doing?" She spat.

"I won't ever leave you alone," Dr. Parker whispered, "not until you are mine." He let go, grabbed the handle and was out the doorway.

Abigail was stunned by his words. He never intended to leave her be as he said he would, that was obvious. She looked over to see Ernest standing a little bit away but close enough to see what happened.

"And you worry about Thomas!" Abigail stormed past him as she took off her apron, headed to the kitchen.

"Abigail-" Ernest darted after her. "I just-"

"Just what?" Abigail was fed up with Ernest not treating Thomas better when there was a threat like Dr. Parker. Not that he would really hurt her but he sure didn't respect her. He didn't love her, he liked the looks of her, and she was certain that's all he cared about.

Abigail sank down in a chair at the kitchen table. Ernest followed suit and sat across from her.

"Why are you so angry?" he coaxed.

"Oh, I am not mad, Ernest." Abigail put her elbows on the table and rested her head in her hands.

"Well, what's wrong?"

"I am tired of Dr. Parker and his inappropriate behaviour and can you give Thomas a break?"

"What do you mean," Ernest looked at Abigail. "First, about the doctor."

"Well, you saw him tonight," Abigail pointed out. "He's been doing that since he came to Abbington Pickets." Abigail proceeded to tell Ernest all about Dr. Parker and how he begged for marriage and told her Jacob was never coming back. She reluctantly explained how he liked to corner her, get real close to her and said she was going to need a man and soon.

"Why didn't you say something?"

"I don't know," Abigail shook her head. "I didn't want anybody to get the wrong idea."

"Well, I will give him a piece of my mind the next-" Ernest piped up.

"Thank you, Ernest," Abigail interrupted with a half-hearted smile. Ernest's brotherly love meant the world to her but Abigail knew Dr. Parker was harmless. He was just a pain. "And who knows, maybe he's right and I should marry him."

"Not a cad like him," Ernest pounded the bottom of his fist on the table. "I'll marry you first."

"Aw, that's the kindest thing I have ever heard, Ernest." Abigail raised her eyebrows as she looked up to him. "I wouldn't make you do such a thing."

"What do you mean 'such a thing?'" Ernest looked surprised.

"As if marrying you was the worst thing in the world."

"I wouldn't tie you down that way." Abigail reached out and put her hand over his. "You have your own life to live, and we owe you so much as it is."

"You owe me nothing," Ernest said plainly. "This was my service to my country, to you and Jacob. It's the least I can do, and I would do more if there was more of me to go around."

"Ernest, you are so honourable, and such a good man." Abigail squeezed his hand. "You will be the best husband. I certainly hope she deserves you."

"Well, we will see about that," Ernest shrugged. "Good women like yourself are hard to find."

"You will, one day."

"'One day' what?" Bert walked in from the bedroom where Alice was resting.

"Oh, nothing," Abigail smiled. "How is Alice?"

"She is sleeping now. I thought I would get the girls ready for bed." Bert headed toward the twins' room.

"Yes, I better get the twins ready too."

"I will load up the stoves," Ernest stood up and began to pick up the wood in the woodbox. Bert had left the room.

"I only want to add one thing." Abigail walked over to Ernest as he held a piece of wood in his hand.

"Please, give Thomas a chance," her eyes pleaded. "He has changed. You can see that. He deserves a second chance."

"Alright, because it's you who's asking," Ernest nodded.

"Thank you."

The next day came and went. Alice was still tired and not herself. Both Bert and Abigail didn't want them to travel. The children had so much fun playing and helping in the kitchen, especially Grace. Grace loved to make breakfast with Abigail in the mornings.

Thankfully, the weather was good. It was cold but it hadn't snowed and the wind was down. The air was crisp, the sun shone brightly in the deep blue sky and reflected off the white snow, nearly blinding a person who walked outside, but the warmth in it felt good.

It was three days after Christmas. Bert, Alice and the girls were still staying with Abigail at The General Store. Alice was beginning to feel better and they thought seriously about packing up and heading home.

"Before you go, I would have Dr. Parker at least have a look at you since Doc is still away," Abigail suggested, even though she didn't care to have him visit quite so soon.

"I agree with Abigail," Bert added.

"Oh, all right," Alice agreed, "but I am sure everything is fine."

"Well, we will let the doctor be the judge of that." Bert smiled at his wife.

"I will tell Mr. Soldier to ask him to come." Abigail walked toward the doorway to the store to go speak with Thomas. She stepped outside but she couldn't see him anywhere. Abigail went back inside, grabbed her coat, and headed toward the hospital.

"Dr. Parker?" Abigail opened the door

"You called?" Dr. Parker came out from the stairway, with a smirk. He knew who was there.

"Can you do a house call?" Abigail began, being more than professional.

"Is everything alright? The twins?" He for once looked somewhat concerned.

"The twins are fine. It's Alice." Abigail stood at the door. "She hasn't been feeling well, and with the baby coming-"

"I wondered why they were still here." Dr. Parker picked up his black leather bag and followed Abigail as they spoke. "Why didn't you say something sooner?" "Alice didn't want to. She said everything was fine." Abigail was two steps ahead of the doctor as they headed toward The General Store.

"Just like a woman to think she knows everything," Dr. Parker grumbled.

"Excuse me?" Abigail looked over her shoulder, "Men aren't so smart. How many babies have you given birth to?"

"None, but I have delivered many," he said sternly.

"Delivering them and birthing them are two entirely different things," Abigail retorted.

"She should have been checked on sooner." Soon his stride was faster than Abigail's and he was almost passing her, but her legs moved faster, determined not to let him be in front of her.

"I was looking after her," Abigail insisted.

"It would have been faster to take the car," he huffed. The puffs of white air coming out of his mouth as he spoke looked like cigarette smoke.

"Ha! If it wasn't stuck in that snow bank," Abigail chuckled. "Besides, by the time you got it started we would be here." Abigail looked up. "See we are here already, so stop your complaining."

"The doctor is here!" Abigail called out as they were getting in the doorway. She took Dr. Parker's coat and hers and hung them up.

"Good. I think something isn't right." Bert came out of the doorway and greeted them.

"That fast?" Abigail looked at him. "I left not that long ago and she was fine."

"Well, she is having pain in her back." Bert explained as they both followed Dr. Parker as he headed directly into the bedroom.

"Well, Mrs. Hibbert." Dr. Parker was very formal as he set the bag on the end of the bed and opened it up to take out his stethoscope. "What seems to be the trouble?"

Alice explained how she had been feeling and how the feeling was better until the pains started a few minutes ago.

"I will go check on the children," Abigail looked at Bert, not wanting to be in the way. Bert nodded and closed the door behind her to let the doctor examine Alice.

Abigail looked in on the four children as they played. They were so content and kept themselves occupied these past few days. Jacob wanted quite a few children, she remembered him telling her. Maybe this was what it was like to have more children. Would they really get along this well as siblings? Her heart skipped a beat with the thought that she may never have any more children, at least not with Jacob. The thought brought tears to her eyes.

She came back to the kitchen, filled the kettle with water and set it on the stove. *Tea was what everyone needed,* is what she thought. *When all else fails, make tea. Besides the hot water may come in handy,* she told herself.

Finally the door opened. Dr. Parker came out first, then Bert. Abigail searched their faces for answers because no one was saying anything. Was this going to be like when Alice gave birth to Grace? She remembered how panicked she was, how awful she felt, and how comforting Jacob was.

"How's Alice?" She blurted out.

"I think you will be stuck with us for a little while longer," Bert grinned.

"I believe Alice is in labour," Dr. Parker pointed out. "It's only the beginning, so no hurry."

"Well, is she doing alright?" Abigail pressed.

"Too early to tell, but as of now, she is fine," Dr. Parker stated.

"I am making tea. Stay for some?" Abigail reluctantly asked as she held the pot in her hand.

"No, I am going back to the hospital to do a few things," he scratched the top of his head. "I will be back to check on Alice, but I am guessing the baby won't be here before tomorrow."

"Thank you for coming, doctor." Bert reached out and shook his hand.

"Send for me if anything changes." He looked at Abigail. He knew she would know what he was meaning.

"I will do." Abigail nodded.

Alice was uncomfortable all night long. Abigail heard Alice moaning quite a lot, and once Abigail got up and asked if she could do anything for her. Bert assured her it was alright.

The sun was rising. Abigail slid out of bed, listened to the quiet of the house and wondered what might be wrong. She hurried to put on her housecoat and slippers and darted out her bedroom doorway to head for the kitchen.

She stopped in her tracks to find Bert sitting at the kitchen table with a baby wrapped in a white cotton blanket.

"What?" Abigail gasped as she ran to Bert's side. "How did I not hear?"

"I don't know," Bert smiled. "You must have gone into a deep sleep."

"I can't believe it! Are you sure I am not dreaming?" She was still stunned.

"To be honest," Bert smiled from ear to ear, "it happened so fast, there was no time for fetching the doctor."

"You mean...you?" Abigail was speechless. "How's Alice?" She looked at the doorway of the bedroom. "Dr. Parker is in with her now. He arrived moments before you got up."

"Maybe that's what woke me," Abigail shook her head in disbelief. "I thought it was the deafening silence."

"Maybe." Bert still looked down at his little baby and rubbed his finger over the little one's forehead.

"Well, what did she have?" Abigail finally got over her awe.

"Another baby girl," Bert beamed.

"Wonderful! She is so beautiful," Abigail admired. "She looks a lot like Annie."

"I was thinking the same thing," Bert nodded. "Would you like to hold her?" He looked at Abigail.

Abigail reached out to pick up the tiny bundle, first scooped her right hand under her back and her left under her head. She cradled the baby in her arms. The baby made funny faces as she stretched and made sweet little baby noises.

"Have you got a name for her yet?" Abigail asked as she rocked the little bundle gently from side to side.

"Mary Edith," Bert stated. "After my mother." Bert's chest seemed to swell a little.

"That's a fine name." Abigail smiled as she watched the baby fall back to sleep.

"Wow," a little voice came from the doorway, "did the baby come?" Grace was standing in her long white nightgown, in awe as she saw the little bundle Abigail was holding.

"She sure did," Bert walked over to Grace. Annie was in tow. "This is little Mary." He crouched down beside Abigail to show the girls their new little sister. "Happy birthday, Annie!" he smiled at his second daughter. "I guess you were right, you now share a birthday!" Annie scowled a little as she looked at the small bundle, not too sure if she liked the idea of a new baby for *her* birthday, but quickly her unsatisfied face turned to a smile.

"A girl!" exclaimed Grace. "We have another baby girl to play with." Grace grabbed Annie's hands and they danced in a circle like Ring Around the Rosie, only singing 'we have a new baby sister,' their own made up song.

Abigail handed the baby back to Bert. "I better get the twins up and make us all some breakfast."

chapter twenty-eight

Bert and Alice and the girls stayed until Alice had the strength for the ride home. One beautiful day in January they packed the wagon and headed east. Abigail sure missed them as they had become part of the routine and besides, it was so nice to have a newborn around. The girls were such little mother hens. Abigail had no doubt they both would be a big help to their mama.

The rest of the winter dragged on with the snow that came early that year. When the snow melted there was a lot of run off which made it nice for the farmers who began to plant their crops. The grass began to grow fast and the annual flowers began to pop out of the ground. Abigail couldn't wait to see her hollyhocks in bloom again. It would remind her of Jacob and how he built the small fence that enclosed the garden which eventually grew the tall annual flowers. Abigail needed something to hold on to, to bring her thoughts closer to Jacob. After all, it had been over a year since she was told he was presumed dead.

Ernest had gone back to his farm and Thomas began to work more in The General Store. With the help of Ernest over the winter, Thomas had learned to do more than haul freight and do yard work.

Dr. Parker was still quite busy at the hospital with new patients coming and mended ones going home. There were always volunteers to help each day, but none gave their heart and soul as much as Abigail did.

The twins were more manageable as they got older and Abigail was able to get her work done with them around. She would take them with her to do some of the work at the hospital. They were now three years old, quite the little chatter boxes and the soldiers sure enjoyed their company. Some of the men would read to them while Abigail stripped and made the beds. Some would try and teach them to play cards, usually ending up being fifty-two pick up, where the children dropped the cards on the floor and had to pick them up. When it was tea time, the soldiers would share their cookies with the twins.

It was a common sight to see Abigail walk between the hospital and The General Store as the twins followed behind, carried little baskets and merrily sang a tune or two.

It was a miserable, windy fall day. Trees banged against the buildings in the village and golden leaves descended to the ground with every gust. *It wasn't supposed to be like this, today of all days,* Abigail thought as she dressed each of the twins for the last church picnic of the year. *How were they expected to eat outside with the wind blowing like this?* She asked herself. Hopefully, the Reverend had a plan.

The church was full that Sunday as each one took the usual pew. Some families could even fill two pews. It was like everyone knew that once harvest was over the weather could turn from bad to worse. It was best to have the last get-together before being stuck inside for the next five months of snow.

Abigail walked the twins down the aisle of the church, sat in their usual spot and said good morning to each one on the way. She hated the sad looks folks gave her as she smiled at them. Abigail knew what they were thinking, 'poor Abigail, left with two little ones while Jacob went off and got himself killed. Now she has to stay alone and look after The General Store.' *Poor Abigail? Poor indeed! I am sick of the word "poor," sick of the pity and tired of the pathetic faces that stare back at me, especially the ones women give me.* Despite the few break downs she had alone in her room, Abigail thought she was handling things quite well. Maybe God didn't do as she asked, or maybe things haven't turned out as she had thought they would, but she still loved her children. Jacob had left her that much. God has always provided, despite the stressful times. She began to muse again. *Is God not faithful? Isn't that what Jacob showed me with his actions? Did not God send me Ernest? Elizabeth? Thomas? Without them, I wouldn't have gotten this far without failure, of* that much she was certain.

Her heart ached for Mrs. Ford on the loss of Elizabeth. She struggled to know why God allowed that to happen, but He had a plan and with all her heart she tried to trust Him. Abigail didn't know what was in store for her and the twins, but knew that when it happened she would know.

When Reverend Young was done his sermon, and the last hymn was sung, he made an announcement.

"With the uncooperative weather out there, we have an offer to spend our last picnic at the Howard's south west of Abbington Pickets. All are welcome." He cleared his throat. "And I hear tell that there will be some music."

The filled room made noise as they looked at each other, oohing and aahing as they smiled at the thought. At that moment Abigail spotted Ernest and Thomas. *They must have snuck in a little late,* Abigail thought. Everyone made their way through the pews and down the aisle to the back of the church and out the doorway. Many held onto their hats as they crossed the threshold as a big gust of wind took hold of their skirts.

"I will hitch up the horses, Mrs. Abigail," Thomas smiled at her as she approached him and Ernest.

"I have my basket all packed," Abigail nodded.

Ernest lifted up Josie and put her on his shoulders. She giggled as he walked. Abigail still held onto Danny's hand

and walked along side of Ernest as the five of them headed toward The General Store.

It was a little more of a ride than simply driving the horses through the village to get to the Howard's. Ernest drove the horses with Abigail in the seat next to him. Thomas rode in the back with a twin on either side of him right at the front of the wagon box. He was holding onto the basket of food and blankets stacked up beside them.

The wind wasn't very kind as it blew fiercely around them. Hats had to be tightly held onto. It felt like the longest ride Abigail had in a long time since she really hadn't left Abbington Pickets much since the war began. It was a nice outing but would have been better without the wind.

As Ernest directed the horses to the front of the house to let Abigail and the twins off, they saw quite a few families were already there. Abigail spied Dr. Parker's tin car among the wagons as they rode past.

Abigail took the twins as Ernest carried the basket and followed her into the house. Thomas tied up the horses and gave them water and hay at the Howard's barn, then joined them inside. Mr. and Mrs. Howard politely greeted their guests at the door. It wasn't as formal as the annual Harvesters' Ball that they hosted every year up until the war began. The community didn't feel right in the celebration with all their loved ones away and felt it was in their best interest to put on hold the fall event.

Folks were in the ballroom with their blankets spread out as if they were in the great outdoors.

"Let's sit over here," Abigail pointed as she walked toward the left corner of the room. She stopped and spread out the quilt on the floor with Ernest's help. The five of them sat down on the colourful blanket.

The sound of people chatting gave the room a sort of humming sound. The Reverend was correct, there was going to be music as Abigail spotted Mr. Thomas and some of his friends setting up to play some tunes. Mr. Thomas played his violin, another played a banjo, one was on the piano and a fellow Abigail didn't recognize had a guitar.

"Good to see you, Abigail." Abigail looked up and saw the face that matched the voice. She quickly stood up to hug Mrs. Ford. She hadn't seen her since Elizabeth's funeral. She was sick over the whole situation and never had the opportunity to tell her so. Mrs. Ford hadn't been to The General Store since. Mr. Ford always came in alone.

"Good to see you, too." Abigail stood back from the embrace. "How are you doing?" She looked into the woman's dark eyes. She looked as though she hadn't slept in weeks and she seemed to have aged somewhat since Abigail saw her last.

"Getting by," she sighed. "It's a struggle, Abigail." She looked at her as she spoke.

Abigail looked down as a feeling of shame washed over her and tears welled up in her eyes. She couldn't imagine how she would have coped, had she lost Daniel that day instead of Elizabeth. She felt ashamed for thinking that.

Mrs. Ford reached out for Abigail's hand and held it with both of hers as she leaned closer to Abigail. "I only wanted you to know, I don't blame you for what happened to Elizabeth." She smiled faintly, but genuinely.

Relief filled Abigail's heart as she placed her free hand over Mrs. Ford's.

"I am so very sorry, Mrs. Ford," Abigail shook her head.

"I know you are, dear, but it wasn't your fault," she whispered. "It wasn't anyone's fault."

Abigail hugged Mrs. Ford again, then both women dabbed the corners of their eyes with their handkerchiefs. Abigail felt grateful for Mrs. Ford's assurance, and more at peace over the death of Elizabeth which had silently haunted her since it happened. God sure has a way of bringing things and people together in difficult times.

The meals were almost done and people were folding up the blankets and quilts to make room for a little dancing on the dance floor as the musicians began to play.

The children danced around the outside of the room to the rhythm of the music while the adults danced the waltz, two step and fox trot. It was a day to forget all their troubles and relax before reality set in. Dealing with the difficult times, this dreadful war, remembering the loved one who were off in it, missing, or perhaps never coming home, was reality. Ernest chatted with Mr. Edwards, while Thomas checked the horses. From a distance Abigail watched her twins dance with the other little ones.

"Good day, Abigail." Dr. Parker approached her. "Can I have this dance?"

"No, thank you." Abigail didn't feel right touching another man that close. "I would rather watch."

"It's alright, Abigail," he insisted. "No one will judge you."

"I am not worried about that," she scowled at him a little. "I don't feel like dancing."

"Ah, why not?" he smiled. "It's kind of fun," he urged.

"Because I don't." He was beginning to irritate her. *Why can't he take no for an answer?* She asked herself.

Dr. Parker reached for her hand and grasped it in his.

"Come on, just one dance," he coaxed.

"I heard the lady say 'no thank you,'" a voice firmly said.

Abigail turned around to see Thomas standing behind her. Dr. Parker immediately let go of her hand. Abigail brought her hand close to her stomach, she held one hand with the other.

She smiled at Thomas and turned back to the doctor.

"If you will excuse me, I have to check on the twins." Abigail walked toward the children.

"Hello, Abigail." She spun around to find Claude holding little Noah, and Jane was carrying a little bundle.

"Oh, my," Abigail reached out to hug her, careful not to squish the baby between them. "I didn't know you were coming. When I didn't see you at church..."

"We had a little... well let's say it took us longer to get here than usual." Jane smiled up at Claude.

"Let me see that new bundle of joy." Abigail bent down to see the baby make faces in her sleep. Abigail was relieved to have heard that Jane had given birth to a healthy baby girl and it was a home birth delivered by Claude himself. Doc had been there to check on Jane and the baby after she had given birth and reported the news to Abigail.

"What is her name?" Abigail looked up at Jane, then over to Claude.

"Katherine Marie, after Claude's mama," Jane beamed.

"What a beautiful name for a beautiful baby," Abigail smiled. "Congratulations, so happy you're here. Jacob would be-" she stopped herself. Too often she found herself saying, Jacob this, Jacob that. She couldn't help it. Every time something happened good or bad, she wanted to tell Jacob about. She shook her head a little and cleared her throat as tears began to fill her eyes.

"I know, Abigail," Jane touched her arm. "It's alright."

Abigail gave her a half smile, then an apologetic look.

"Excuse me." Abigail quickly backed up, headed toward the hallway and then the outside doorway. She stepped outside and took in a deep breath. She needed some air. Abigail didn't even notice that the wind had gone down quite a bit and it was rather nice outside. She began to walk around the back side of the house.

"Abigail, wait!" Dr. Parker called after her.

Abigail stopped abruptly in her tracks without turning around. The young doctor dashed toward her and walked in front to face her. He looked down into her brown eyes, as he grabbed her hand. Abigail was about to pull it back, but he held on tight.

"I am in love with you, Abigail." His eyes seemed to soften as he spoke. "I always have, from the first time we met in The General Store."

Abigail's heart pounded hard in her chest, so hard, she thought he would be able to hear it as well.

"But-" the tears that filled her eyes, spilled down her cheeks.

"Shhh." He put his finger to his lips, "don't say anything." He lowered his voice as he put his head down and looked at the ground. "I know you don't feel the same way. I know where your heart is." He took in a deep breath. "But with time, you could learn to love me. I will be patient," he smiled and looked up at her again. "Heck, I have waited this long, I can wait for you to love me back."

Abigail was speechless, she had no idea what to say. He was absolutely right, her heart was with Jacob. She couldn't ever see that changing, no matter if Jacob came back or not.

"You need a father for your children, a husband to take care of you," he added gently. For once he sounded caring, not arrogant or loud, but affectionate.

"How can you love someone who loves another?" Abigail whispered. "You know I will always love Jacob." Tears once again welled up in her eyes at the thought of betraying the only true love of her life.

"I believe in time you will start to love me," Dr. Parker's eyes pleaded. "Promise me you will think about it? At least give me a chance?" He then fell down to one knee, still holding her hand in his.

"Will you marry me, Abigail?" His eyes pleaded with hers as she stared back at him in shock.

Abigail took in an involuntarily sobbing breath. She wanted to burst into tears, but feared if she did, she wouldn't be able to stop. Slowly she pulled her hand back from his. She didn't have any words. She began to back away, but as she turned around to walk back to the house, he again called after her, still on one knee.

"Please, think about it."

"Alright, I will." Abigail said. She didn't know if he heard her or not. She kept walking. The children would be wondering where she was.

Abigail couldn't get the look of Dr. Parker's face out of her mind as the five of them rode back to Abbington Pickets. The ride was much more enjoyable than when they drove to the Howard's, since the wind had died down and the sun was still shining warmly. No one knew how many more nice days there would be and there was still much to be done before the snow flew. Abigail tried to think about that instead of her conversation with Dr. Parker.

Ernest helped Abigail off the wagon. Thomas passed each of the twins to her, she set them down on the ground and they ran toward the store.

"I am going to finish chopping that load of wood," Ernest pointed out as Thomas took the horses to the stable to unhitch, feed and water them.

"I will start supper," Abigail smiled back at him. Her mind was full and her stomach ached as she followed the twins to the store, carrying the basket and quilts they took on the picnic. Supper was the last thing she wanted to think about.

chapter twenty-nine

"Did you hear?" A loud voice sounded as the door flew open and Ernest plunged inside, "The war has ended! Germany has surrendered!" He ran up to Abigail who was still holding the broom from sweeping. He put his arms around her waist, picked her up, and spun her around in a circle several times. Abigail dropped the broom on the floor.

"Are you sure?" Abigail's eyes widened as she held onto Ernest's shirt to keep her balance. "How do you know?"

"The lad from the city says it's in the paper." Ernest stopped and set Abigail back on her feet. "We should be getting our shipment of papers soon."

Abigail bent down to pick up the broom and leaned on it as she stood up straight, still dizzy from Ernest's outburst. *Could this be real? The war really over?* Abigail's mind raced as she thought of the news Ernest had told her. Her heart ached for Jacob. It was this terrible war that took him from her. She felt relief and bitterness at the same time.

What a celebration the nation would be having, not to mention Abbington Pickets. Local soldiers would be coming home. It was a joyous day. It should be one to remember for a lifetime, but Abigail's heart didn't feel the joy. It felt nothing but heartache.

Word spread quickly that the war had ended. The newspaper headline across the nation read 'GERMANY SIGNS ARMISTICE, WAR ENDED!' The official day of Armistice was on the eleventh hour of the eleventh day of the eleventh month in 1918. Germany had signed an armistice with the Allies at Le Francport, France.

Abbington Pickets took on a new countenance since the news that the war had ended. The village main street seemed busier and people were smiling instead of the usual sombre faces that they wore to town. Villagers were beginning to plan their spring, like painting their homes or putting in more flowers for colour. It was a time of encouragement and looking forward to getting back to normal.

It was a particularly warm Sunday morning at the beginning of December. The birds chirped outside without a care. It was like they, too, knew the war had ended and liberty was here at last. It had only been weeks since the war was declared over, but everyone still felt the effects of it. Soldiers were slowly coming back from Europe and returning to their lives. It wasn't as easy for some men as it was for others. Some came back wounded and missing limbs and would never be the same, which made it harder for them to make a living. Other soldiers were still in need of medical attention and Jacabig Hospital was busier than ever. Dr. Parker and Doc spent many sleepless nights tending to patients.

Ernest was the only one at the store that day. He put away yesterday's freight, cut wood for the week and hauled water to the kitchen for the next few days' household chores. Although it was a busy day for Ernest, there was something quite tranquil in the air. He knew where he should be instead of working but there seemed to be so many things to do and not enough hours in the day to get them finished. Sunday was supposed to be a day of rest but he found it hard to have any sort of break when there were things to do.

Ernest piled the papers on the front counter for purchase. As he put the last paper down, he wished he could have stayed with Jacob longer to do his part. He resented the fact that he was wounded enough to be sent home. Despite his vision not being perfect anymore, he didn't care. He would go back in a minute if he could save the life of only one person.

Ernest was standing on the top half of the wooden ladder in the shadowed storage room when he heard the store door open. The only light in the room was the oil lamp Ernest had set on the shelf near the door.

"I will be right there." Ernest shouted as he placed the last box on the top shelf. He began to climb down and stepped on each rung carefully as he held onto the rails on either side. "Coming." He reminded his unknown guest as he set his foot down on the floor, turned around and saw a shadow standing in the doorway.

"I am sorry, I was way up-" Ernest pointed to the loft he had just finished putting stuff in, then looked back at the man in the dark uniform, who walked closer. The light glowed over the man's bearded face. His hair was overgrown and rather messy as he stood holding his forage cap. Ernest squinted his eyes.

"Jacob?" He squinted tighter as he got closer. "Is that you?"

"Ernest, lad. Good to see you." Jacob smiled at the familiar face. "Where's Abigail?"

"Ah, my boy, it's so great to see you," Ernest grasped him by the upper arms, smiled as he looked him up and down, then he gave him a slap on the back. "The church!"

"The church?" Jacob tightened the grip on his hat, then began to put it on his head, darted for the door and pushed it open.

"Go!" Ernest pointed east. "Hurry!"

Jacob ran as fast has his legs would take him until he got to the church doorway. He took a deep breath, removed his cap, grasped the door latch, pulled open the door and walked inside. The silence was broken right before Jacob entered the back of the church.

"We are gathered here-" Reverend Young stopped abruptly and looked up at the man in the back. "Can I help you?"

The wooden pews creaked as everyone turned around in their seats to see who was standing there. Abigail and Jane stood at the front of the church along with Claude and Peter.

Abigail turned around quickly. "Jacob!" She gasped and brought her hand to her mouth. She was holding Jane and Claude's new baby in her arms. "Praise The Lord." She shouted as she passed the baby to Jane. She stepped past Claude, and ran down the aisle as everyone in the congregation watched without blinking an eye. It was as though she was moving in slow motion. It seemed to take forever for her to reach the back of the church. Jacob quickly stepped forward to meet Abigail part way, as she ran into his outstretched arms. Her hair flowed down her back and Jacob could feel the soft tickle of her locks as they brushed against his hand. Abigail held him as tightly as her arms could squeeze.

"I knew you would come back to us," Abigail whispered against his chest, not wanting to let go. Tears of joy streamed down both cheeks. Abigail tipped her head back to look at Jacob's war-ridden face. There were a few extra lines near his eyes, but they twinkled as they always did. His bristly hair shadowed his face, but his smile shone through.

"You are all I thought about," Jacob whispered. "You and the babies kept me going, kept me alive." He nestled his head in her hair close to her ear. Abigail didn't want to ever let go, but she could feel the eyes of their audience behind them.

"Oh, my lad," Jacob smiled as he saw that Alice and Bert were each holding the twins behind them as they patiently waited for the couple to stop embracing.

"You must be Daniel Andrew," he looked at the children. "And you must be Josephine Lucy." He took Danny from Bert and Abigail took Josie from Alice. "They're more beautiful than I imagined." Jacob couldn't stop smiling. He kissed the top of Danny's head, then leaned over and kissed the top of Josie's head. Josie shyly turned her head, while Danny only stared at whom he thought was a stranger to them both. Although Abigail had told the twins every detail about their father, they were unsure of the smiling face before them, so eager to hold them.

"Wow, brother, it's so good to see you," Peter slapped Jacob on the back of the shoulder. "I see you're all in one piece."

"Thanks. It's so good to be home."

"Jacob, you always know how to stir up things," Jane spoke up as she held her little baby. Claude stood behind her holding little Noah.

"And who is this?" Jacob beamed while watching Jane with her little one.

"This, dear brother," Jane couldn't keep from grinning either, "is your niece, Katherine Marie, named after Claude's mama."

"Congratulations!" He stepped toward his sister and reached out to hug Jane with his free arm as he continued to hold Danny with his other. He turned toward Claude and reached out his hand.

"And this is Noah Benjamin," Claude smiled while holding two-year-old Noah. He was dark like his father but had a seemingly resemblance to his uncle with the one dimple on his cheek.

"Thank you. It's good to see you're alright." Claude took his hand and shook it firmly.

"What a joyous day this is," announced Reverend Young loudly for the congregation to hear. "God has answered our prayers, and we must say thanks. Let us bow our heads in prayer."

Everyone stood still as the Reverend prayed.

"Dear Heavenly Father, we thank You for this day and for bringing us our Jacob home safely. Bless Jacob, Abigail and family as they come together after years of being apart. In Jesus' Name, Amen."

"Amen," everyone said all together.

Everyone began to chatter all at once amongst themselves as they were gathered around Jacob and Abigail like a cluster of wild flowers.

"This is little Katherine's Christening," Abigail beamed.

"Yes, and now that you're here, you can officially be her Godfather," Jane informed Jacob.

"Sorry we are late," came a voice from behind Jacob and Abigail. Everyone turned to see who it was. There stood both doctors and Mrs. Johnson.

"What did we miss?" Dr. Parker looked at Abigail as he raised his eyebrow with his usual smirk.

"Hello, sir." Jacob stepped forward and put out his hand to the doctor. "You must be Dr. Parker. I am Jacob Hudson."

THE END

discussion questions

1. How would you have handled Dr. Parker and his attention had you been in Abigail's position?

2. In today's society our day is full of multi-tasking. How much more difficult do you think it was for Abigail who was running a store, looking after her family, helping at the hospital and all without a husband.

3. First Jacob was absent at war, then missing in action, then presumed dead! All this added to Abigail's stress. How would you handle Abigail's stress in today's world?

4. Throughout the book Abigail realized God was still working in her life. How is God working in your life and world today?

5. Mrs. Johnson, Doc's wife, has a particular role in Abbington Pickets by helping patients and their loved ones plus being Doc's assistant, not to mention the person who cleans up after every emergency. Do you know someone today who represents her personality and responsibility?

6. Are there people in the Abbington Pickets community with whom you would like to spend time today? Why?

7. Abigail found it difficult to pray out loud but persevered. Do you find it difficult to share prayer out loud? If so, what would help you to become more comfortable with this? If not, how can you help others to become more comfortable with this?

8. Do you bake? Do you hand sew? With all our modern day technology do you think it is more enjoyable today or do you think years ago the passion for it was as pleasurable?

9. What teaching did you take away from reading this book? Do you feel Abigail encouraged you to become a better person?

10. Today we communicate with modern technologies, such as email, texting and social media options. Discuss some of the advantages to handwritten letters – both 100 years ago and sending letters today.

11. When Abigail felt low, disappointed, or discouraged, her response was to write to Jacob. Even when he was missing in action, she still called out to him through letter writing. How do we cope today in this age of technology? Have you a special person you turn to in times of crisis? Do others rely on you for encouragement?

12. Abigail's establishment of A.P.L.G. was not unique but certainly was new to Abbington Pickets. Do you know anyone involved today in projects to help our communities? Are you aware of their goals?

13. What can you do to help others in today's world who may feel their hope is lost?

14. Abigail's heart is so big. She wants to help everyone and make a difference, first with the A.P.L.G. then the cribbage benefit. Discuss how her interaction with the town's people also shows her love and Christian sharing.

15. Mr. Soldier went through an awful lot throughout the war years. How do you think he feels when Abigail is shot, when he meets Abigail at the hospital, when he is caught in Jacob's shop, when she takes him in and helps him?

16. Discuss how Abigail's faith grows throughout the years while Jacob is gone.

17. For all we feel about Dr. Parker, God still shows Dr. Parker has redeeming values. Name a few of these.

about the author

H. C. Hewitt grew up on a farm in Southeastern Saskatchewan where she developed a deep appreciation for the rural prairie landscape and the people who live there. She has been passionate about reading and writing from an early age and always knew that she would someday write a historical romance. Her grandmother's extensive knowledge of Saskatchewan history and her grandfather's collection  of antiques sparked an enduring love of history, especially of the era in which her story unfolds. Her story's setting in the series of *Abbington Pickets* was inspired by a historic park near where she grew up, founded in 1882 by an Englishman who set out to create a Victorian village in Canada.

H. C. Hewitt's other passion is quilting. She owns and operates a quilt shop where she designs and makes quilt patterns. Her four children have grown up and moved away, giving her more time for writing and quilting. She also has six grandchildren and loves to spend time with them. H. C. Hewitt lives in rural East-Central Alberta with her husband, dog, two cats, and nine miniature donkeys.

Corinne owns and operates a quilt shop in Hanna, Alberta, and also designs quilt patterns. Corinne designs quilt and embroidery patterns to coincide with her novel series. Check out these and many other patterns including patriotic designs, at: www.hchewittauthor.com or connect with her at: hchewittauthor@gmail.com.

H. Corinne Hewitt
Pattern designer/Author

More books in the Abbington Pickets Series by H. C. Hewitt. You can find these on her website: www.hchewittauthor.com or wherever books are sold.

Connect with other Abbington Pickets fans or share by using:
#abbingtonpicketsseries
#jacobofabbingtonpickets
#jacobsplace
#lettersfromjacob
#jacoblovesabigail

You can also connect with Corinne on Facebook, Instagram, and Twitter
@hchewittauthor

CPSIA information can be obtained
at www.ICGtesting.com
Printed in the USA
LVHW040849270720
661612LV00003B/171/J

9 781640 859494